Mischief
with the Marquis

ROGUES OUT OF TIME
BOOK 2

PATRICIA BARLETTA

Published Internationally by
Patricia Barletta
Boston, MA, USA
Copyright © 2026 Patricia Barletta

PRINT ISBN 978-1-7355994-6-5
EBOOK ISBN 978-1-7355994-7-2

Exclusive Cover and Interior Formatting and Design: Joanna D'Angelo

Editor: Joanna D'Angelo

For permissions or inquiries, please contact: patricia@patriciabarletta.com
patriciabarletta.com

PATRICIABARLETTA.COM

Mischief with the Marquis

ROGUES OUT OF TIME
BOOK TWO

PATRICIA BARLETTA

"Come out of the circle of time
And into the circle of love."

— RUMI

Prologue

BOSTON, PRESENT DAY

Maggie Blake stood in the middle of her antique shop on Newbury Street in Boston and stared down at the old journal in her hand. She had found it in an escritoire, a small writing desk with a cabinet above for books. The piece had arrived two days ago in a shipment of several other pieces from England, all dating from the time of Prince George, Regent to his father, King George III. The escritoire was exquisite and valuable, but the journal was a historical document, written, it appeared, in 1814 by a woman named Emma, coincidentally the same name as her older sister. Who had disappeared days ago.

Maggie had become worried about her sister as the days passed, and she hadn't been able to contact her. She'd texted her, called, left voicemails, and even emailed. But her sister hadn't answered any of them. Emma had gone silent before, when she'd been researching some obscure bit of history for the historical romance she was working on, but she'd always texted after a day or so to check in and say she was okay. Not this time.

Maggie had contacted everyone she could think of who might have heard from her sister since she'd finished her manuscript and sent it off to her editor. No one had. Not Darcy, their youngest sister, who was doing an internship in Milan with a high-end fashion designer, not Emma's author assistant, not her agent, not her editor. None of her friends.

Maggie had contacted the authorities — the police, Scotland Yard, the American Embassy. They had all been sympathetic and began a search for Emma, but a week had gone by and they hadn't found her. Maggie felt that she needed to go to London herself. With a glance around the antique shop, she sighed out the anxiety.

She would have to leave her business in Boston, the shop that had been their father's before his untimely death in a plane crash six months ago, and fly to London to find Emma. Would she still have the business when she came back? She'd hired a new assistant only a few weeks ago. Would the young woman be able to run the shop on her own while Maggie was away? Pushing that worry aside for the moment, she focused instead on travel details — plane ticket, packing, transportation to the airport.

She ran her fingers over the lovely, embossed, leather cover of the journal. For some illogical reason, she suspected the diary had something to do with Emma's disappearance. Because the woman who wrote it sounded like Emma. But that was crazy. This woman had lived over two hundred years ago. It had to be a coincidence.

The entries in the journal began with a narration of her husband's quest for his rightful title, discovering secret notes, unraveling a secret code, and revealing the treachery of her husband's half-brother. The other entries were mostly descriptions of life in London and on a grand estate, the day-to-day experiences of a genteel woman of the time, but also about the lady's frustrations over the restrictions of society. The author included her deep feelings for her husband, whom she referred to as her hero, as well as several comments about how much and how often he pleased her. And on the first page was a date and a dedication: *30 June 1814. To my sisters, whom I miss greatly. Even though we are separated, know that I hold you in my heart.*

Those two sentences brought tears to Maggie's eyes every time she read them. They sounded like something Emma might write in one of her historical romances. But Maggie decided that was just happenstance. The woman who had authored the journal couldn't possibly be her sister, because that would mean she had traveled back in time. Which was preposterous. Impossible. An absurd idea.

One

London, Present Day

After an overnight flight to London, Maggie relished the freedom of a jog through Hyde Park. Directly from Heathrow Airport, she had gone to her dad's flat, the one he had owned so he would have a place to stay on his extended buying trips to England. It was where Emma had been staying, and when Maggie walked in, she half-expected to see Emma sitting at the desk and staring at her computer. But her sister wasn't there.

After a quick search through the rooms, she discovered Emma's clothes and her purse, with her passport and money still inside. The flat looked like her sister might show up any minute and apologize for not being there to welcome

Maggie. As she contacted the police and Scotland Yard and the American Embassy to let them know she was in London, she waited for her sister to come sailing in the door. But Emma never appeared. Where was she?

That question ran through Maggie's head in a loop as she jogged, but she had no answer. Distracted by trying to figure out where her sister might be, she slowly became aware that the tiny, delicate gold key hanging on a thin chain around her neck had turned warm, then suddenly scorching hot. Burning where it touched her skin. She stopped short as a hiss of pain whistled through her teeth. Pulling the key from beneath her tee shirt, she let it dangle in the breeze to cool it down and wondered what had caused it to turn so hot.

Hanging next to the key on the chain was the sapphire and diamond pendant, shaped like a flower bud, that had come from a necklace belonging to her mother. She had died when Maggie was barely a toddler. Her other two sisters each had a pendant exactly like it. As it dangled, a ray of sun pierced the deep shade thrown by the huge oak tree next to her and lit up the jeweled pendant, as if some magical element had been triggered. The effect was mesmerizing. Other-worldly. Then it faded. Weird.

Maggie glanced around to see if anyone had noticed, if anyone else seemed as shocked as she was by the phenomenon. But the few people nearby appeared unaffected. Located in the middle of London, Hyde Park looked as it always did in mid-morning in early summer. People ambled along the paths, a few nannies pushed their young charges in strollers, several diplomatic types hurried across the freshly mowed lawn. No one seemed to have noticed anything out of the ordinary. She stepped off the path and flopped onto the grass beneath the enormous old oak tree that looked like it might house a whole colony of elves. Pulling the chain over her head, she checked beneath her tee shirt for signs of a burn on her skin. Nothing was there, not even a red mark. Weird again.

Holding up the chain, she watched the key swing slowly next to the pendant, as if the two were dancing together. The little key was a lovely thing, its head an intricate filigree of gold. She imagined that it fit into the lock on a beautiful, antique, carved wooden box that held a lady's jewels.

For her last birthday, just months before her father's untimely death, he had told her to choose anything she wanted from his antique shop, the one she had inherited and now owned, stocked with only the best antiques, high-end items that sold in the thousands, occasionally in the tens of thousands. The key had lain in a dusty corner of the single display case in the shop for as long as she could remember, an anomaly that contrasted sharply with the other exquisite items for sale. She had always wanted the tiny trinket from the time she had first spied it when she was a little girl.

When he'd given it to her, he told her it was the key to her heart, to be given away to the man of her dreams. She'd laughed because she didn't see any "hero" in her future, despite the fact that her older sister, who made her living writing about romance heroes, kept telling her that everyone should have a happily-ever-after. Maggie's relationships with men had been minimal and brief, either ending in disappointment or fading into nothing, for which she was glad because she couldn't see herself spending the rest of her life with any of the men she'd dated. She hadn't been with a man for over a year.

The key was a cherished reminder of her dad. The sapphire pendant hanging on the chain beside it was a keepsake from the mother she didn't remember, because she had been too young when her mom died. But her dad had always spoken of her as if a part of his heart was missing. For some reason, Maggie felt that the two items, the pendant and the key, needed to be together.

With a sigh, she closed her fingers around the trinkets and leaned back on her elbows. She blinked back tears as that tug of loss assailed her again.

The loss of her mother, whom she never knew, was a void that her dad did his best to try to fill. Then she'd lost him a year ago when the small, two-seater plane he'd been piloting crashed into Cape Cod Bay. Now Emma, who had come to London to finish her historical romance, had gone missing. The last time Maggie had talked with her, Emma had said that she was working furiously on her manuscript because her editor wanted it earlier than the original due date. And then she had mysteriously disappeared.

When Maggie saw that all of Emma's belongings were still at the flat, as if she had just stepped out for a moment, a chill went through her. Emma had been gone for days. Was she injured and lying in a ditch somewhere? Had she been kidnapped? Maggie didn't want to think about the worst possibility—that she was gone. The police hadn't been able to pick up any clues to her whereabouts, and she'd heard nothing from Scotland Yard or the American Embassy. Maggie missed her sister and worried about her. Something terrible might have happened to her. But wouldn't she know in her heart if Emma was dead?

The key warmed in her palm, then turned very hot again.

Sitting up, she opened her fingers and let the chain swing in the air.

"What the devil...?"

The man's voice came from somewhere nearby. Maggie glanced over her shoulder, but the expanse of grass behind her was empty.

"What the devil...!"

The agitated exclamation came again, this time from above. The branches of the oak tree over her head thrashed wildly, as if they were in the middle of a mini storm, but she felt no wind. The sun still shone brightly, and the sky was blue. Something whizzed past her. Ducking, she threw her arms over her head for protection. She heard a thud on the ground and a grunt of pain.

"WHAT THE DEVIL...?!"

She peeked between her fingers. A man lay sprawled on the grass in front of her. Where had he come from? Maybe he had fallen out of the tree. That would explain the thrashing branches. But what had he been doing up there? Spying? He rolled to his hands and knees and shook his head as if to clear it, then climbed to his feet and brushed himself off as he surveyed his surroundings.

Maggie slipped her chain back over her head, scrambled up and backed away a step, just in case she needed to run. Strangers falling out of trees didn't happen every day. He might have been up there for a perfectly innocent reason. Or not.

He was quite tall, probably about six feet, maybe a little more, and he was dressed — Wait. How was he dressed? She blinked, then squinted, trying to decide if her eyes were playing tricks. No, she wasn't seeing things. He was dressed in tight, buckskin breeches tucked into high boots and a soft, white, full-sleeved linen shirt, open at the neck. He looked all decked out for a historical costume drama. Maybe he was an actor and had been hiding from the film crew working on that historical costume drama.

"Hi," she said. "Are you all right?"

He swung around, took one look at her, and immediately turned his back. "I beg your pardon. I did not mean to intrude upon your — your —" He gave a helpless wave of his hand.

"It's okay. You didn't interrupt anything."

"No?" Peeking over his shoulder, he quickly turned away again. "Then why are you...?" He took a deep breath. "Where are the rest of your clothes?"

Glancing down at her tee shirt and running shorts, she saw nothing was missing. "These are all my clothes."

He swiveled to face her. "Good God, woman, you cannot wander about London like that."

She frowned. "Why not?"

"Why not? *Why not?* Because—Because—," he sputtered, then stopped, scowled, and took two steps closer. Then two more. To within arm's reach.

She fell back, but before she could turn and run, his hand whipped out and captured both the pendant and the key. The chain bit into the back of her neck. She was caught.

"Hey! Let go of that!" She took hold of the length of chain that wasn't in his large fist and tugged. Of course, he didn't release it.

"Where did you get this?" he growled.

Alarmed and angry, she tugged on the chain again. "None of your business."

He inched closer, towering over her. "It is very much my business."

She tilted her head back to look up at him. If he didn't look so threatening, he would have been quite handsome, with dark green eyes, straight nose, square chin, and strong jaw that was covered in a thick scruff. Hair, a bit unkempt and too long, the color of mahogany with light streaks, brushed his neck and fell across his brow. His shirt showed signs of hard wear, and dirt smudged one shoulder. He smelled sweaty, as if he'd been working out, with a trace of salty caramel, but, damn, that smelled good. Then she scolded herself for thinking such a thing because he could be a dangerous criminal. If he was involved in making a movie, he must have been playing a fugitive. But that was a fleeting thought amidst all the other thoughts that were flashing through her head, the loudest and most insistent being to get away as fast as possible.

"Why is it your business where I got the key and pendant?" she asked. Maybe if she kept him talking, he would be distracted enough to release his hold on the chain so she could escape.

At that moment, a skateboarder followed by a friend on roller blades sped past. They caught the stranger's attention. As they disappeared down the lane, he stepped off the grass to watch them zoom away and dragged Maggie at the end of her chain along with him.

He turned to her with a suspicious squint. "What manner of conveyance was that?"

Hadn't he ever seen a skateboard or roller blades? Where was he from?

Maggie opened her mouth to answer, but before she had the chance, the sound of a distant police siren pierced the air. He startled and froze, then as the noise faded into the distance, he glared at her.

"What was that confounded noise? A banshee? Are you a witch?" he growled. "Have you conjured me into a nightmare?"

She stared in disbelief. "What? No! I haven't conjured you into anything!" Although the fact that he seemed to have fallen from the sky might be considered conjuring. But that was just crazy.

"Never mind." He tugged twice on the trinkets in his fist. "Where did you get this?"

"None of your business," she repeated, this time allowing annoyance to color her words, as she tried to pry open his fingers. "Let go of my necklace."

"*Your* necklace," he scoffed. "You have no right to it."

Was he deranged? On drugs? A thief? "I have every right."

"You do not." Anger darkened those green eyes.

"Why not?" Maggie was angry now, too, and her shock began to morph into fear.

"Because the key is mine." With another tug, he brought her up against his body.

Maggie was aware of two very distinct things. The stranger's body was hard and muscular. And she was suddenly and quite dizzyingly falling...spiraling down, as if she had stepped into a very, very deep, dark hole.

Smack!

Simon Herrington, Marquis of Wildford, sucked air into his lungs and blinked. How in hell had he wound up on his back in the middle of a lane in Hyde Park with a very lovely woman sprawled on top of him? A woman who was wearing little more than his key on a chain around her neck. One minute, he was upright and confronting the young woman, whose curves, he noticed, fit very nicely against him. The next minute, he was falling through space and slamming into the earth on his back. How the devil had that happened?

That was the second time something very, very strange had occurred. The first had happened just moments before, as he had been silently raging against the fates that had put him in a prison cell. Between one blink and the next, he was falling through the air, bouncing through tree limbs, and landing on his face in Hyde Park. His brain was having trouble keeping up.

The woman squirmed and wriggled her way off him, jamming her knee against his privates in the process. He grunted in pain, but she gave no indication she realized what she had done. Instead, she hissed with annoyance.

"Let go," she demanded, as she tried to pry his fingers from his key.

Her face was only inches above his, caught as she was by the length of chain around her neck. He looked into her eyes, the same blue as the sapphire pendant hanging next to his key. Lovely eyes, surrounded by thick lashes, but at this moment, stormy eyes, because she was angry. A tiny beauty mark sat just at the corner of her left eye, as if the artist who created her had left his mark. Her dark hair was scraped back from her face and tied in a manner resembling a horse's tail and just as luxurious. The rest of her was quite delightful as well, for he had seen much, much more than was proper for the middle of Hyde Park. And he had felt her delicious curves when she landed on top of him. But he knew very well that an attractive exterior could hide an ugly, treacherous heart.

"I will not let go," he said quite equitably, considering she was most likely a thief. Or a witch. "You are in possession of a key that belongs to me."

Her eyes widened, then narrowed. "That's impossible. The key is hundreds of years old. It's an antique. My father had it in his shop for years before he gave it to me, just before —" Her words halted on a catch in her throat.

Something about her father upset her, but he put away that tidbit of information for later. Instead, he focused on the rest of her words.

"Hundreds of years old?" he scoffed. "Your father must have been mistaken. How did he gain possession of it? Was he a thief as well?"

Insult made her rear back to the length of the chain. "How dare you! My father was no thief!" She began to pummel his chest. "Let go of me, you weirdo!" Raising her head, she yelled, "Help! Help!"

Simon clapped his hand over her mouth. "Shush. I will not harm you."

Her cries didn't stop, but at least they were muffled. He ignored the blows she rained on his chest and ribs. The last thing he needed was to attract attention, especially from the authorities. He caught sight of a horse and rider far down the path, trotting in their direction. He didn't want to be seen, especially with a woman dressed in odd undergarments, and in their compromising position.

"If I release the chain, will you remain quiet?" he asked.

She stopped hitting him, studied him a moment, then nodded.

"Will you promise not to run away?" he pressed.

Her nod of agreement was much too quick, indicating she had no intention of remaining where she was.

He held back a sigh of exasperation. "I will not harm you. I just wish to straighten out this misunderstanding. Please, don't run away."

Her nod came more slowly.

Carefully, he unclenched his fist from around the key and pendant. She held very still, her eyes — those magnificent eyes — never leaving his face. Still not trusting that she wouldn't run, in a single, fluid motion, he rolled to his feet, wrapped his hand around her arm and pulled her up with him.

She tried to jerk away. "I said I wouldn't run."

"Sh," he warned, glanced down the path at the horse and rider, then dragged her behind the huge oak. For some reason, he had the impression the tree was much larger and older when he had fallen through its branches and first encountered the woman. But he had just been pulled from his prison cell and tumbled through the air, so maybe he was mistaken.

The rider came abreast of the tree. "Wildford, is that you?"

Simon winced. He knew that voice. Brandon Connaught, a schoolmate, a friend, whom he hadn't seen in several years. If he remained behind the tree and didn't speak to him, the man would think he was giving him the cut. With a warning glance to the woman to remain hidden, he mouthed, *Stay here.* Then he stepped out from behind the tree while keeping a firm grip on the woman's wrist.

"Hello, Connaught," he said.

Connaught's eyes widened a bit at Simon's disheveled appearance, but instead of commenting on that, he said, "It's been years since I've seen you. Where have you been?"

Simon gave a casual shrug. "Doing a bit of the King's business. And you? Still fighting for your birthright?"

His friend's mouth ticked up at the corner. "All settled. A

bit of bad business with my half-brother. The old man is dead. The title is mine."

"Congratulations. And condolences on your father's death." Simon suspected that his friend's brief sentences hid a great deal of drama.

"I have also taken a wife." A happy, smug smile creased Connaught's face.

Simon grinned. "I thought you had sworn off marriage."

"When the right woman appears, a man must submit to the inevitable," Connaught — now the Earl of Cranleigh — said with good humor.

At that moment, a large group of riders, both men and women, approached and surrounded the earl. Simon stepped back behind the tree. He had recognized several of the newcomers, but he didn't want to interact with them. One of them, he was sure, perhaps more, had been instrumental in his arrest. He needed to make a plan before he accused anyone of treason.

The woman peeked around the trunk of the tree, then glanced back at him. "Look at all those gorgeous costumes. Are you shooting a movie?" she asked, her eyes lit with excitement. "What's the title?"

"I'm not shooting at anything." He frowned at her very odd words and questions. "What is a moo-vey?"

She frowned back. "You're kidding, right? You don't know what a movie is?"

Simon heard the words, but most of them made no sense.

Perhaps the woman was deranged and speaking gibberish. Or perhaps some spell was wound up in her odd way of speaking. Even so, he was not about to let her out of his sight until she turned over his key. Cranleigh and the other riders moved off, so he felt safe to emerge from hiding. Without answering, he pulled the woman in the direction of one of the exits from the park.

"Wait," she said, hanging back. "Where are you taking me?"

"Some place where we can come to an understanding about the ownership of my key," he said and dragged her along.

"It's my key," she argued, as she tried to pull from his grip. "And I'm not going anywhere with you. I have no idea who you are. You could be a rapist or a murderer."

Simon halted so quickly that she ran into him, then she immediately backed away as far as she could with his hand still wrapped around her wrist.

"I am neither a rapist, nor a murderer," he said tightly, deciding that the men he'd killed in the name of his king and country didn't count as murder. "My apologies for not introducing myself earlier. I am Simon Herrington, Marquis of Wildford." He executed an abbreviated bow, since he still had hold of the woman.

"Oh," she said, appearing a bit shocked. Then her eyes narrowed. "Of course you're a marquis. You play your role very well. You must have the lead in the movie."

There was that word again: *movie*. And she said he had the lead. Well, of course he did. He was leading her and they were moving — *movie* was how she pronounced it. Annoyingly, she did not introduce herself in return, nor nod acknowledgment of his introduction, or even extend a hand for him to bow over. Well, he did have hold of her wrist, so maybe extending a hand wasn't possible. But obviously, she was not a woman of quality. He didn't care. All he wanted was his key. If he had to, he would pay her an exorbitant amount for it, then send her on her way.

They came in sight of the road with its carriages and coaches and drays and riders on horses, and ladies shopping with their maids, and gentlemen making their way to their clubs, and delivery boys and messengers — all the usual traffic. The woman's reluctant steps halted abruptly. When he turned to see what the problem was, she was staring at the road.

"That's quite a movie set," she said.

He gazed at the scene before them as he tried to figure out what she was talking about. "Moo-vey set?"

"Yeah, you know, a fake background so the actors look like they're in a real place." She continued to stare at the road and its traffic as if fascinated.

"I assure you, there is nothing fake about the congestion of London," he said.

At that moment, a nightsoil man, out much too late in the morning with his odoriferous wagon, rolled by. The woman gasped and covered her nose and mouth. After watching the wagon a moment, she turned to him. Her cheeks had turned quite pale, her eyes wide with shock.

"Wha—Wha—What year is this?" she asked, her words barely above a whisper.

"1814," he said, curious why she wouldn't know that.

And then she collapsed in a dead faint.

Two

The first thing Maggie noticed was the warm, muscular chest she leaned against and the two strong arms that held her. The next thing was that she was in some sort of conveyance, and it was moving. Opening her eyes, she saw she was in a coach. And she was sitting on the lap of Simon Herrington, Marquis of Wildford.

With a yelp, she rolled off his knees onto the floor, covered in dried mud and other stuff she didn't want to think about. "What do you think you're doing?"

"Trying to care for you after you fainted," he said.

She had fainted? She'd never done that before. But then she'd never traveled back in time, either. How had that happened? Maybe she was dreaming. That was the answer. She had fallen asleep under the oak tree, and her brain was making up this story, because she had found that journal and she had come to London to find Emma. Could someone faint in the middle of a dream? And who was this man who was in the dream with her? He'd introduced himself as Simon Herrington, Marquis of Wildford. Didn't people dream about someone they knew? She couldn't ever remember meeting anyone like the man seated before her.

She peeked at him. He didn't appear to be threatening at the moment. In fact, he'd been considerate to care for her after she'd fainted, but she didn't like the idea of being taken anywhere without her consent, nor the fact that he had seemed quite content holding her on his lap. Not even in a dream.

"Where are you taking me?" she demanded.

"We are on our way to my townhouse where we might come to some understanding about my key," he said with a challenging lift of one brow.

"I'm not going to your house. How do I know you won't keep me prisoner or murder me?" She scrambled up, sat on the worn and cracked leather seat opposite, as far away from him as she could get, and rubbed her hands on her shorts to get rid of whatever she had touched on the floor.

Suspicion narrowed his eyes. "How do I know you are not a witch and will not turn me into a frog?"

"A witch?" Her voice rose an octave or two with insult. "If I were a witch, I'd have abracadabra-ed my way out of this coach."

He emitted a sigh of great forbearance. "I am an honorable man. On my word, I will not harm you. I have already introduced myself, which, by the way, you have not."

Maggie crossed her arms and scowled. Should she tell him her name? Even in a dream she wasn't sure she should do that. Glancing out the window of the coach, she watched nineteenth-century London pass by. Why was she dreaming about the past? Why had the man sitting across from her fallen into her life, appearing out of nowhere? She certainly wasn't a witch. If she could dream her way back to Hyde Park and the ancient oak tree, she could wake up and return to the twenty-first century where her life was. But until that happened, she had to deal with this moment in time.

She had no money, no clothes except what she was wearing, no credit cards. She had her cell phone, but that wouldn't work, and neither would her credit cards, even if she had them. The only resource she had was the man sitting across from her. But since she was dreaming, he had to take care of her. Didn't he? Mr. Simon Herrington, Marquis of Wildford. At least, that's what he said his name was, sounding all noble and snooty. How had her brain come up with that name?

He wasn't dressed like a marquis. She expected a nobleman to be well-groomed, wearing well-tailored clothes, not buckskin breeches and a shirt that looked like he'd been wearing the clothes for days, weeks even. And the coach they were in looked like it might be ready for the junkyard, not her idea of the type of transport a marquis might own.

Except he spoke and acted as if he had been entitled his whole life. Maybe he had. Or maybe he was a really good actor.

On the other hand, he hadn't taken advantage of her when she'd fainted. He hadn't hurt her or tried to steal the key that he said was his, even though he could have easily over-powered her or taken it while she was unconscious. Maybe he was as honorable as he said. Maybe she shouldn't make an enemy of him. Maybe he could help her get back to her own time. Or help her wake up from her dream.

She lowered her chin and took a quick peek at him from beneath her lashes. He was watching her with those green eyes the color of spruce trees. Those eyes seemed to bore into her. She shifted on the seat.

"My name," she said, "is Maggie Blake."

His lips twitched and he nodded once. "A pleasure to meet you, Miss Blake."

"How do you know I'm a Miss?" she demanded. "I could be a Mrs. Blake, or a Lady Blake, or even a Countess or Duchess Blake."

His eyes danced with amusement. "You have no wedding band, so I assumed you were unwed. I apologize if I was mistaken. And if you are a countess or a duchess, then I am quite contrite. Please forgive me." He placed his hand over his heart and bowed his head.

Annoyed at his teasing, she grumbled, "Just a miss." She wasn't ready to allow him to call her by her first name.

The carriage slowed, turned through a pair of iron gates, then stopped before a large, imposing, stone mansion. The man across from her glanced out the window.

"Excellent. We've arrived," he said.

The door to the carriage opened, and a footman, dressed better than Simon Herrington, Marquis of Wildford, said, "Welcome home, my lord."

The marquis thanked the man, stepped down from the carriage, then held out his hand to Maggie. She looked at the huge house, then back at the man who said he was a marquis, then back at the house. He acted as if he belonged there. And the footman seemed to know who he was.

Befuddled that she was dreaming about being in the company of a nobleman who appeared to be living in a huge home, Maggie placed her hand in his and stepped down. She craned her neck to look up at the mansion. To live in such a home implied the man beside her must be incredibly wealthy. Of course he was. She wouldn't have made up anything else in her dream.

"Welcome to my London home, Miss Blake," he said, then led her up the stairs.

The front door swung wide and a very large man, who looked like he could play for the New England Patriots, dressed in clothing similar to the footman's, except nicer, stood in the opening. His bald head gleamed, and a triangular scar puckered the dark skin on his left cheek. When he saw the marquis, his eyes widened, then narrowed.

"I thought you were in pris—." He cleared his throat. "We were coming to get you, sir." His words held the musical lilt of someone from the Caribbean.

Maggie's gaze swung from the giant to the man beside her. "Prison? Was he about to say you were in *prison?*" She stepped away from him, but his fingers clenched tightly around her hand. Now she knew why he looked so disheveled and perhaps even disreputable. Why would she dream up a man like that?

"Do not run away," he commanded, then his tone modulated. "Please. A misunderstanding. I will explain everything." He glared at the man who had opened the door, then he dropped her hand. "My butler, Kelwin, exaggerates."

"Nice to meet you, Kelwin," she said, then turning back to her captor, she demanded, "How can he exaggerate prison?"

The marquis and his butler exchanged a glance, then the man who had fallen into her life said, "I was mistaken for someone else. Please, Miss Blake, will you listen to what I have to say?"

Maggie had a suspicion he might be lying. She wrapped her fingers around the key and the pendant to protect them. Both pieces were very dear to her, and she was not about to give up either of them, not even in a dream. But she was also curious about why the marquis seemed to think that one of the pieces belonged to him. And how a mistaken identity had landed him in prison. She loved a good story, even one that wasn't true, so she jerked a nod.

The marquis smiled, and Maggie was entranced. Maybe that's why she had dreamed him. A rogue with a great smile was a weakness of hers.

"Excellent," he said.

She turned away from that smile because it was too distracting and instead took in her surroundings. They were standing in a grand, two-story, entrance hall painted in soft ivory. Elegant crown moldings bordered the ceiling, and plaster curlicues decorated the corners. The finishing touch was a huge, crystal chandelier suspended from the center. A graceful, central staircase led up to a gallery on the second floor, and several doors opened off to the right and left. The floor beneath her feet consisted of wide strips of highly polished parquet in a herringbone pattern. Against the walls, several side tables held vases, candlesticks and knickknacks, and directly opposite the front door, a long case clock slowly ticked each second. The impressive exterior of the house hadn't prepared her for the opulence of the interior. The marquis was obviously a very wealthy man.

As he waved her toward an open doorway off the entrance hall, Maggie hid a sigh. Why couldn't the man who wanted her key, be homely and awkward...not charming? Or polite. Or considerate. Not mouth-wateringly hot. And rich as Croesus. She didn't want to be attracted to him. She wanted to tell him to get lost. But she couldn't, because she was in another century and he was the only one who could help her. And if this was a dream, it was turning out to be a long and involved one.

Or maybe, he was the reason she was in another time, if that's where she really was. Maybe her travel through time had been his fault. She'd have to mull that over.

She stepped into a sitting room decorated in green and ivory and gold. It was quite small and inviting compared to the enormous entry hall, and furnished with silk and velvet covered chairs and delicate tables. A lovely Aubusson rug covered the floor, and several paintings adorned the wall. She took in the furnishings and the artwork with a practiced eye. They were all authentic pieces. A portrait by Thomas Lawrence hung on one wall, and a J.M.W. Turner landscape hung above the fireplace. Those two artworks alone were worth a fortune. In fact, if she sold even one piece of furniture or one of the other knickknacks, like the ormolu clock on the mantel, the set of matching silver candlesticks, or any of the other items in the room, she could retire and live very comfortably. In fact, she could have someone else manage the shop full-time and she could pursue her ambition to design furniture. But in this room, in this time, they weren't antiques. She had to remember that. Besides, they weren't real. They were figments that her subconscious mind was creating. She was dreaming.

"Please, Miss Blake, sit down," the marquis said.

Maggie perched on the edge of a handsome, green, velvet-covered wing chair. The marquis leaned an elbow on the mantel. He looked like a pirate, ready to casually lop off the head of anyone who dared defy him. All he needed was a cutlass hanging at his side.

"Would you care for some tea?" he asked. "Or perhaps something more fortifying?"

Maggie wanted a shot of something very, very strong, like tequila or vodka, just to calm her nerves, but she shook her head. "I'm fine, thanks. Let's just get on with it."

He studied her a moment, as if trying to figure her out, then gave a nod. "Very well. Then perhaps you can explain to me how you came to be in possession of my key."

"I told you, my father gave it to me." She went on to elaborate a bit on what she had first told him. "He had it in his shop, and I always liked it, from when I was little. Then he gifted it to me on my birthday." She left out the part about it being the key to her heart, because that was just some made-up, Dad stuff.

"What sort of shop did he have?"

"He sold antiques—high quality antiques—like these chairs, and those paintings." She indicated the items.

"Those are not antiques," he said, looking a bit insulted. "I acquired both paintings from the artists, who are very much alive."

"Well, in my time, they're really, really valuable. Museum pieces, actually."

His brows drew together. "Your time? What, exactly, is your time?"

Maggie's brows crunched together as well. If he was in her dream, wouldn't he know that? "The twenty-first century. I'm from the future."

He stared for a moment, then barked a laugh. "Of course, you are. That is a very droll story. Now, tell me who you really are and how you came into possession of my key."

Offended that he didn't believe her, Maggie shot to her feet. "I'm not lying. You were there, too, just for a few minutes. And then you dragged me back here, to your time. So, it's your fault that I'm here."

As she spoke, something clicked into place. The weird light in the pendant. The ancient oak tree. That hole she fell into. Maybe she wasn't dreaming. Maybe she really had time traveled...

Oh, no! No! No! No!

She was dreaming. She had to be. The stuff that her sister Darcy believed in about ghosts and time travel and all that paranormal mumbo jumbo was nonsense. It had to be. All she had to do was get back to the oak tree. That was where she'd fallen asleep and gone into this strange dream. Maybe then, she'd wake up and be back to cars and cell phones and the internet.

She stomped toward the door. "I'm going back to Hyde Park. I'm going to wake up and go back to my own time."

"Wait."

His abrupt command made her pause and turn back.

He straightened and took a step toward her. "Those strange modes of transportation that I saw —"

"Yeah, a skateboard and roller blades."

"Strange names, although quite appropriate," he mused. "I did not imagine those."

"Nope." Actually, she imagined them in her dream.

"And your scanty mode of dress—" He swallowed and averted his eyes. "I take it, you are not — not — a woman of ill repute."

At first, she was affronted at his suggestion, then she grinned at his obvious discomfort. "Nope. We dress like this a lot, especially when we're jogging."

"Jogging?" His brow arched.

"Yup. Running for exercise."

"I see."

She felt his warm glance slip over her like a feather's touch. Holy moly. That had never happened in any of her dreams before. But if she wasn't dreaming, he *was* taking liberties. She crossed her arms and straightened her spine, resisting the impulse to melt beneath those sensual eyes.

His gaze skittered away and he cleared his throat. "I apologize for thinking you were anything other than virtuous."

Not ready to let him off the hook for that, she said nothing.

With a bow, he said, "Forgive me."

She sort of forgave him. How could she not with that

bow? But his accusation still rankled. "I didn't steal your key. I'm not a thief."

"I'm beginning to believe you."

Maggie narrowed her eyes at him. Beginning to believe her? What more proof did he need?

"But I do believe you might be a witch," he added.

"I'm not a witch," she stated. Again. Then she sighed, threw up her hands in defeat and swung toward the door. "Whatever. I'm going back to Hyde Park to try to get back to my own time." *And wake up from this ridiculous dream.*

"No." He lunged forward, caught her by the wrist, and dragged her up against his body.

Maggie yelped, frightened into immobility, and stared up into those green eyes that had gone as hard as jade. She abruptly understood why he had been in prison. He might be a marquis, and charming and handsome, but at that moment, he was definitely the pirate. Dangerous.

And he might be about to murder her to get what he wanted.

This dream was turning into a nightmare.

Furious and frustrated, Simon had done the only thing he could think of in the moment. He had grabbed the woman to prevent her from leaving. He needed that key. Desperately. In the next second, he realized what he had done. She was frightened, because he had reverted to his piratical ways. Damn it, he had to remember he was back in civilized society.

Immediately, he backed away, but in a tiny corner of his mind, he missed the press of her warm, delightful curves against him. No. That was insanity. She was from another century. How could that be? And she had his key that, somehow, he had to liberate from her possession. Honorably. Before she returned to her own time.

"I did not mean to frighten you, Miss Blake," he said, guilt pricking him for alarming her, but he refused to relinquish his hold on her. "But we need to come to an understanding about my key."

As soon as he allowed her space, she backed away the length of her arm. Her eyes were still wide with fright, and they had turned the most amazing bright blue. He forced himself to glance away. To her nose — adorable and sweet. To her cheeks — rosy with color. To her lips — plump and kissable. Very kissable. No, none of those. All of them made him want to draw her close, cup her face, and taste her. He finally settled on a spot in the middle of her forehead.

She jerked and twisted against his hold. And growled. Growled? He didn't think he'd ever heard a woman growl at him before. The sound sent a tingle straight to his privates. God's teeth! He needed to focus. He'd never been so distracted by a woman in his life. All he wanted was his key, and then she could go back to whatever century she came from.

He took a deep breath to steady himself, then tried again. "Miss Blake, I will not harm you." Hadn't he told her that already? Why did she not believe him? Oh, yes, his grip on her wrist. But he couldn't let go and allow her to run away. "Please, what can I give you in exchange for my key?"

She stared at him a moment, then her glance traveled around the room. "The Turner painting," she said, her tone adamant. "And the Lawrence."

He made a tiny choking sound in the back of his throat at her audacity. She was robbing him. But he was desperate.

"You may have the Turner, but I'm afraid the Lawrence shall remain with me," he said. "It is a portrait of my father."

She glanced at the portrait, then nodded. "Deal."

"Deal?" Did she wish to play cards and wanted him to deal them?

Her forehead wrinkled, then her expression cleared and she explained. "I agree. I'll take the Turner. We have a bargain. A deal."

"Yes. Quite. A deal." Slowly, he loosened his grip on her wrist. "Please remain here while I ask Kelwin to summon my coach."

She glanced out the window. "Isn't it right there out front?"

"That is a hired coach," he said, his lips twisting in

distaste, "and it should have moved on by now. It was the only means at hand to get you somewhere safe when you fainted." He watched her digest that bit of information, then asked, "Do I have your word you will not try to run away?"

She nodded again, which he supposed was close to giving her word. Then she smiled. Not a warm, inviting smile, or even a conciliatory smile, but a cool, victorious one. Well, she could have her victory and the painting, but he would get his key — and his life — in return. Stepping around her, he went to summon Kelwin.

As soon as the marquis left, Maggie headed toward the fireplace and the painting that hung above it. Visions of selling it for millions flashed in her brain. Her ambition of creating exciting, comfortable furniture would come true. And if she somehow forgot to exchange the key for it, well, she was in a dream, after all, and nothing was real anyway.

She ignored the fact that she was reneging on the deal she had made with the man who had fallen from the sky. And she ignored the cool bracelet of air around her wrist where his warm fingers had been. He was from the past. Or a figment of her imagination. He'd be long gone as soon as she returned to her own time, so no point in getting flustered by a phantom who only existed in her own mind. Besides, even though she had seen nineteenth century London with her own eyes, she was convinced she was dreaming. She must have surely fallen asleep on the grass under that huge oak tree.

That painting was hers. Anything was allowed in a dream.

Dragging a small stool over to the fireplace, she positioned it and stepped up so she could reach the painting. It was huge, as wide as the spread of both her arms and nearly as tall as she was. The frame was beautifully carved wood covered in gilt. She tried lifting it from the wall, but besides being enormous, it was also impossibly heavy. It didn't budge.

"What, may I ask, are you doing?"

The chilly question came from behind her. It was a very good question. What *was* she doing? She imagined her good angel shaking her head in deep disappointment. Glancing over her shoulder, she saw the marquis with a furrow between his brows. Guilt dug a hole in her chest. Shame flowed over her in a hot wave. That flood of emotions made her think that maybe she wasn't in a dream after all. But of course, she was. The alternative explanation, that she really was in the year 1814, was just too implausible to even consider. But dream or not, she had to contend with the annoyed man who had just walked in and discovered her trying to steal his painting.

She stepped down from the stool. "I — ah — thought I'd try to help. With the painting. Getting it off the wall."

"I employ people for those types of things, Miss Blake." He tipped his head, his glance narrowing with suspicion. "You weren't trying to steal it, were you?"

"Of course not!" *Liar, liar, pants on fire.* "We made a deal, after all."

"A deal. Quite." Although his words said he believed her, his tone suggested otherwise.

Two footmen entered the room, and he pointed at the painting. "That one. And please wrap it securely. It will be traveling some distance."

Maggie stepped out of the way as the two men hefted it off the wall and carried it out. As soon as they were through the door, the marquis shut it behind them. Then he turned to her.

"I believe you have something to give me."

She wrapped her fingers around the key and pendant. "I don't have the painting yet. Get me to Hyde Park and the oak tree first."

He shot her a hard stare, then he nodded abruptly. "Very well. But if you double-cross me, Miss Maggie Blake, I will hunt you down until I get what is rightfully mine."

The threat sent a shiver down her spine. But he'd never find her, because she was going to jump back to her own time, or rather wake up from her dream. Confident that she'd be safe, she blithely agreed. "Okay."

His eyes narrowed. "I'm assuming that word means you understand that I am serious."

The stern look he gave her sent another shiver down her spine. "Yes." She didn't want to think about what he might do if this wasn't a dream.

"Excellent. We will have tea while we wait for my coach to be brought around and the painting prepared for travel," he declared, his threatening demeanor abruptly switching to one of polite graciousness.

As if on cue, a footman entered carrying a tray loaded with teapot, cups and a plate of tiny sandwiches. Another footman followed and moved a small table between the two chairs framing the fireplace. They set out the tea things, then left.

Disconcerted at the marquis's swift change from dangerous pirate to cordial host, Maggie just stood and watched, not sure what to do.

He indicated one of the chairs. "Please, countess, make yourself comfortable." His lips twitched with amusement.

Maggie narrowed her eyes at him, not pleased at his teasing. She was certain she would never be comfortable in his presence, but she once again perched on the edge of the chair opposite him.

"Would you care to pour, Miss Blake?" he asked, as he sat as well.

No, she really didn't, but decided that she should placate him since she'd already tried to steal his painting. She discovered he took his tea with cream no sugar, while she added a bit of sugar to hers. He piled a plate with biscuits and the tiny sandwiches of bread and butter. She couldn't bear the thought of eating anything.

After he had devoured four of the sandwiches and two biscuits, and when they had each sipped from their cups, he asked, "If you don't mind my asking, where are you from?" At her surprised glance, he smiled. "Your accent indicates you are not from London."

"Boston, in America," she said.

"Do you have family there?"

Maggie swallowed back her grief. "Yes. Well, I used to. My father died in a —." she stopped, realizing he'd never understand what a plane was. "An accident," she finished.

"My deepest condolences," he murmured.

She nodded, accepting his sympathy, then added, "My sister lived there too until she came to London to finish her book."

"Her book?" A single brow rose at his question.

"Yes, she's an author, like Jane Austen."

"I'm afraid I'm not familiar with that author," he said, taking another sip of tea.

Maggie remembered that Austen's books were first published anonymously. "She wrote *Sense and Sensibility* and *Pride and Prejudice*."

"Ah, that author," he said. "Did you come to London to visit your sister?"

Another stab of grief assailed her, this time with the added weight of worry. "I came to find her. She disappeared. And now I'm here in the past, and I have no idea how to find her, and my younger sister, who used to live in Boston with me and who now lives in Milan, is alone and must be worried about me, and I don't know how to let her know that I'm all right."

The words tumbled out before she could stop herself. Why was she telling this man about her troubles? He couldn't help her find Emma.

Sympathy entered his eyes. "Perhaps your sister is in the past, as well."

"What? No, she couldn't be." Even though she'd thought of that herself, she'd dismissed the idea as impossible. But maybe not. There was that journal she'd found. Had Emma time traveled to the past? If she had, was she in this past, or some other past? Emma couldn't be in this past, because Maggie was dreaming it. She was so confused. Besides, time travel was impossible.

Before she could worry over the answer to that question, Kelwin knocked on the door. "Your coach is ready, m'lord."

With relief, Maggie set down her teacup. The marquis waved her toward the door, and she headed out to the coach with the hope that soon, she'd be back in her own time.

Three

As soon as they arrived at the oak tree in Hyde Park, Maggie scrambled out of the clean and elegant coach with the comfortable leather seats and crystal-clear windows, a vast difference from the shabby vehicle that took them to the marquis's huge house. During the short ride, he had kept up a commentary on the residents of the mansions and townhouses they passed along the way. They even drove by the building where her father's flat was located, where her sister was living and where Maggie had been staying. She craned her neck as they passed it, to get a better view of the elegant brick mansion. A pair of trees flanked the front door and ivy climbed the walls, nearly obscuring one of the windows. The house appeared empty, as if no one lived there, but then she spotted an open window on one of the upper floors.

"It belongs to a widow, a recluse," the marquis told her. "A Mrs. Edwards."

The house intrigued her, and she wondered about the woman who lived in it. Why was she a recluse? Sorrow for the woman landed heavily in her chest, but she dismissed the sensation as only part of her dream. Besides, she had to get back to the spot where she had fallen into the past. Or fallen asleep. She was anxious to continue her search for Emma and to talk to Darcy.

The marquis lapsed into silence, but his gaze remained fixed on her. She could feel it like a physical touch. She didn't understand why she should have such a reaction, for she had only just met him. Besides, she was dreaming. She supposed anything was possible in a dream. But she was grateful he didn't attempt to ask her any questions. She'd told him enough. They entered Hyde Park and wound through the lanes until they came to the ancient oak tree. Maggie peered at it from her seat in the coach. She thought it was bigger, thicker through the trunk and more gnarly. But she was in a dream, and things in a dream always seemed a little different than in real life.

The marquis stepped down from the coach and guided her down, then directed his two footmen as they untied the huge painting from the top of the coach and set it carefully on the ground. He turned to her with a quizzical lift to his brow.

"Where would you like my men to place the painting?" he asked. "And how, pray tell, are you going to carry it?"

"I'm just going to hold onto it. It should travel with me, right?" Maggie hoped that was the case, even if she was dreaming.

"I have no idea whether it will travel with you or not," he said, a hint of exasperation underlying his words. "As a witch, don't you know such things?"

"I told you, I'm not a witch," she grumbled.

"As you say," he agreed without conviction. "I assure you that before today, I had no acquaintance with time travel, so I will leave it up to your expertise."

She gave a vague nod, because she certainly wasn't a witch and had no idea how to time travel either. But she needed to get back to her own time. Or wake up. So, she began examining the ground with a stomp here and a jump there. The hole she stepped into that brought her to the nineteenth century must be somewhere nearby. The oak tree was right there, so the hole had to be close. It had to be. As soon as she found it, she'd grab the painting, and — POOF! — she'd be gone. And wake up in the twenty-first century.

He watched her in silence for a few moments, then said, "Before you tumble back to your own time, countess, I would like my key, if you don't mind."

"Oh, sure." She ignored his teasing nickname.

Maggie slipped the chain over her head and held it up. The

last time, the pendant was glowing, and the key was very hot. Neither was happening. Maybe she wasn't in the right place. She glanced around. The tree was to her right, where it had been before. And she had been sitting on the grass right about in this spot when the marquis fell from the sky. And then—

Drat! She hadn't been sitting on the grass when they traveled back to his time. He'd had hold of her necklace, and she — Maggie gulped. He'd grabbed her necklace and dragged her up against his body. That muscular, hard body, with broad shoulders and sinewy thighs encased in tight buckskin. So, it *was* his fault that she had time traveled.

She peeked a glance at him. Her cheeks burned at the memory of him pressed against her. No, she wouldn't, couldn't ask him to do that again. Besides the embarrassment of the intimate position, he might end up travelling to the twenty-first century with her, and then what would she do with him? She'd feel obligated to teach him about her century and take care of him. Nope, she wasn't taking him back with her, not even in a dream.

But if she was dreaming, he would disappear as soon as she returned to her own time. So, she wouldn't have to watch out for him. A twinge of regret twisted through her at that thought. Then giving herself a mental shake, she told herself to get over it. He was only a figment of her imagination.

She slipped the chain back over her head.

"Miss Blake!" Her name was an annoyed reprimand.

"I know," she said, putting him off. "I just want to find the hole to step through first."

His eyes narrowed, his lips thinned, and he crossed his arms, but he lapsed into silence.

The time travel — or waking up — had to work without his looming presence against her, without his large, masculine body with its hard planes and shallow hollows pressed close. It just had to. Because no way was she going to let him get that near again.

Keeping the chain around her neck, she held it up with the pendant and key dangling. She walked back and forth, around the tree, onto the path, and back again. Hoping the pendant would start to glow and the key begin to warm, she jumped and stomped. She stepped softly. Over and over. Here, and there. Back and forth and around the tree. But nothing happened.

Absolutely nothing.

She didn't time travel, and she didn't wake up.

The pendant and key slipped from her fingers and fell against her chest. They felt as heavy as a lead weight. Disheartened, she sank to the grass beneath the tree.

"I can't find the hole!" she wailed. "It's disappeared! What am I going to do? This is all your fault!"

"It is not my fault," he said, affront coloring his tone. "I had nothing to do with this." He waved his hand back and forth between them. "Whatever this is."

"Of course it's your fault," she snapped, as she tried to

keep from crying. "I was minding my own business when—Bam! —you landed on the grass in front of me. And if you hadn't grabbed my key—"

"*My* key," he grated.

"—then I wouldn't be here in the past!"

The tears she had been holding back gathered and started to slip down her cheeks. Wrapping her arms around her head, she let it fall forward onto her knees. Her mind reeled. She couldn't wake up. This wasn't a dream. She really had traveled through time. It wasn't impossible. She was stuck. In the nineteenth century. With a man who claimed to be a marquis, but looked like a pirate. Who wanted her key. Because he said it was his.

What had she done to make Fate trick her like this?

SIMON FELT A PANG OF GUILT, DESPITE KNOWING HE'D HAD nothing to do with bringing her into his time. He'd watched the woman stomp and jump and tiptoe around the ancient oak, and he knew exactly what she was doing. She was going to double-cross him and take both the painting and his key back to her century. And that infuriated him, more than making him feel guilty. But beneath her antics and seemingly calm demeanor and her intent to cheat him, he could sense her desperation. He knew that feeling. Because he had been just as desperate not so long ago. So, he had let her try to find the hole back to her own time. He was ready to jump into that hole with her, so he wouldn't lose his key.

But now she sat dejected on the grass and unable to find her way back. Empathy stirred in his chest. If she truly were from another time, and he suspected she was, which amazed him, then she was completely alone, with no friends or family to help her. But her accusation that it was his fault that she had traveled through time? Absolutely not. Despite that, his honor demanded that he help her.

He stepped forward. "Miss Blake."

"What?" she mumbled without raising her head.

"Miss Blake," he repeated, this time with an edge, and held out his hand.

She looked up, her blue eyes a bit misty.

"First of all, I want to reiterate and make perfectly clear that I had nothing to do with your landing in my century," he said.

Behind the mistiness in her eyes, he saw an argument begin to form. Before she could voice it, he said, "It appears that you have not found the hole to take you back to wherever you came from. I am offering my assistance."

The argument in her eyes faded away. She squinted at his hand, then met his gaze. "To help me stand, or to help me live."

His lips quirked. He couldn't help himself. She was so

suspicious, so self-sufficient, so wily. So adorable. Despite his annoyance, knowing she was attempting to dupe him, he had enjoyed watching her stomp and jump and tiptoe.

"I am offering whatever help you may need," he said.

After a moment, she placed her hand, delicate and smooth, into his, and he pulled her to her feet. "Thanks," she said, the word clipped, indicating her reluctance.

"I think we should return to my house and discuss how we might resolve this very strange situation." He gestured at the coach. "Perhaps we might help each other."

Her glance cut from him to the coach and back again. "I don't see how I can help you. I don't know a soul in this time."

He cleared his throat. "If I may be so bold to suggest— You know me. And you have possession of my key."

Her fingers curled around it.

"And," he added for good measure, "you were about to try to steal my painting without proper payment. I believe you were trying to bilk me."

Her cheeks flamed and her glance slid away. "Sorry. I didn't think you'd mind because time travel is impossible, and I thought I was dreaming, and it was your fault I was here, and when I got back to my own time, centuries from now, you'd be de— Um, I didn't think you'd mind."

"I mind quite a bit, Miss Blake. I do not appreciate someone who tries to cheat. Since you are a woman, I will not call you out." He frowned.

Her eyes widened in horror. "Call me out? As in a duel? With pistols?"

"Or rapiers. I would accommodate the weapon of your choice." He shrugged with indifference.

A little choking sound came from her and her cheeks paled. "I don't — I don't —"

With an annoyed scowl, he declared, "I said I would not, Miss Blake. You need not concern yourself."

She blew out a breath and her shoulders dropped.

Did she truly believe that he would have challenged her to a duel? What sort of man did she think he was? But of course, she knew nothing about him. Likewise, he knew little about her. Which was why he would give no quarter in this battle of wits until he gained what was rightfully his. Using his sternest tone, he said, "But you have tried to steal from me, and you have possession of my property."

"Why do you need the key?"

The direct question surprised him. The women he knew would never be so forthright or abrupt. They would consider a man's business to be beyond their purview. And that key was very much his business. His *secret* business. Not to be discussed with anyone, especially a woman. A woman who was something other than what she appeared. Like a spy. Or a cunning baggage. Or a witch. But she was from another time, so her motive in wanting to know his business had to be something besides malicious mischief.

"I do not discuss my private affairs," he said stiffly.

She huffed. "Look, my dad gave me the key, just before he died. I told you that. So, it's sort of precious to me. I'm not going to give it up just because you want it. How do I know that it's really yours? It might belong to someone else who needs it just as much as you do. You could be lying."

He sputtered. "Lying? I do not lie. I am an honorable man."

"Prove it."

"Prove it?!" He was so incensed at the demand that he spun away and stalked a few steps before he said or did something he would regret. His honor had never been questioned before. Except, of course, when he had been arrested. But that was different. He'd been set up. Betrayed. Taking a calming breath, he turned back to her. "This is not the place for me to explain. Will you come back to my house, so we may discuss this in private?"

She said nothing.

"I could have you arrested for robbery." It was an empty threat, but he saw her eyes widen in fear.

"You wouldn't."

Shrugging a nonchalant shoulder, he said, "I am a marquis, Miss Blake. I can do anything I wish." Although he was who he said he was, the other part of that statement wasn't quite true.

Her shoulders sagged. "All right. I'll go back to your house." Then she sent him a hard look. "But no funny business."

"Funny business?"

"Yeah, like trying to take the key without my permission, or — or *funny business.*"

The way she emphasized those last two words made her meaning very clear. Instead of being insulted, sympathy crashed through him. The woman was alone, in a strange century, with no one to help or support her. Except him. And although filmy visions and wayward thoughts of what he would like to do with this woman flitted through his head, he definitely would not commit any *funny business.* Unless she consented.

Placing his hand over his heart, he said, "You have my solemn promise there will be no funny business." Then he indicated his coach. "Please, Miss Blake."

She studied him for a moment, then with a nod, she walked to the vehicle as if she were a countess.

Simon held back his smile. If nothing else, Miss Maggie Blake would be a challenge. And he liked nothing more than a challenge. Especially with a beautiful woman.

As soon as they arrived back at the house, the marquis ushered Maggie into the green, ivory and gold sitting room. The tea things had been cleared away, and the room appeared as pristine as when she had stepped into it earlier. Except for the empty space above the fireplace where the painting had hung. The two footmen wrestled the painting through the door, but instead of hanging it, the marquis directed them to leave it someplace out of the way.

She looked at the empty wall and shame scratched at her. She had never stolen anything before, and the magnitude of what she had tried to do nearly overwhelmed her. What had she been thinking? Maybe the disorientation of being in a century other than the one where she belonged had rattled her brain.

"Miss Blake."

Maggie jumped, because her name on his lips was a stern bark. But she couldn't let him see she was intimidated. Her chin tipped up.

"I'm sorry I tried to steal your painting," she said before he could chastise her — or have her arrested. "I've never done that before."

His gaze narrowed.

She ducked her head. "I didn't think I had really time traveled. I thought I was dreaming."

"Dreaming," he repeated, as if thinking over the concept. "About stealing. Then you must have some thievery in your blood." He was silent for a moment, then breathed out a sigh. "Apology accepted." He tipped his head, as if thinking over something. "What am I going to do about you?"

"You know, I'm not some inconvenient package that suddenly arrived on your doorstep," she huffed.

"You most certainly did arrive at an inconvenient time." His hands went to his hips as he studied her.

Maggie had the distinct impression that he was forming some plan and that she was going to be part of it. She backed away a step. "What are you thinking?"

He smiled, the smile of a predator. The smile of a pirate. "I think I have found the answer to our problem."

She didn't like the sound of that. "Yes? What is it?"

"We are going to enter society," he said. "And you will be my new wife."

"What?!" Maggie shook her head vehemently. "Absolutely not. No. No way."

The idea of being married made her itch because of her past experiences. The idea of being married to him made her break out in a cold sweat. She hardly knew him. He made her feel a smorgasbord of emotions. Unease with a dash of fear. Curiosity with a heap of fascination. Attraction with a generous helping of arousal. She definitely needed to stay away. Besides, what kind of marriage proposal was that? She dreamed of being swept off her feet when the man she finally fell in love with proposed to her. But no love was involved here. He didn't love her. And she certainly didn't love him.

He scowled. "I am not asking for your hand in marriage, Miss Blake. I am suggesting a deception."

"Oh." Relieved, she sank onto the green velvet chair. "Why?"

His mouth thinned. "I have been betrayed. By a scheming she-devil who would see me destroyed."

"What did you do to her to make her so angry?"

"I did nothing except believe her lies." Those green eyes snapped in fury.

She leaned away, very glad that his anger wasn't directed at her. Whatever this woman had done must have been horrible. Then something clicked into place.

On a gasp, she said, "Was she the reason you were in prison?"

His lips thinned and a muscle ticked in his jaw. "Yes," he hissed. Glancing away, he swallowed, and when he turned back to her, he had calmed. "She was my mistress, and she stole a very important document from me. I was unable to produce that document, so I was arrested and thrown into prison."

"What document?" She tried to think of any piece of paper that might get him arrested if he couldn't show it. A passport, maybe? But she didn't think people had those in 1814.

His eyes bored into her. "The one that was in the box that is opened by the key hanging on the chain around your neck."

"Oh." Maggie wrapped her fingers around the two trinkets dangling from her chain. Maybe the key did belong to him. "Where's the box?"

"That is a very good question, one that I would very much like to answer," he said. "Unfortunately, I don't know where it is. I would like your help to find it."

Maggie wasn't sure she wanted to get involved in a lover's quarrel, especially one that sounded deadly. His mistress must have been very, very angry with him to steal something that would put him in jail.

She shook her head, intending to tell him that she couldn't possibly help. Before she could say anything, he went down on one knee before her. And looked like a man about to propose marriage. Astounded, she found her words evaporate.

"Miss Blake." He took her hand. "Please. We will make a deal. If you help me, I will help you. I'll search for a way to send you back to your own time, and I will give you any painting you wish. I'll give you all the paintings and every stick of furniture in the house. Please."

His generous offer overwhelmed her. How desperate was he to offer so much? His thumb rubbed softly across the back of her hand. The sensation distracted her. It soothed. It sent a tingle up her arm. Glancing down at her hand, she watched his thumb as it traced back and forth, then around in a circle. Why did that feel so good?

It felt too good. She couldn't think straight. Slipping her

hand from his grasp, she sat back and found her brain worked again. She had many questions. And objections.

"But —"

Before she could say anything else, he placed a gentle finger across her lips. "Sh. If you agree, I will take care of everything," he said. "You will live here. As my wife, no one will question your presence in my house."

His finger stopped her protest, but it also created the strangest urge to lick it. Why ever would she want to do that? She jerked back, disconcerted at the impulse.

Frowning, she said, "If I live here, there'll be no funny business."

"Absolutely. No funny business." He placed his hand over his heart. "I promise."

Maggie thought she caught a twitch of his lips, but she couldn't be certain. Since he'd been a gentleman so far, she decided she'd be safe. Besides, she had nowhere else to go.

"And I keep the key until we find your box," she added.

His hesitation lasted only for a fraction of a second. "Very well."

"All right," she said with a nod. "I'll pretend to be your wife. Maybe if we find your box, the tree will send me back to my own time."

"Perhaps it will." He smiled, stood, and offered his hand.

Maggie was perfectly capable of standing on her own, but having a man act like a gentleman made her melt. She placed her hand in his, and he led her out of the room and up the grand staircase.

THEY STOPPED BEFORE A DOOR ON AN UPPER FLOOR AND HE flung it wide. The room beyond was dim, with the drapes drawn tight across the windows. Maggie could see the shape of a four-poster bed looming to one side, but the rest of the pieces of furniture were only vague, dark shadows. The marquis strode into the room and pulled open the drapes. Sunlight streamed in, and Maggie looked around in dismay. All the furniture was swathed in covers, and the carpet had been rolled up. Obviously, the room hadn't been used in quite a while.

The marquis surveyed the room with a frown. "I had forgotten this room had been closed up. I'll have Mrs. Alsop put it to rights. This was my sister's room."

"You have a sister?" she asked. For some reason, she had imagined him with no family, a man alone, forging a single path through the world.

A wry smile twisted his lips. "Yes. She was the scourge of my childhood, always pestering me. She is married now, wed to a viscount, and with a babe."

"I have two sisters," she said. "One younger, one older."

He looked at her, his gaze sympathetic. "One disappeared, one left behind."

"Yes." Maggie swallowed back her sorrow.

His chin dipped. "I am sorry. I did not mean to drag you to my time."

"Thank you." She smiled sadly. "I don't think it was really your fault."

"No? That eases my conscience." He opened a wardrobe against the wall to Maggie's right. "My sister left some frocks. They will do until we can get you to a modiste."

"A modiste? How long do you think I'll be here?" A surge of panic ran through her.

"I have no idea." His eyes had gone serious, and he lifted a hand as if to comfort her.

Before he could do that, which would surely make her dissolve into a sobbing lump, she turned to the clothes in the wardrobe. The dresses were filmy, frilly things, such as a young, unwed girl might wear. She took one out and held it up against her. The dress looked like it was at least two sizes too small, and the hem only reached the middle of her shin.

"Um, I think the reason your sister left them was because she had outgrown them," she said.

Looking befuddled and a bit embarrassed, he said, "Oh, of course." He glanced around the room again. "I've been away a long time."

Intrigued, she asked, "How long?"

"Two years and a bit more," he mused, as he stared into the room.

"Were you in prison all that time?"

His attention returned to her. "No."

The abrupt answer made her think he was hiding something, like the reason he needed the document in the box that her key opened. What had he been doing before being tossed into prison? Before she could quiz him again, he swung away.

"This room won't do. I believe there is a better option," he announced and strode out the door.

Maggie trailed him down the hall to a set of double doors that he flung open. Across a small sitting room were two other doors side by side, and he opened the one on the right.

"Ah," he said. "This is more appropriate." He waved her into the room.

Maggie stepped into a large, beautiful room, with the palest of pink walls and a Chinese carpet in pastel colors covering the floor. A tester bed dominated the room, its canopy and coverlet embroidered with colorful birds and flowers. A fainting couch upholstered with the same material lounged near the windows. Various small tables and a couple of elegant chairs were scattered in other spaces. Several windows draped in white damask let in the sunshine. A fireplace opened in the wall to her left.

The marquis strode to a doorway in the far corner and

looked into the space beyond. "Yes, the dressing room, just as I remember. This will do."

Maggie had never seen such an elegant bedroom, not even in the historical houses with their reconstructed furnishings that she had visited. She couldn't imagine staying in it and messing it up.

"This is a beautiful room," she said. "But it's much too nice. I'll stay in the other one."

He shook his head. "No, no. You need to stay in this one. As my wife, you should inhabit the bed chamber of the mistress of the house."

Maggie gulped. "This is your mother's room?"

"Well, not any longer. She died quite some time ago."

"I'm sorry." Maggie wasn't sure if she felt better about staying in the room or not.

"Thank you." He glanced around. "She was hardly here. She preferred to stay in the country. My housekeeper, Mrs. Alsop, keeps up the room in the hope that I'll bring home a wife." His lips twisted wryly. "I suppose I have." That green gaze landed on her with warm speculation.

"Um, yeah, I guess." Uncomfortable with the idea, Maggie pretended to examine her surroundings.

A knock on the door distracted her.

A middle-aged woman with a ring of keys hanging from a belt at her waist stood in the tiny hall. "Pardon, my lord." Two footmen carrying a brass hip tub stood behind her, along with several maids carrying two buckets each. The woman waved them to the door on the left.

"Thank you, Mrs. Alsop," the marquis said. "But I did not order a bath."

"Yes, my lord." Her mouth pursed. "That man you call a valet ordered it as soon as you walked through the front door."

"Ah, of course. Deems," he said, amusement lighting his eyes. "I do hope you haven't been badgering him too much, Mrs. Alsop. He does enjoy his outlandish cravats."

Intrigued by the exchange, Maggie wanted to meet the valet with the wild cravats, but most of her attention focused on the footmen and maids as they disappeared through the door in the corner of the room. She longed for that bath. With a surreptitious sniff, she checked her armpit. Yup, stinky, just as she thought, because she'd jogged, and traveled through time, and landed on the disgusting floor of a hired coach, and tried to steal a painting, and failed to get back to her own time, and—

The marquis diverted her attention. "Mrs. Alsop, this is Maggie Blake. She is — ah — she will be staying with us for a while."

"Of course, my lord," Mrs. Alsop said calmly, but her glance held a tiny chill.

Maggie wasn't sure what to do. Should she shake hands? The woman intimidated her. Impulsively, she dipped a tiny curtsey.

Mrs. Alsop's eyes widened in shock, and the marquis coughed, clearly covering a chuckle. Maggie's cheeks burned. Obviously, she'd committed a terrible faux pas.

"Miss Blake," the marquis said, sliding over her mistake, "will be acting as the marchioness for a time."

"Of course, my lord," the housekeeper said evenly, accepting his declaration as if he had merely requested bacon instead of ham for breakfast.

"Unfortunately, she has lost all her luggage." He made the statement sound like her suitcase had been put on a plane to San Diego while she had been flying to London. "Can you suggest a modiste that might be available?"

Mrs. Alsop's glance took in Maggie's shorts and tee shirt, then her gaze skittered away as if she were embarrassed. "I will send to Madame Fanchon straight away. Perhaps she will be able to accommodate the lady this afternoon."

"Excellent." The marquis nodded approval. "That will be all, Mrs. Alsop."

Maggie gripped her courage with two hands. "Um—Do you think—That is, if it's not too much trouble—Could I have a bath, too?" After all, if she was going to be stuck in this century, she might as well be clean.

Mrs. Alsop gave a nod. "Of course, miss."

The marquis cleared his throat. "Since Miss Blake is supposed to be my wife, I think you should use the proper title, Mrs. Alsop."

A line appeared between the woman's brows but quickly disappeared. "As you wish, my lord. I will instruct the staff."

Maggie opened her mouth to protest. She wasn't his wife, and she felt uncomfortable being addressed by anything except her name. But something about his declaration made her swallow her words. How much danger was he in if even the staff didn't know who she really was? How much danger was she in by agreeing to the deception?

Four

W rapped in a towel after her bath, Maggie stood in a corner of the bed chamber and watched in awe as Madame Fanchon and two girls unpacked a truck load of boxes and packages. Every piece of furniture was covered with dresses and underthings. Linen, silk, voile, cambric, all in pastel shades or white, with an occasional glimpse of something in a deeper hue. While Madame shook out and arranged, the two girls untied and unfolded. Occasionally, they whispered together in French. Maggie didn't remember much from her high school French class, but she understood when one of the girls cast a surreptitious glance her way and whispered, "*Elle est comme l'autre.*"

"Like the other one?" she asked. "What other one?" Did the girl mean Emma? No, that couldn't be.

"Oh, no, no, no." Madame waved away the question with

a charming chuckle, then sent the girls a stern look. "These young ones, they do not know when they should not wag their tongues. We do not speak of our other clients. Come, now, let us look at you."

The modiste indicated that Maggie should drop her towel.

Maggie clutched it tightly and shook her head. She'd always felt self-conscious about her body. She wasn't petite, like Emma, her older sister, and she wasn't willowy like Darcy, her younger sister. Jogging kept the weight off, but she didn't love the exercise like Emma. Her hips were too wide, and her breasts were bigger than she would have liked. So, she was not going to allow Madame Fanchon to take away the only protection she had against appraising eyes.

"Ah," the woman said with a discerning look. She snapped her fingers at one of the girls and spoke rapidly in French. As the girl handed her a filmy garment, she said to Maggie, "You are a beautiful woman. You should not hide it." She slipped a chemise over Maggie's head. "*Eh, voilà!*" Then she tugged away the towel.

A bit more comfortable in the chemise, even though it didn't hide much because the material was so fine, Maggie resigned herself to the ordeal of being measured from head to toe, trying on frock after frock, of being tucked and pinned and corseted. Hours later, the modiste left, and exhausted, Maggie sank into one of the chairs before the fireplace. She had two dresses, one a day dress of yellow striped cambric, and a dinner dress of pale violet silk. Madame Fanchon assured her that more would be coming. When she protested, the modiste told her that the Marquis of Wildford would want his marchioness to be *ravissent*. Ravishing.

She didn't feel ravishing. In fact, she felt rather silly. She plucked at the skirt of the day dress the modiste had insisted she wear. Madame Fanchon had added two rows of white eyelet at the hem so the dress would be long enough. Frilly wasn't Maggie's style, and certainly not long dresses that made her look like she was playing dress-up. She was used to wearing simple, business casual attire. But she was in the nineteenth century now and had to dress accordingly. Her tee shirt and shorts had been whisked away by one of the maids to be laundered. No telling when she'd see them again. She glanced longingly at her sneakers, tossed uncere-moniously into a corner. They would look ridiculous with the frock she was wearing.

What was she doing here? Why had Fate thrust her into the past? How was she going to return to her own time?

A knock came from the back corner of the room. When she investigated, she found another door, partially hidden beyond the bed, that she hadn't noticed. She opened it and saw the marquis standing on the other side.

He had bathed and changed his clothes while she had been busy with the modiste. A burgundy coat hugged his broad shoulders and beneath it was a dark blue, damask waistcoat. A black neckcloth tied in a simple knot accentuated the white of his shirt. Tight gray trousers were tucked into shiny hessians. He had shaved and brushed back his hair, which showed off his sharp cheekbones and square jaw. Her breath caught in her throat. He was the most attractive, the hottest man she'd ever seen. And he looked like a marquis, a vast difference from the way he had looked when he landed on the grass in front of her. She wanted to devour him with her eyes, but that would be rude.

Casting around for somewhere to look, she noticed that behind him was another bedroom. His bedroom. And the door she'd just opened connected the two rooms. The implications of that rattled around in her head. She'd definitely need to lock that door.

"Miss Blake," he said in greeting.

"Mr—" she halted, stumped. "What do I call you?"

Amusement lit his eyes. "I should be addressed as 'my lord.' Or by my title, Wildford. But I would be delighted if you called me Simon."

Something made her think that she shouldn't be calling him by his given name. "How about I call you Mr. Marquis?"

He chuckled. "Quite unusual, but then, you are an unusual lady. And looking splendid, by the way."

Although his glance didn't wander from her face, she tugged up the neckline of her gown. It was quite low, and with the stays acting as a push-up bra, showed off some cleavage. More than she'd ever shown off, even in a bathing suit.

"I thought we should promenade through Hyde Park," he said. "I would like to show off my new marchioness."

Maggie thought that sounded like she was his new toy, and he wanted to brag to the boys. She wanted no part of that.

Sticking out her bare foot, she said, "No promenading for me. No shoes. Unless you want me to wear those." She indicated her cast away sneakers.

He glanced at the sneakers, grimaced, turned back to contemplate her foot, then smiled. "It is a very lovely foot, but we certainly do not want to dirty it. We shall ride through Hyde Park in my phaeton, instead."

"But—"

He cut off her protest with a raised brow. "Are you reneging on our deal, Miss Blake?"

She really wanted to go back on the deal. But she had nowhere else to go. If she didn't go along with his plan, whatever that was, he would throw her out.

"All right," she grumbled. "I'll go for a ride with you."

"Excellent. I'll have the horses and phaeton brought around." As he turned to leave, he tossed over his shoulder, "Mrs. Alsop will provide you with anything else you might need."

Maggie watched him stride across his room to the door that led into the hall. As she admired his muscular back and the coat that fit perfectly across his shoulders, she wondered what else she might need, besides a pair of shoes. Although she was very familiar with the style of house furnishings of the different historical periods, her knowledge of the fashion of the time was superficial. But her curiosity about the upcoming ride through Hyde Park dissolved as she gazed at the empty bed chamber before her.

It was a masculine room, decorated in plum and red. A tester bed that appeared even larger than the one in her room dominated the space. A wardrobe towered against one wall, and two wing chairs bracketed the fireplace. She itched to examine the room more closely to discover more about the man who occupied it, but if she didn't appear downstairs, she knew that the marquis would come looking for her. Instead of stepping forward into the room, she backed away, firmly closing and locking the door.

Learning about the Marquis of Wildford would take more than the few minutes she had. It would take hours, maybe even days, weeks, months. Of course, she wouldn't be in the nineteenth century for that long, because she didn't belong here. But in the little time she had, she would learn as much as she could about the mysterious man who had dropped from the sky.

Simon slowly paced across the entry hall, turned when he reached the wall, and paced back. Tapping his gloves against his thigh, he glanced up the staircase. Where was she? His phaeton was waiting out front. The horses were getting restless. When he had left her, she seemed ready to go on a drive. Perfectly put together, except for missing a pair of shoes. The memory of her bare toes peeking out from beneath her frock made him swallow.

He'd had the most indecent urge to cup her foot in his hand and suck on each one of those little pink toes. Why would he want to do that? Especially with her. The woman was the most exasperating creature he had ever met. He must be suffering some effect of being tossed from century to century. That was the only answer.

She appeared at the top of the stairs. Finally. She had a shawl draped over her shoulders and awkwardly held a closed parasol. A bonnet with an absurdly large brim sat on her head. Mrs. Alsop must have rummaged through his sister's left-behind belongings, because he remembered that bonnet and teasing his sister about it. For some reason, it looked quite becoming on Miss Blake.

As she stepped down the stairs, her bare toes peeked out from beneath her frock, and he found himself staring, wondering how she would react to his taking each one into his mouth and—. No, no, that would not do. He thought his housekeeper might have found something to cover those intriguing toes.

"Mrs. Alsop!" he bellowed.

Kelwin emerged from one of the rooms nearby. "Sir? I believe Mrs. Alsop is above stairs. She mentioned searching for something." He glanced up and a smile pulled at his mouth. "Appears she found it," he murmured.

Simon's exasperation was reaching the breaking point. "Just because you served as my first mate and saved my life, does not give you the right to comment on *her*."

Kelwin coughed, clearly covering a laugh. "Of course not, sir."

"And I would appreciate if you would use the correct form of address while you are serving as my butler," Simon snapped.

"Of course, my lord," Kelwin responded with a straight face. Then, as he turned away, he said with a grin, "Aye, aye, captain, sir."

Simon gritted his teeth. Kelwin knew him too well, and not only as the Marquis of Wildford. But he would deal with his butler later, for Miss Blake, his counterfeit marchioness, had reached the bottom of the stairs.

Just as she began to step off the last step, he said, "Wait, please."

He tucked his gloves into his pocket, a practice that Deems, his valet, would highly disapprove because they ruined the line of his coat, and strode to meet her. She stood on the lowest step, so was nearly the same height as he was.

He made the mistake of looking into those incredible blue eyes.

"I — ah—" For a moment, he couldn't remember what he was about to say.

A line appeared between her brows. "Yes? I thought you wanted to go for a ride through Hyde Park. Well, here I am, ready for a ride. I've got my umbrella and my shawl, and your housekeeper plunked this ridiculous hat on my head."

At her vexed comment, his brain cleared. A corner of his mouth tugged up. "You are a vision in that hat. But you should not be walking out with no shoes. Allow me." Before she could protest, he swept her up into his arms.

Her cry of surprise echoed in his ear, but the sensation of her arm around his neck made him smile. She was a delightful armful, and thoughts of carrying her to his bed without layers of clothing between them rose up in his head. God's teeth! No! Absolutely not! He was not going to entangle himself with her. Not like that. She was from another century. She might be a witch. She had his key. Which he very much wanted, and she had refused to give him. And which lay very nicely in the valley between her lovely breasts.

With resolve, he dragged his gaze away from that intriguing sight and focused on the door, which Kelwin held open.

"Enjoy your ride, my lord, my lady," his butler said.

Simon ignored the amused glint in Kelwin's eyes as Miss

Blake thanked him. After setting her on the seat of his phaeton, he climbed up, donned his driving gloves and snapped the reins.

"I could have walked, you know," she said.

"As I said, no shoes." He focused on steering the horses onto the street.

"I've walked barefoot before." She stuck out a foot and wiggled her toes.

At that sight, he jerked on the reins, nearly causing the horses to veer off the street. Why did those toes fascinate him so?

He concentrated on driving the horses as he said, "Please keep your feet covered. You will scandalize anyone who sees them."

"If you didn't want to scandalize anyone, why did you insist that we go for a ride through Hyde Park?" she asked as she tucked the skirt of her frock over her toes.

"I wish to make it known that I have returned to London," he said.

"Why? Where have you been? Besides prison?"

He hesitated. Was her question merely curiosity, or was it motivated by something more sinister? She had already tried to steal from him. What would she do with the information if he told her where he had been? Sell that as well? He decided to be vague until he learned if he could trust her.

"I've been out of the country," he said. Then, with relief, he turned into Hyde Park and changed the subject before she could ask anything else. "If we meet any acquaintances, you will only have to nod and smile when I introduce you, and perhaps offer your hand."

"So, I'm to be your sweet, adoring wife who doesn't have a thought in her head," she said.

He sent her a grin. "You may have all the thoughts you wish, Miss Blake. And I would enjoy hearing them. Just don't reveal them to anyone else unless you can trust them."

Simon wondered if he were warning her against himself. He'd been playing a role for far too long and wasn't sure he wouldn't revert back to the loose morals he'd practiced while executing that role. She'd tried to steal from him and still wore his key about her neck, so perhaps he couldn't trust himself to be completely honorable. He could part with a painting, but the key would save his life. If he didn't retrieve it— He was distracted by the snap of her parasol opening.

"I can keep my thoughts to myself," she declared, and lifted her nose in the air.

Simon swallowed a chuckle. She had transformed into a prim lady, acting as if even the trees should bow as she passed.

A carriage approached, accompanied by two riders. He recognized the men, and his jaw clenched. One of them was the Baron Cuthbert, who had ridiculed every proposal he had ever raised when he occupied his seat in the House of Lords several years ago. Not only that, the man disagreed with the war against Napoleon, a cause that Simon supported.

The other man was someone he disliked nearly as much. Roger Bowker, who was as lively as a stone wall, but seemed to be acquainted with every member of the ton. He ingratiated himself into the most exclusive places. Simon remembered him from his school days as knavish and mean.

Riding in the carriage were Cuthbert's wife and daughter, two of the most disagreeable females he had ever met. He glanced at Miss Blake. Would she be able to play her part? If she didn't, both of the men, and especially the women, would know immediately that something was amiss. The last thing he needed was for them to be suspicious.

Because he did not want to go back to prison.

Five

Maggie gripped her parasol and sat up very straight as the carriage approached. She noticed her companion's hands tighten on the reins and felt him stiffen, even though his calm expression never changed. Meeting this group disturbed him in some way. Intrigued, she decided to pay close attention. Maybe she would learn something about the enigmatic marquis.

The two carriages came abreast of each other and slowed. The older man on a horse nodded a cool, polite greeting.

"Wildford," he said. "We have not seen you in Lords for quite some time."

"I have been traveling," the marquis said. "And I have wed. Allow me to introduce the Marchioness of Wildford." He took Maggie's hand and sent her a warm smile.

Maggie smiled back. She couldn't help herself when he looked at her with those eyes.

And his warm fingers wrapped around her hand made her both want to hold on forever and pull away immediately. What was wrong with her? His smile and his gentle grip were all an act. She had to remember that and not let her hormones mess up her thinking.

He introduced the older man as the Baron Cuthbert and the women in the carriage. Maggie barely heard him, focused as she was on the warm, calloused feeling of his fingers, but she gathered the women were connected to the baron.

"I am very pleased to meet you," she said in the most snobbish tone she could muster.

The marquis raised an amused brow at her, then he introduced the other man, Roger Bowker, the most nondescript man she had ever seen. Everything about him seemed beige. Even his eyes. But those eyes, even though they were nearly colorless, sent a chill up her back. He nodded and smiled and was perfectly polite, but she felt as if he wanted to dissect her.

The baroness sniffed loudly, raised her lorgnette, and examined Maggie from her head to her toes, which she tucked farther beneath her skirt. "We are quite surprised to hear you have wed so suddenly, Wildford," she said. "I understood that you were not in the market for a wife. But here you are, leg-shackled, and with a foreigner." She sniffed again.

"The marchioness is from America," he said. "Not exactly a foreigner."

"Nevertheless," the baroness said. "Well, you must come to visit. A dinner party, I think, so we may get to know your little marchioness. I will send round a note."

"Of course," he said, tipping his hat. "We shall look forward to it." Then he released her hand, snapped the reins and they rolled away.

Maggie's shoulders slumped in relief, from both his liberating her hand and escaping from the strangers. "What disagreeable people! Do we really have to go to dinner? And their daughter looked as if she was about to burst into tears at any moment. Or claw my eyes out. I couldn't decide. I didn't even get her name."

He chuckled. "She is the Honorable Agnes Cuthbert."

Maggie cast a teasing glance at him. "She has a thing for you."

"A thing?"

"She likes you." At his confounded expression, Maggie laughed. "I think she was disappointed that you introduced me as your wife."

"Good God! I have never shown the slightest interest in her. I would never — I couldn't possibly —" A muscle jumped in his jaw, and he retreated into grumpy silence.

Entertained at his disconcerted response, Maggie turned her attention to the park around her. The birds twittered and flew from branch to branch. Swans glided on the Serpentine, the large pond in the middle of the park. The breeze was soft. Despite being wary about the man beside her, the ride in the phaeton was very enjoyable. They passed several other groups of people out for an afternoon ride or stroll. Since the marquis didn't stop to chat, all she had to do was smile and nod a greeting. And then they headed back to the house.

The closer they got, the more apprehensive Maggie grew. What would be expected of her as the "wife" of the marquis? Perhaps she could plead an illness. But she'd go crazy if she had to stay in the house all day. Maybe she could sneak out in disguise. After all, no one really knew her.

They turned through the impressive iron gates of his house and stopped before the steps leading up to the front door. Maggie drew a breath to steady her nerves. The day had been busy and distracting and so she'd had little time to think about her situation. But night was coming soon. And then the next day. And the day after that. How long would she be in the past? Her fingers curled into her skirt in worry and anxiety.

A boy ran forward to catch the bridles of the horses. The marquis jumped down, strode around to her side of the phaeton, and before she could protest, scooped her up in his arms. Again.

"Don't say a word, Miss Blake," he murmured. "There's no telling who is watching, and we don't want to start gossip about discord in our marriage."

Maggie wasn't sure if he was serious, but she glanced around at the quiet street. Not one person was out. But maybe they watched from behind curtained windows. She slipped her arm around his neck. Despite feeling a bit silly about being carried, she couldn't deny the pleasant way his chest supported her, nor the strength of his arms.

"Do all husbands tote their new wives around like this?" she asked.

His lips twitched. "Only those who are smitten."

Maggie couldn't resist asking, "Are you smitten, Mr. Marquis?" She touched a teasing finger to his chest.

"Definitely." He turned his head, and she caught the full impact of that gaze. "Would you like to know how smitten I am?"

She gulped. "Ah—"

The corners of his eyes crinkled and he glanced away. "My answer isn't for polite company, and Kelwin is holding the door for us. Perhaps another time."

Both relieved and frustrated, Maggie forced a smile at the butler. She suspected the marquis wasn't smitten at all, that he would remind her she had tried to steal from him and that he wanted his key. At the same time, the strength of his arms and the warmth from his body made her wonder what he would have said if he were smitten with her. Because if she were smitten with him, she'd be climbing all over him. And touching, and kissing, and—*Stop. Just stop.* She wasn't going to do any of those things.

Because she was going to return to her own time and forget about him.

SOON AFTER, SIMON SAT AT ONE END OF THE DINING ROOM table and gazed to the other end where his houseguest-thief-counterfeit marchioness-possible witch sat eating her dinner. She tucked into her meal like a sailor who was having his first meal ashore after being at sea for months. He had never seen a woman enjoy her food quite so much. Every woman with whom he had dined, including his mother and his sister, had nibbled at the food on their plates as if afraid it might come back to life. Miss Blake, on the other hand, appeared to enjoy eating. Both amused and in awe, he put down his fork and enjoyed the show.

His cook had prepared a simple meal of roast chicken stuffed with herbed rice, boiled buttered potatoes, and creamed celery. He had relished the good food after being in prison and had ignored good manners by eating in silence rather than holding a conversation with his table companion. But Miss Blake didn't seem to mind, for she was completely focused on her meal.

She picked up a chicken leg with her fingers, rested her

elbows on the table, and took a bite. Juice from the meat escaped at the corner of her mouth and her pink tongue swiped it up. Ignoring her atrocious manners, he imagined licking at the same spot, then running his tongue across that pouty bottom lip. Dismay at where his thoughts roamed jolted him, and he gave himself a mental kick. What was it about this woman that prompted him to conjure up such images? He should be suspicious of her and keep her at arm's length, which was the exact opposite of where he wanted her to be.

She glanced up, saw him watching, and placed the chicken leg on her plate. A blush spread across her cheeks. After using her napkin, she snapped, "What?"

The abrupt demand made his lips quirk. "I think before I take you out in public, you will have to learn some manners, Miss Blake."

"I know manners," she said, sitting up straight. "I was hungry. I hadn't eaten all day."

"I offered you tea earlier."

Her brows snapped together. "I had just tumbled through centuries and been bundled into a coach without my knowledge by a man who wanted something that was mine. How could I eat anything?"

"My apologies," he said with a nod. "But you will have to learn our manners if we are to embark on our charade."

"That wasn't part of the deal." Her bottom lip set mulishly.

"I could have you arrested for thievery." He raised a challenging brow.

The look she sent him held knives. Then her shoulders slumped. "Fine. Whatever you want, Mr. Marquis."

Smothering his chuckle, he took a sip of wine. "If you were at a dinner party, how would you deport yourself?"

Her eyes narrowed. "Is this a test?"

"Let's call it an inquiry." He smiled. "I would like to know if you could pass for my marchioness."

"A little late for that now," she grumbled. "What if I can't?"

It was a little late. He'd already introduced her to the Baroness Cuthbert, who would surely spread the gossip about his marriage, and they'd passed several of his acquaintances in Hyde Park, who had seen her beside him in the phaeton. That had been his objective, of course, to let London know he had returned. But as he watched her eat, doubts had slipped into his head. He'd been much too impulsive to suggest the ruse, something that went against his normal mode of behavior. But he was also very good at rethinking his position and getting out of any difficulty. Like now.

He smiled smoothly. "You will need lessons in deportment."

"Lessons in —" Her words ended in a sputter of indignation, then she clamped her lips together and sent him a calculating gaze. She wiped her fingers and mouth with her napkin, placed it across her lap and sat up straight. Picking up her fork, she stabbed a chunk of celery. "This is a very delicious dish, Mr. Marquis," she said in a tone that sounded like she was encased in ice. "I must have your cook send the recipe round to my cook." Then she popped the celery into her mouth and chewed delicately.

With difficulty, Simon contained the bubble of laughter that wanted to burst forth. He hadn't had the urge to laugh in a long time, and he was afraid if he let it go, he would lose control. This wasn't the time to do that. Not before this woman, who was from the future and had tried to steal from him. He needed to know he could trust her before he allowed himself to feel easy around her.

"Very well, Miss Blake," he acceded. "You've answered my inquiry. Lessons in deportment aren't required." But he wasn't done. "Can you dance?"

A mischievous glint entered her eyes. Without a word, she stood, closed her eyes a moment, then hummed some notes. Her eyes snapped open, and she began swaying her hips and weaving her arms above her head. The movements were sinuous and enthralling and the most erotic thing Simon had ever seen. Blood rushed to his privates, and all he could think of was having her move like that beneath him. Or above him. Anywhere she wanted to be, just as long as it was against him.

Bloody hell, no! He shifted and lowered his brows as he forced his thoughts away from those dangerous shores.

"What," he asked, "are you doing?" He congratulated himself on sounding so normal.

She froze. Her arms dropped. She blinked. "Isn't that what you meant? That's how we dance in my time." Her tone was pure innocence. "Oh," she said, her mouth a perfect oval. "I know what you mean." She posed as if holding something quite large, like a man's body.

He saw himself in the other half of that pose, one of her delicate hands on his shoulder, her other hand cupped in his palm. Blinking away the vision, he gripped a random spoon to ground himself and waited to see what she would do.

She counted, "1-2-3, 1-2-3, 1-2-3—." Then she waltzed around the dining table.

Enthralled, Simon watched her. She seemed to float. As she passed behind him, he caught a whiff of something lightly sweet, like roses, and he dragged it into his lungs. Her bare toes peeked out as her frock swirled around her. Closing his eyes, he counted as well, only his numbers went to ten, then twenty, then thirty, as he fought the urge to dance with her. And sweep her up in his arms and lay her out across his bed so he could suck on those toes.

"That's enough, Miss Blake," he barked. "Tomorrow, we visit a shoemaker."

Stopping abruptly, she asked in honeyed tones, "Have I passed your test, Mr. Marquis?"

Foregoing an answer, he stood and bowed, desperately hiding the erection in his pantaloons. "I bid you good evening, Miss Blake." Then he escaped as quickly and with as much dignity as he possessed.

Her delighted laughter followed him up the stairs. Only after he shut himself in his bedchamber did he feel safe. The woman was a witch of the highest order. She could have her sport for now, but tomorrow was a new day. He could think of any number of ways to torment her.

With a smile, he called to Deems to bring his banyan. He had hours left to contemplate his revenge.

LAUGHING, MAGGIE WATCHED HIM ABRUPTLY STRIDE OUT OF the room. He had asked if she could dance, so she'd shown him. Well, maybe she had teased just a tiny bit, especially when she had that rock song playing in her head. She chuckled as she thought about the expression on his face, awe with a flash of heat in his eyes. When he had bowed, she caught a glimpse of the bulge in his pants.

Knowing he had been aware made her own body heat up. As she had twirled around the table, the intensity in his jade eyes had set off tiny sparks along her skin. Her nipples had pressed against her clothing with wanting—the pinch of his fingers, the slide of his tongue, the suck of his mouth. Why did that aggravating man do that to her? Her amusement fading, with a huff, she left the dining room and headed up to her own bedchamber. She hoped he was already shut up behind his door.

As quietly as possible, she opened the door to her side of the suite. A maid was there to help her undress, which she did as quickly as possible, then dismissed the girl. She'd never had a maid in her life, and having someone wait on her made her uncomfortable, but she needed the help to unlace from the stays and undergarments. After climbing into bed, she turned on her side. A strip of soft light peeped beneath the door into his room. He was still awake.

She watched a shadow pass through the light, then back again. If she listened very hard, she could hear his muffled footsteps. Back and forth. And again. He was pacing. The light to dark to light beneath the door annoyed her, so she flipped to her other side. But when she closed her eyes, she imagined that door opening, those quiet footfalls coming closer, a gentle touch to her cheek, a kiss to the sensitive spot at the curve of her shoulder. The cup of his hand on her breast.

Her eyes snapped open, and she flounced onto her back. She reminded herself that she was in the past, living in the house of a mysterious marquis-pirate, pretending to be his wife for a short time. Surely, she'd be able to get back to her own time soon, and he would only be a memory. So, she wasn't going to allow her hormones to overcome her good sense. She closed her eyes, but he rose up behind her eyelids in the form she had first seen him, disheveled and annoyed and steely. And sizzling hot.

Since he'd transformed from pirate to marquis, his blatant sexuality had toned down with structured clothing, but she knew what was lurking beneath the wool and linen and damask. Blowing out a breath, she rolled to her side and saw his shadow passing back and forth again beneath the door.

Hours passed. Or minutes. She wasn't sure which. Eventually, the strip of light seeping under the door went out. She heard the creak of his bed and absolutely did not want to imagine what acrobatics the two of them could perform on that huge mattress. Trying to distract herself with designing a chair in her head, she ended up with a rocker for two that could have been used in a porn movie. What was wrong with her?

She scrambled out of bed. This time, it was her turn to pace. After working off some of her excess energy, she flopped into one of the chairs near the fireplace, where she eventually dozed off and on until morning.

Six

Maggie again sat next to the marquis in his phaeton as they made their way to the shoemaker. A headache throbbed dully behind her eyes from her sleepless night. Of course, it was his fault she was so grumpy. If he hadn't quizzed her so arrogantly about her manners, she wouldn't have teased him with her dancing. If that green gaze of his hadn't watched her so intently, she wouldn't have felt it like a touch. Annoyed she hadn't slept, she blamed her headache on him. If he wasn't so gorgeously sexy, she would have been able to sleep. And she wouldn't have a headache. And she wouldn't have teased him. And had him look like he wanted to do all sorts of naughty things to her. Which kept her awake all night. And gave her a headache. Her brain kept spiraling around and around.

She had taken advantage of the luxury of breakfast in her

room, so she could stay away from him as long as possible. A cowardly thing to do, but necessary for her sanity. They were going shoe shopping, and she was riding with him in his phaeton, sitting right next to him, his muscular thigh barely inches away. The heat from his body seeped through her layers of petticoat and skirt, but the seat was too narrow to allow her to inch away.

She had slipped on her sneakers because she was done with him carrying her around. If someone commented on her strange footwear, she'd find some explanation. As much as she liked the feel of his arms and chest against her, she didn't enjoy the sense of helplessness. She ran a business for goodness' sake. She wasn't a weak female.

When she descended the stairs, his glance went to her sneaker-covered feet, and a strange expression flashed through his eyes before he covered it up with bland courtesy. Had it been irritation? Disappointment? Anger? She couldn't decipher it, so she ignored it.

The air was cool as they rode along, and she was glad for the short little jacket, called a spencer, that Madame Fanchon had delivered early that morning, along with two more dresses and a pair of stockings. She wore one of the dresses, a lovely walking dress of creamy muslin printed with tiny green leaves, and left the other of pink-striped cotton for another time.

Their drive out of the marquis's quiet neighborhood and into increasingly busier streets, lined with shops and small businesses was made in near silence between them. He concentrated on the horses, and she watched the passing scenery. They finally stopped before a shoe shop with a sign hanging above the door proclaiming, "Wood. Cordwainer. Ladies Shoes."

Cordwainer? she wondered. As in cords of wood? "Are all shoes made out of wood?" she asked. If that were the case, then she'd wear her sneakers, no matter what strange looks she received.

Mr. Marquis glanced at her as if trying to decide if she were serious or joking. "No," he said, then glanced up at the sign. His mouth twitched. "Wood is the man's name. He is a cordwainer, someone who makes shoes."

"Oh." Her cheeks heated. She'd have to learn the different terms for things.

Politely ignoring her embarrassment, he reached under the seat and pulled out a pair of clogs, which were made of wood, with ribbon ties. "These are to protect ladies' shoes from that." He motioned to the mud of the road spotted with horse dung. "I thought they would be more acceptable than your footwear," he said. "What you are wearing might cause questions that you don't wish to answer. I borrowed these from one of the maids."

Maggie looked from her comfortable sneakers to the clogs, little more than a thick wooden sole and a piece of leather that tied across the instep. Her sneakers were high-tech runners, designed on a computer and manufactured by a robot, a vast difference from the handmade clogs that he held out to her. But she needed to fit in. With a nod, she took the clogs and changed.

He helped her down from the phaeton and she clattered across the cobblestones to the entrance. When they entered the shoe shop, the scent of leather and polish filled her nose. Shelves along one wall held wooden forms shaped like feet, each labeled with a name or initials. A counter at the back stood before other shelves with boots and shoes of every color and size. Two small chairs with tables next to them took up the other wall.

A man hustled out from the back room. "I am Joseph Wood. May I help you, sir?" he asked.

The marquis introduced himself, then said, "The marchioness is in need of shoes. A thief stole her valise when we landed on the docks."

"Of course, my lord." He indicated one of the chairs. "If the lady would be so kind as to sit, I can measure her foot."

Maggie sat in one of the chairs. Used to trying on shoes by herself, she bent to untie one of the clogs. Mr. Wood hurriedly went down on one knee before her.

"Please, my lady, allow me," he said. With business-like efficiency, he untied her clog and slipped it off, then placed her foot on his bent knee. He pulled out a measuring tape and hummed as he wrote down every measurement of her foot on a slip of paper.

As he finished, Mr. Marquis said, "We will need everyday

shoes, half-boots and dancing slippers. Madame Fanchon is making frocks, so please consult with her about color. The marchioness will also need something immediately. Do you have anything available?"

Maggie sat in stunned silence at the generosity of the marquis.

Mr. Wood rose. "I will see what I have in the back." With a bow, he excused himself.

Just as he did, the bell above the door tinkled, announcing a new arrival. The Baroness Cuthbert swept in, followed by her daughter, the Honorable Agnes.

"Wildford," the baroness greeted.

The marquis grimaced, then his expression went bland as he turned to greet the woman. "Baroness. Always a pleasure."

Maggie ducked her head to hide her smile.

"What a surprise to see you here," the woman said. "I thought you got your boots from Hoby."

"The marchioness needed shoes," the marquis said smoothly. "One of her valises was stolen at the docks."

While the baroness made sympathetic noises and a conversation about the audacity of thieves ensued, her daughter stepped closer to Maggie.

"How did you land him?" Agnes whispered. "He had sworn off marriage."

Maggie glanced up at her in surprise. "Land him? He's not a fish."

"He was the biggest catch three seasons ago. And then he disappeared." Her eyes glittered with wild emotion. "Where did you find him?"

"Um." *Finding* wasn't exactly the right term. But Maggie wasn't going there. She wanted to say Hyde Park, but she had the feeling that would require too much explanation, so she improvised. "America. In Boston."

"Impossible," Agnes snapped. "He would never be in Boston. We're at war with America."

Maggie nearly slapped her forehead. Of course. She was in the year 1814. England and America were involved in the War of 1812 that didn't end until 1815. "Um, he was on a diplomatic mission." The fabrications kept piling up. She had to tell the marquis about them so they could keep their story straight.

Agnes's eyes narrowed into slits. "He was supposed to be mine," she hissed. "And I mean to have him."

The girl's animosity was palpable. Speechless, Maggie blinked. From what the marquis had said when they met the family in the park, he'd never had any intentions toward her. Thankfully, before Maggie needed to respond, Mr. Wood popped out from the back of the shop.

"I have the perfect footwear," he announced.

Agnes drifted away, and the process of trying on a pair of half-boots and then making arrangements to have the other shoes delivered as quickly as possible took Maggie's attention. Even though the baroness and her daughter examined the ready-made shoes displayed on the back wall, she felt as though the two of them were hanging on her every word and action.

When Maggie and Mr. Marquis turned to leave, the baroness called out, "My invitation will be arriving soon, Wildford. I hope you will be able to accept."

The marquis merely tipped his hat, took Maggie by the elbow and hurried her out the door. She was glad to escape, because the Honorable Agnes unnerved her.

Simon was relieved to be out of the presence of Baroness Cuthbert and her daughter, and it appeared Miss Blake was as well, as he helped her up to the seat of his phaeton. After he got the horses going, her stiff posture indicated something was amiss. She no longer swayed comfortably as they rolled along, but instead she sat ramrod straight, gripping the seat rail. What had upset her?

Surely not the Honorable Agnes. The girl was harmless and cloyingly sweet. She had made her come out three seasons past, just before he had left London. He wondered why she hadn't snagged a husband by now. Although she wasn't beautiful, she was passably attractive and had an interesting dimple in her chin. He remembered dancing with her once or twice at a ball and at Almack's, but found her sweetness over-powering and her conversation boring. Besides, he wasn't in the market for a wife.

He glanced at the woman beside him. In contrast, Miss Blake had a presence that drew the eye. She was vibrant and fearless. And sassy. That set her apart from other women, as if she was very aware of who she was and what she wanted. Far from boring, she intrigued him. Her dancing the night before had been riveting. More than that. Sensual. Seductive. Arousing. And those toes—

He gulped and snuck a quick peek down. Thankfully, they were demurely covered now. He'd never been so aware of a woman's toes, not even those of his previous mistresses. Before he had glimpsed Miss Blake's, toes were merely appendages at the end of a woman's foot. But her toes fascinated him. And her toes were connected to her feet, which were dainty, and then her ankles, slim and nicely formed. Above those ankles were her lovely legs, shapely and long, and those led up... Good God!

Maybe she *was* a witch, and had cast a spell on him. No, that was just foolishness. Keeping his eyes on the road, he decided his brain must have been rattled around a bit when he was pulled from his prison cell, dropped into the future, and then whisked back to his own time. That was the only explanation.

He remembered his decision to get retribution for her teasing dance the night before, but that was for later. Something had upset her, and he wanted to know what it was. He didn't like that she was distressed. Whatever it was, he wanted to fix it.

Stopping at the edge of St. James Park, he turned to her. "Is something bothering you, Miss Blake?"

She swung to him as if surprised to hear him speak. "What? Oh, no. Nothing." Then she looked out over the park.

"I know the baroness is not the most pleasant of people, but I try not to offend her," he said.

She shook her head. "No, it wasn't the baroness."

"Then tell me." He took her hand and noticed with disappointment that of course she wore gloves. No touching that soft skin, but at the edge of the glove, he caught a tempting glimpse of creamy skin.

Her teeth caught her bottom lip, and she cast a speculative glance at him.

Something had occurred at the cordwainer's, and he wanted to know what it was. "Please, tell me what troubles you."

She looked as if she were about to say something, then merely shook her head.

"Do the shoes not please you?"

A tiny smile curved her lips. "You have been very generous. Thank you for the shoes, and the dresses, and everything."

She wouldn't tell him. Instead of prying it out of her, he embarked on his plan for revenge. "You are most welcome."

He raised her hand to his mouth, but instead of kissing the air above her knuckles, he touched his tongue to the tiny sliver of skin visible between her glove and her sleeve. Her tiny indrawn breath was his reward. Still bent over her wrist, he chanced a glance up at her. But rather than startled affront, which was what he expected, her look was one of suspicious speculation.

"Are you trying to seduce me, Mr. Marquis?"

He feigned shock. "Miss Blake, you wound me."

"Ha." That single syllable indicated her complete disbelief. "How many women have you seduced?"

Surprised at her audacious question, he blinked. He had to remember she wasn't a retiring miss. She was bold and brave and wily. And that invited some taunting. Leaning in, he murmured, "How many men have you seduced?"

Her eyes widened just the tiniest bit, but she didn't look away. Instead, she appeared mesmerized, those sapphire eyes staring into his. He felt himself falling into them. Time stretched. An hour passed. Or a minute. Or a second. Then she laughed.

"Oh, dozens," she said. "I've lost count of the number of men I've seduced."

"A vixen, then," he murmured, falling in with her play, because he didn't believe her for even a moment. "Are you trying to seduce *me*, Miss Blake?"

She gave him a look from beneath her lashes that sent heat to his groin. "A woman never tells her secrets, Mr.

Marquis. Would you be disappointed if I didn't try to seduce you?"

"Would you be disappointed if I likewise refrained?" he dared. He didn't want to forego the enjoyment of the chase, but he would if she wished it.

Tipping her head, she studied him with a smile playing around those pouty lips. "I think you are challenging me."

"Will you accept?"

"Another deal?"

He huffed a laugh. "No, vixen. A duel. To the climax. To death."

Her lips parted on a breath. "The French have a name for that."

"*La petite mort.* The little death." He brushed a stray curl of chestnut hair away from her cheek and watched her slow blink. So, she liked his touch. "Well?" he pressed. "Do you accept?"

Her gaze traveled over his face. Leaning in, she placed her hand on his thigh. His muscles bunched in response. He ignored that response of his body with every fiber. Would she accept his challenge? Or would she turn and run?

A sly smile curved her lips. "Yes," she whispered. "I accept. To the death. *La petite mort.*"

With a satisfied smile, he brought her hand to his lips and sealed the challenge with a kiss. But not to the back of her hand. No, that was too proper for this arrangement. Instead, turning her hand over, he placed his kiss in the palm of her hand. More intimate, more memorable. Then he snapped the reins and guided the horses back to the house.

This woman enticed him like no other ever had. The challenge before him brought a rush of heat. And he intended to be the victor.

As they drove away from the park, Maggie gnawed her bottom lip. What had she done? Made a deal with the devil, that's what.

The man tied her up in knots and made her lose all perspective. He was engaging, charming, handsome, and unlike any other man she'd ever met. Maybe that was because he was from a different century. But that didn't matter. She should have used her common sense and told him: NO. She should have scrambled down from his carriage and run. Very far and very fast. But she didn't. Because that girl Agnes with hatred in her eyes had tried to claim him. As if he would allow that. As if she would. Because she knew, without a doubt, that the Honorable Agnes was not honorable in the least.

Some protective instinct had risen up inside her, which was why she didn't tell him about the Honorable Agnes and her vitriol. And why she had accepted his challenge. Because in some deep, cockeyed part of her, she wanted him for herself. Which was stupid, because she couldn't have him either. He lived in the nineteenth century. She lived in the twenty-first. At least, she used to. And she had to go back. Sometime.

Coming from different centuries was only one of many reasons why she shouldn't have taken up his challenge. She barely knew him. While he obviously was a marquis and owned a beautiful house in the middle of London and appeared to be quite wealthy, she didn't know the man. He had been kind and generous, tolerant when she tried to steal his painting, but she'd only been with him a couple of days. Maybe he was just conning her to get his key back. Or not.

She wanted to learn more about him. What did he enjoy? What annoyed him? What made him laugh? What foods did he like?

Besides those questions, she wondered what he had been involved in that had put him in prison. Who was the devious woman who had stolen his locked box? What was the document inside? She placed her hand over the key and pendant hanging beneath her spencer. He could have taken the key by force. But he hadn't.

She stole a glance at him. He had clothed and fed and housed her. He could have easily tossed her out on the street. He was a man with presence. Besides being handsome, and tall, and lithely muscular, he was charismatic. She could see him as a leader of men. A seducer of women. She closed her eyes, remembering the touch of his finger as he swiped a hair from her cheek, and the feel of his lips on the skin above her glove. The kiss on her palm. Even through her glove she had felt the heat of him. Had he already seduced her? Her eyes snapped open. No. She had merely accepted his challenge. She could seduce him as easily as the other way around. This was a game they played. It would be over when she returned to her own time, and she would have a pleasant memory.

But that touch of his finger against her cheek remained on her skin like a brand. Her thighs clenched in anticipation. She had never played such a dangerous game. Her life had been staid, predictable. Now everything was new. Excitement made her blood race.

Both of her sisters had struck out on their own, each focused on their own passion. Emma had her writing. Darcy had her fashion design. But she had taken the easy route and become her father's assistant, and then, when he died, she'd taken over the shop. Perhaps, it was time to rebel, to live life on the wild side.

She shifted on the seat, pressed closer to his hip as if by accident, then away. Even though he didn't move, didn't take his eyes from the horses, she knew he had felt the contact. A smile curved her lips. Let the games begin.

Seven

Two nights later, Maggie slowly descended the stairs to the entry hall. She and the marquis had been invited to a ball. When they had returned from the cordwainer's, a silver tray on the table just inside the door had been overflowing with notes and invitations, so his plan to ride through Hyde Park to be seen had worked. He had pulled an envelope out of the pile, taken one look at it, grinned like a pirate discovering booty, and declared, "Perfect."

After that, she had seen little of him for the next two days, for he had engaged a dancing coach and an etiquette coach for her. She had lessons in all the different dances, and lessons in table manners, and introductions, and how to address the peers and royalty, and visits, which were called morning visits but were always in the afternoon, and a number of other nineteenth-century life skills that she was sure she'd forget. But even as she followed the dance master's counting and tried to remember which fork to use for which dish, she plotted and planned her seduction of the marquis.

It began when she descended the stairs to leave for the evening. Madame Fanchon had delivered a gorgeous gown of silvery white silk that shimmered in the candlelight and skimmed her body in all the right places. The neckline dipped dangerously low. She watched the marquis's eyes widen fractionally when he saw her, then narrow just the tiniest bit.

Game on.

He was breathtaking as well in his black evening clothes, his coat fitting just so across those wide shoulders, his narrow trousers hugging his muscular thighs. The pristine white of his shirt was decorated with a neckcloth tied in some intricate knot, held in place with a ruby stickpin, and a waistcoat of ivory brocade embroidered in red covered his flat stomach. She was stunned at his devilishly handsome looks. While he was dressed as a civilized gentleman, his aura suggested dangerous pirate. Her knees went weak, and she might have tumbled down the stairs if not for the leg muscles she'd gained from all that jogging.

When she stepped off the last stair, he held out his hand. "You are looking splendid this evening, marchioness."

Smiling, she placed her hand in his. "And you are dashing, Mr. Marquis."

He huffed a pleased laugh and placed her shawl about her shoulders.

Kelwin held the door for them. "Have a pleasant evening, my lord, my lady." While his words were completely proper, his eyes glinted with humor.

Maggie sent him a cheeky grin. "Thank you, Kelwin. We'll try our best."

Mr. Marquis helped her step up into the coach and they set off. As he settled beside her, she could feel the warmth of his thigh through his trousers and her petticoats. She had the urge to scoot closer, but that would reveal her need to feel him. Not going to happen.

"This ball," he explained, "is the most sought-after invitation of the season. It's being hosted by the Duke and Duchess of Wyndham. Rumors and speculation abound about how they met. Some say that they were both spies on opposite sides, and others say that she cheated him at the gaming tables."

"Scandalous," Maggie said wryly. She touched the back of his hand with one gloved finger. "What's your opinion, Mr. Marquis?"

His hand jerked just the tiniest bit, and he glanced down at her finger. "I believe that the gossip mongers should leave them alone." His gaze turned to the window. "Ah, we've arrived."

Maggie wasn't fooled by his change of subject. Her light touch on his hand had affected him. One point to her. She smiled at her small victory as he helped her down from the coach, but when she gazed up at the imposing London mansion, her confidence fled. Would she make a fool of herself in front of all these people? This was a different time from what she was used to, with different expectations, and with different ways of acting and speaking. She tried to remember all the dancing and etiquette lessons she'd had over the last couple of days, but she couldn't recall a single one. The marquis held out his arm and his lips tipped up at the corners. That tiny smile reassured her. Placing her hand on the arm of her pseudo-husband, she climbed the stairs to the front door.

This house was even grander than Wildford's. The entry was two stories with a gallery that ran around three sides. A wide, elegant staircase swept up to the second floor. Several doors opened off the entry hall, and guests stood chatting or meandered from room to room. Music drifted from an open pair of double doors, where she caught glimpses of a glittering crowd.

The host and hostess stood off to one side, greeting their guests, and Mr. Marquis escorted Maggie over to them. The duchess was a petite woman with a crown of black curls, woven through with a single strand of diamonds, and striking, light blue eyes, while the duke had golden hair and intense green eyes. With their coloring, they could have been relatives of both Maggie and the marquis.

Maggie dipped a curtsy, as she had been schooled to do

by one of the tutors. "Your grace," she murmured, feeling a bit awkward.

The duchess took her hand and smiled warmly. "So, you are Wildford's new marchioness." She threw a teasing glance in his direction. "We had no idea you were courting, Simon, and this is what you were doing during your absence from London."

The marquis smiled thinly. "You must allow me my secrets, dear Jessica."

The duchess pouted prettily and slanted a glance at her husband. "Oh, you men and your secrets. They will be the death of me."

The duke took his wife's hand and kissed her fingers. "Secrets make the world go round, my love." He shared a look with the marquis.

Maggie wondered if Mr. Marquis had told the duke about their sham marriage, and she also got the impression that the two men shared other secrets as well. Then the Duke of Wyndham turned to her with a bow and a warm smile.

"Welcome to our house, marchioness, and welcome to England," he said. Although his gaze was bland, he seemed to be evaluating her. "We are very glad to meet you." Then he turned to the marquis. "Come share a brandy with me later."

Although the invitation was cordial, Maggie had the impression that if the marquis didn't show up, the duke would not be pleased. Remembering that England and

America were at war, she wondered if the duke would quiz Mr. Marquis about bringing an enemy into his house.

With a wink at Maggie, the duchess said, "Then we will share a glass of Madeira. I want to hear all about America."

Maggie smiled and nodded, trying to hide her nerves and trying to remember what America was like in 1814 from her history lessons in school. Her thoughts scattered as the marquis swept her away into the ballroom. It was a glittering kaleidoscope of moving parts and breathtaking décor. Two large chandeliers, sparkling with candlelight, hung from the ceiling, and sconces on the walls added to the glow. The parquet floor gleamed and the walls were covered in a pale blue silk. Small chairs, their seats upholstered in rosy brocade, sat along the wall or in small groups in the corners. In the center of the room, the guests danced in intricate formations. The women were dressed in sumptuous, frothy gowns of white or pastels, and the men were tailored to the hilt in their dark evening wear. About the periphery, those guests not dancing milled about, chatting or just watching the dancers. The orchestra played an upbeat tune. Conversation flowed.

Maggie clutched the marquis's arm. "I can't do this," she said, anxiety pulling her muscles tight.

"Yes, you can." Mr. Marquis placed his hand over her white knuckles as she wrinkled his sleeve in her grip. "You tried to steal a painting from me. Surely, you are bold enough to face Society."

She shook her head. "I thought I was dreaming when I did that. This is real." Staring at the crowd before her, she abruptly realized how different their two worlds were. She would never have been invited to such a glittering gala in her time. Yet, the marquis appeared quite comfortable in these surroundings. He was acquainted with a duke, and most likely with many more titled gentlemen, maybe even the Prince Regent. What was she doing here? The goal of seducing the man beside her was a far-fetched idea. How could she ever have thought she'd be brave enough to do that or live in his world?

"Real is so much better than a dream," he murmured. "Don't you think?"

Glancing up at him, she found his warm gaze on her. Caught in those eyes, disconcerted, she swallowed and mumbled, "Um, sure."

"Real is breath and movement and heat," he said, the low timbre of his voice skipping along her spine.

"Ah—" Mesmerized, she couldn't come up with a single thought.

A corner of his mouth tilted up. Looking out over the crowd, he asked, "Would you honor me with this dance?"

She blinked and took a breath. He gazed down at her, an inquisitive brow lifted. His eyes challenged. The music had changed tempo and became a waltz, a more intricate version of what she had danced around the dining table.

Glancing back at the room before her, she saw couples

start to gather in the middle of the floor. She could do this. The dance master had taught her the steps. Mr. Marquis waited for her answer. And she had a suspicion that he had just beguiled her.

"I will be devastated if you say no," he said, his hand over his heart.

She sent him a narrow look. Was he being serious? No, absolutely not. Even though his expression was solemn, his eyes teased and dared.

"Yes," she said, taking the dare. "All right."

His mouth twitched. "The proper response would be, 'I'd be delighted to dance with you, my lord.'"

She scoffed, but his flirting helped to release some of her tension. "I said I'd dance with you. That's all you get."

With a grin, he led her into the middle of the ballroom. He was a wonderful dancer, and she found herself relaxing into the music. But she was very aware of his strong hands guiding her and the scent of him tickling her nose, like sea salt and caramel. He smelled delicious, and she wanted to dance with him forever, so she could breathe him in.

"Now that we're dancing together, everyone will want to meet you," he said, forcing her brain back to reality.

"Everyone?" She glanced at the guests standing or sitting around the wall — matronly ladies, older gentlemen, a few wallflowers, and several groups of young men, who interrupted their enthusiastic conversations now and again with speculative glances at the young debutantes who stood in clusters, pretending to ignore them. Then her gaze traveled over the other couples dancing. "Why would they want to meet me?"

He ducked his head closer. "Because you are my marchioness, and you are a mystery they wish to solve."

Although he spoke of the members of Society, she somehow felt his statement was much more personal. His warm breath wafted across her ear and a tingle ran down her spine. Distracted, she went left instead of right and stepped on his foot.

"Sorry," she mumbled, heat blooming in her cheeks.

"Perhaps a few more dancing lessons are in order," he suggested mildly.

She shook her head. "I don't think I can stand hearing the dance master tell me to lift my chin and stand up straight one more time."

"I would be happy to offer my services," he murmured.

The thought of having him in such close proximity for such an extended amount of time sent panic through her. She couldn't. In the time they had been dancing, she discovered that being so close to him was doing strange things to her. She wanted to run her fingers through his hair to see if those bright highlights warmed beneath her touch. She wanted to press against him and feel those muscles along the length of her. She wanted to untie that lovely neckcloth, unbutton his shirt, and kiss the hollow of his throat. And below that. Her thigh muscles clenched. Her nipples puckered. She prayed for the end of the dance. This evening's goal of coolly seducing him had been flipped around.

He had seduced her.

With one dance.

She was not going to let him win. Tightening her jaw, telling her hormones to behave, she sent him a bright smile.

"I would love to have you teach me," she said. "How soon can we start? Tomorrow?"

His gaze froze on her for a split second before a sly smile curved his lips. "Tomorrow would be perfect. Just before we go out to make a call."

Maggie kept the smile on her face, but she really wanted to stamp her foot in frustration. He had called her bluff. Besides that, he said they had to make a call on someone, and his tone of voice implied she couldn't get out of it. She didn't want to make a call. She wanted to try to figure out how she was going to get back to her own time. But that problem was for tomorrow. Right now, she needed to distance herself from the man who messed with her mind and messed with her hormones.

As soon as the dance ended, he escorted her off the dance floor. Then she excused herself to escape to the room reserved for the ladies' privacy.

SIMON WATCHED HER SASHAY ACROSS THE FRONT HALL AND start up the stairs. When she had nearly reached the top, she fled the rest of the way as if demons chased her. A smile hovered around his lips. He'd called Miss Maggie Blake's bluff, and she had run. Point to him. But it wasn't a complete victory because she had snuck beneath his guard.

When he had danced with her, the feel of her had sent his blood racing. She felt perfect. More than perfect. He ached for her.

What was wrong with him? He didn't trust her. She had tried to steal from him. He shouldn't be yearning after a woman who refused to give up the key that would lead to clearing his name. Besides that, she was from the future. She could disappear at any moment, even though her witchy attempt hadn't worked the last time.

Thoughtfully, he stared up at the empty staircase. He had to keep her in his time until he could retrieve his key. For now, the only way he could think to do that was to distract her. Their duel of seduction seemed to be working, because she seemed quite distracted.

Pleased with the evening so far, he turned back to the ballroom, where the Duke of Wyndham caught his eye. The duke jerked his chin in the direction of his library just before he turned with a smile to an elderly lady beside him. Simon sighed. That invitation to share a brandy was more than a friendly gesture. Wyndham wanted to know about his abrupt appearance in society and his sudden marriage.

As Simon made his way to the duke's library, he tried to concoct a plausible story about Miss Maggie Blake and his return to London. He doubted Wyndham would believe that he had traveled through time and back again, bringing the delicious Maggie with him. But he did want to discuss his arrest and confinement in prison with his friend. Despite the embarrassment of being duped by that woman who stole his key, he needed to alert Wyndham about her and the possible existence of a spy ring.

And then he wondered how soon he could escape the duke's library and invite his counterfeit wife to dance once more.

IN THE LADIES' RETIRING ROOM, MAGGIE STOOD BEFORE THE cheval mirror and pretended to tuck a lock of hair into place. Two young ladies whispered and giggled behind her about the good points and bad points of several eligible bachelors in the ballroom. One young man was a crack horseman. Another was a perfect dance partner. A third had already inherited his title. A fourth would inherit one very soon. The two young ladies finally left in a froth of titters and a flurry of skirts.

With a sigh, she stepped back from the mirror. She didn't

need to fix her hairdo or touch up the kohl the maid had applied to her lashes. What she needed was time away from the devastatingly attractive and aggravating man who was waiting for her in the ballroom.

"We try to appear perfect, but there is always a flaw somewhere," a woman said from behind her.

Startled, Maggie spun around. She thought she had been alone. The woman rose from a chair set back into a dim corner of the room. A few years older than Maggie, she was beautiful, with deeply golden curls piled atop her head and dramatically dark eyes. Her dress was a rose silk that plunged daringly at the neckline and flowed over her svelte figure like water.

"Forgive me," the woman said with a smile. "I didn't mean to startle you. I am Rosalind Hornley. And you are Wildford's new marchioness."

"Yes, I am." Maggie wondered how the woman knew that.

Rosalind winked. "I saw you arrive with him, and everyone has been buzzing about his marriage. It seemed quite sudden. I had heard he had sworn off marriage."

Maggie forced a smile. "I suppose he changed his mind."

"Well, the poor girls in the market for a husband are devastated." Rosalind turned to the mirror and patted at her perfect hairdo.

"I'm sure they'll find someone suitable," Maggie murmured, wondering if Rosalind had set her sights on the marquis for herself.

"Yes, I'm sure they will." The woman turned back to her and her gaze landed on Maggie's chain holding the sapphire pendant and the key. "That is a very interesting piece you are wearing. I'm surprised Wildford hasn't presented you with the family jewels."

Maggie placed a defensive hand over the charms and spun a story. "Oh, these have a very sentimental value, so I convinced him to let me wear these instead. Besides, it would have been so troublesome for him to retrieve the jewels." Did the marquis really own family jewels? How wealthy was he?

"How did you meet?" Rosalind asked. "I understand you are from America."

"It is quite a tale." Maggie frantically fabricated a fantasy out of reality. "We met beneath an old oak tree. We sort of bumped into each other."

"How romantic. Was that in America?" One of Rosalind's perfectly sculpted brows lifted.

Since she had already told Agnes that they had met while the marquis was on a diplomatic mission, she decided to stick with that. "Yes, in Boston. He was there to meet with several important men. To try to end the war."

"So that is where he has been," Rosalind mused. "I did wonder where he had disappeared to. I could have sworn I'd heard he was in prison."

"Prison?" Maggie forced a laugh. "Oh, my goodness. Wherever did you hear that?"

"From the source, dear Marchioness, if that is who you

truly are." Rosalind's smile turned coldly cruel. "Because, you see, I put him there." She swung about with a swish of skirts and left.

Stunned, Maggie stared at the door that Rosalind closed behind her. She'd just had a conversation with the marquis's former mistress. The woman who had stolen his document. The reason he had landed in prison.

Why had Rosalind revealed herself? How had the woman received an invitation to such an exclusive ball? Why had she wanted the marquis to be arrested? If she had his locked box with his document, she no doubt wanted the key. Was the woman's revelation about who she was a threat?

Maggie wrapped her fingers around the two charms. The encounter left her shaken. Did Mr. Marquis know Rosalind was at the ball? She had to let him know. Rosalind might have him arrested again. Even if he belonged in prison, that was the last place Maggie wanted him to be. He'd done nothing illegal while she'd been with him, and he was her only friend in this century. If he were arrested... She didn't want to speculate about that. Her urgent need to warn him wiped everything else from her mind as she rushed from the room to search for him.

Simon sat across from the Duke of Wyndham in the library. They each held a snifter of brandy, the outward sign of their friendship, but Simon knew this conversation would not be completely amicable. Wyndham was his superior. The duke had been a spy in the years before his marriage and now worked with the Foreign Office. But they had been friends since their school days at Eton, despite Wyndham being several years older. Besides that, Wyndham had saved his life.

When Simon had learned he was to inherit the title of Marquis after the death of his older brother, he had wanted no part of the title, not the honor, nor the responsibility, so he had spent his days at his club and his nights at various gaming hells. After one disastrous night at the tables, Wyndham had found him at the club with a mostly empty bottle of brandy at his elbow. The duke offered him another option besides drinking and gambling, to sail for England against France. That was the day Simon decided to live and became a privateer.

Wyndham took a sip of brandy and placed the snifter on the table beside him. "I was surprised to hear you were in London," he said. "The last communication I received from the Mediterranean mentioned you were in Malta."

"I was. We had put in there for supplies, and I wanted to give the crew some liberty ashore. Our last encounter with a French frigate had been intense, even though we had persevered and come away the victor." Simon shifted uneasily.

"Then I met Mrs. Rosalind Hornley, a young, beautiful widow who was staying with the British Envoy and his wife. We became—ah—interested in each other." He glanced away, embarrassed at his foolishness.

"Please do not tell me she duped you," Wyndham said with a frown.

Simon leveled a look on him. His friend had recounted numerous stories of his own affairs before he married. It was no secret the duke and his wife were deeply in love, despite their tempestuous beginning.

With a sigh, Wyndham relented. "Yes, I know. How can one resist a beautiful woman? What did she do?"

"She stole a box from me, a box that contained my letter of marque and documents I had taken from the French frigate. I never had the chance to pass them along to the British Envoy." Simon gritted his teeth. If — when he crossed paths with Rosalind again, he wanted to strangle her. Or at least send her to prison.

"What documents?" Wyndham's gaze sharpened.

Simon grinned. "Plans for the deployment of the French fleet in the Mediterranean."

"Good god! Those are like gold!" He shot to his feet and began to pace. "If we could get those back—"

Simon watched his friend stride back and forth in front of him. He knew Wyndham's frustration, because he had felt the same, along with rage at Rosalind and embarrassment for being so blind.

"Impossible, unless I can find my box." He continued his tale. "After I discovered it was missing, I went to confront Rosalind, but I learned she had sailed for London. I rounded up my crew and came after her." Simon's fingers curled into a fist on his knee. "When we docked, I was boarded by the customs officers, arrested for piracy, and thrown into prison."

Wyndham stopped pacing. "Piracy! Why would you be boarded? What would cause the officers to be suspicious of you?"

"Someone obviously whispered lies about me." Simon suspected Rosalind, but he couldn't figure out how she could have convinced the customs authorities. What proof did she have? Why would she have been believed?

The duke started pacing again, deep in thought, then turned unexpectedly to confront him. "If you were arrested, how are you out in society? What of your sudden marriage? Where and how did you meet your new marchioness?"

Surprised at the abrupt change of subject, Simon blinked and floundered for an answer. Did Wyndham suspect that Maggie was another spy, like Rosalind? His friend would never believe the truth, that she was from the future.

Taking a breath to give himself a moment to think, he decided half-truths would satisfy Wyndham. "The woman I introduced as my marchioness is Miss Maggie Blake and not my wife. She came into possession of the key which opens my box, and in order to keep her close as well as protect her, I decided on the deception."

Wyndham frowned. "But who is she? Can you trust her?"

Could he? She had tried to steal a painting. But his instincts told him she was honorable.

"Yes," he said. "We have an agreement. My marriage to her is a ruse to draw out Rosalind and anyone else she might be working with."

"A clever ruse," the duke agreed. "And that will keep the key close."

Simon nodded, relieved that his friend believed him.

Wyndham said. "What are your intentions concerning Miss Blake after you retrieve your box?"

Simon had no idea, except he wanted to postpone Maggie's return to her own time for as long as possible. He wondered how he could do that, because he very much wanted to continue their duel of seduction to the very end.

Eight

When Maggie entered the ballroom, she saw no sign of the marquis. She threaded her way through the guests around the edge of the room, but he wasn't chatting with any of the men, nor was he dancing with anyone. Where had he gone?

"Are you looking for Wildford?" a woman asked from behind her.

Maggie startled, thinking that Rosalind had sought her out for more cattiness. Instead, she was relieved to see her hostess, the Duchess of Wyndham, standing beside her. "Yes, I seem to have lost him."

A dimple appeared in the duchess's cheek. "You know, it is very bad form to be so attached to your husband. Not the thing, you know."

"Oh, I didn't realize—" Maggie wondered if she'd ever learn all the unspoken rules of nineteenth century society.

The duchess waved a graceful hand as if swiping away an annoying bug. "Don't concern yourself. You are newly wed. I find myself frequently searching out Damien at these affairs."

"Damien? Your husband? The duke?"

With a grin, the duchess leaned closer. "Don't tell anyone, but we use each other's Christian names. Something else that is not done. I should call him Wyndham. Please, call me Jessica."

"I'm Maggie." Disarmed by the woman's disclosure, she confided, "I'm not quite comfortable calling the marquis by his first name."

"I have the feeling you will be soon." Jessica's eyes teased. "Come, have that glass of Madeira with me. And to satisfy your curiosity, Wildford is drinking brandy with my husband in the library."

Despite her urgency to find Mr. Marquis to warn him of Rosalind's presence at the ball, she felt she couldn't decline the invitation. Besides, he was safely shut away with the duke. Maggie followed the duchess through the ballroom to a cozy sitting room near a back corner of the house. She felt as if she had found a friend.

As the duchess poured the wine into two crystal glasses about the size of a child's teacup, she said, "I always find the stories of how couples meet fascinating. Even if they meet in the usual way, at a ball or at Almack's, there is usually an incident that brings them together." She handed Maggie a glass of wine. "Don't you agree?"

"Oh, yes," Maggie said. Before Jessica could ask about how she met the marquis, she asked, "How did you and the duke meet? I heard an outrageous story that you cheated during a card game with him."

Jessica laughed and invited Maggie to sit with her on a sofa. "Yes, I did. He was quite put out. But it is a long story, and I wish to hear how you and Wildford met."

Maggie knew that request was coming, so she elaborated on the story she had told Rosalind. "We bumped into each other under an old oak tree. It had begun to rain, and we both ran to get under cover."

The duchess took a sip and studied Maggie over the rim of her glass. "I want to hear more. Why were you in London?"

"We were in America, in Boston, not in London," Maggie said, keeping to her story. "The marquis was on a diplomatic mission."

Jessica blinked. "How fascinating." She casually placed her glass on a table beside her. "I believe I heard that the American coast was blockaded. You were very fortunate to escape and sail to England."

With a sinking feeling, Maggie realized the woman was skeptical of her story. But she couldn't tell Jessica that she had time-traveled from the twenty-first century. The duchess would think she was deranged. The only thing she could do was to keep bluffing.

"Yes, we were very lucky," Maggie agreed, then wove more lies to get Jessica to believe her. "We sailed out of the harbor at night. I was very frightened."

"Well, you are here now, quite safe," Jessica said, then stood. "I believe we should join the men. I am sure Damien will want to hear your story and how brave your husband was."

As Maggie stood as well, she wondered why she had to relate the story to the duke, then panicked when she realized she hadn't shared any of it with Mr. Marquis. What was he telling the duke about their fake marriage? If he was telling a different story, then the duke and duchess would know they both lied. What would they do? Would they throw them out of their party? Would they send for the authorities? Would they have the marquis arrested? What would happen to her?

Nervously, she followed the duchess out of the room and began to wonder if Jessica was actually as kind as she appeared, or if she was just pretending. Rosalind had seemed nice at first, then revealed she was the one who instigated the marquis's arrest. Did the duchess know about that, or was she also an enemy? How much did she know?

Maggie's brain whirled with anxious questions as they stopped before a door and the duchess knocked. A man's voice bade them enter. She followed her hostess into a very masculine room, paneled in rich, dark wood with shelves of books taking up one wall. A huge desk of gorgeous, carved mahogany hulked in one corner, and a plush oriental rug covered the floor. The men sat in chairs on either side of the fireplace. They both rose when Maggie and the duchess entered. Maggie thought the marquis seemed a bit tense.

"We're sorry to disturb you," Jessica said, "but I thought you would be interested in a story."

"I enjoy a good story," Wyndham said with a fond smile at his wife.

Jessica beamed back at him. "Lady Wildford was telling me how she met her husband in Boston while he was on a diplomatic mission."

With a raised brow, the duke turned to Mr. Marquis. "Boston? A bit far off course for you, wouldn't you say?"

"Off course? As in sailing off course?" Maggie asked, suddenly apprehensive. Had Mr. Marquis told a different story about how they met?

The marquis shifted his weight and glanced at the duke. "She doesn't know."

Already on edge, feeling as if she'd just stepped into quicksand, Maggie blurted, "What don't I know?"

Three pairs of eyes regarded her. Two assessed, as if trying to decide if they had a dangerous felon in their house. The third pair of jade-green eye appeared—guilty?—apologetic?

Maggie's sense of being the center of attention faded as

the duke said to Mr. Marquis, "I believe it's only fair that we enlighten her. Would you like to tell her?"

The marquis shifted again, then drew himself up. "I am a privateer," he said, as if daring her to deride his declaration.

She took a moment to absorb what that meant. Visions sailed through her head of a daring, swashbuckling man, wielding a cutlass, standing on the rail of a ship as he grasped the rigging in his fist and stared out across the sea. She remembered her first impression of the marquis when he fell from the tree. Dangerous. Sexy. And looking very much like a pirate.

She gasped. "You're a pirate?!"

"A privateer," the marquis said between clenched teeth. "I raid the enemy's ships. Legally."

"The enemy? Like America?" She had a moment of dismay. Since England and America were at war, she and the marquis were supposed to be enemies.

"No," he said. "France."

"Oh." Maggie was relieved he wasn't raiding American ships, but then another thought popped into her head. "Then you're not really a marquis?"

"He is most definitely who he says he is," the duke said. "But he was never in Boston."

This time, Maggie shifted uncomfortably. She met the marquis's gaze and wondered what he had told the duke. He remained stubbornly silent. Of course he did. If she revealed that she was from the future and that he had fallen from the sky and out of a tree, the duke and duchess would no doubt think she was delusional.

"Would you sit for a moment, please, Miss Blake?" the duke asked as he indicated one of the chairs near the fireplace.

Maggie took a step in that direction, then halted. "You know my name?" she asked faintly. She cast a scorching glance at the marquis. Was she about to be thrown out for not being married to him and for impersonating a marchioness?

"Yes. We have all played different roles at times." The duke glanced quickly at Jessica and an amused, silent message seemed to pass between them. Then he turned back to Maggie. "Wildford told me that you are helping him regain an important document."

As she sat, Maggie made an indistinct sound, not agreeing but not disagreeing either. She hadn't decided what she was going to do about the key.

The duke sat in the chair opposite her. "I am not interested in how exactly you met Wildford."

Maggie glanced at Mr. Marquis. His shrug confirmed he had made up some fanciful tale. Or had he? Had he told the duke the truth?

Wyndham regained her attention. "I believe that your story about meeting him on a diplomatic mission is a perfect explanation of his absence for the past several years. I would encourage you to keep to that story."

"Okay." Maggie wondered what the connection was between the duke and the marquis. The duke seemed to know a lot about what the Marquis of Wildford had been doing.

He went on, "Certain people would like to do him harm, and your presence will help to deter that."

"Like Rosalind Hornley?" Maggie asked.

The marquis stiffened and his face darkened. "How do you know that name?"

Knowing what Rosalind had done to him, she made her words gentle. "She's here. I met her."

Stunned silence dropped into the room.

The marquis took a step forward, his gaze intense. "Where is she?"

"I would not advise you to confront her here, Wildford," the duke said and placed a restraining hand on his arm.

Jessica's mouth tightened. "I never invited her. I wonder who her escort is."

"Maybe she crashed the party," Maggie suggested.

Three people looked at her with various degrees of confusion. Mr. Marquis's face was the first to clear.

"Ah, you mean she came uninvited," he said. Then with a wry twist to his lips, he said to the duke and duchess, "An American expression."

Jessica chuckled. "That certainly explains what Rosalind did this evening."

"How are we going to keep her from going to the authorities?" Maggie asked.

"If she does, she will have to reveal that she is working for the French," the duke said. "I don't believe she'll wish to do that. Wildford is safe for now, but he does need to retrieve his letters of marque."

"His letters of marque?" Maggie asked.

"A document that allows him to legally raid French vessels," the duke explained.

Maggie surmised that document was in the box that Rosalind had stolen. And she had the key. No wonder he wanted it. She placed a protective hand over her chain.

"But we will act as if nothing is amiss," Jessica said with a smile at Maggie. "In a day or two, you and I will go shopping. People will see us together, and you will be accepted everywhere. Perhaps, you might meet up with Rosalind again."

Maggie forced a smile as the thought of being invited to another ball or social event gave her indigestion, not to mention the unpleasantness of running into the marquis's former mistress. Fortunately, he suggested that they leave the ball, and she was thrilled to comply.

SIMON WATCHED WYNDHAM HOUSE DISAPPEAR FROM VIEW AS their carriage drove away from the ball. Beside him on the seat, Miss Maggie Blake was quiet. He was furious with his former mistress, and he needed to get his anger under control before it erupted all over the woman who sat next to him.

How had he not seen that Rosalind was a conniving jade from the beginning? How could he have been so easily duped? A tiny voice in the back of his head reminded him he had been grieving over his brother's death and had just become the new Marquis of Wildford. He had been running away from everything. But he silenced the voice. He should have known what she was.

"Did you love her?"

He startled at the question and turned to Miss Blake. "I beg your pardon?"

"Rosalind. Did you love her?"

He frowned, disturbed by the suggestion. "No. We found satisfaction with each other. I suppose I was fond of her. But I never expected her to—" Uncomfortable with the confession, he turned back to the window.

He felt a touch of her fingers on his hand laying on the seat between them. It was a sweet gesture, comforting, sending warmth up his arm.

"I'm sorry she did that to you." Her words held an offering of sympathy.

He didn't want sympathy. He wanted revenge. Turning to

face her, he declared, "I will find her. She will get what she deserves."

"Of course you'll find her." Then her lips tipped teasingly. "Because you are a pirate."

"Privateer," he grumbled.

"Yes, a privateer. But in my time, the pirates of old times are romantic," she said, as if giving a lesson. "They are swash-buckling. Audacious, adventurous. Scoundrels with hearts of gold."

He huffed a laugh, some of his anger fading. "Truly?"

"Truly."

"I do not have a heart of gold."

"What sort of heart do you have?" she teased.

He thought for a moment. "Perhaps you should decide."

"That will require some investigation." She tipped her head. "What about the scoundrel part?"

He flashed a grin. "Definitely a scoundrel."

"Hm."

Her hum sent a pleasant vibration through his chest. He realized she had distracted him from his dark thoughts. Who was this woman who had magically pulled him from his dank prison cell? Was she truly a witch? Or just a woman who had been caught up in a very strange set of circum-stances? Whoever she was, he was glad for her presence.

"How did you become a privateer?" Her voice came quietly out of the dark.

The question took him back to the old grief that had

nearly swallowed him. "Wyndham suggested it. He has worked for the Foreign Office for quite a few years, started his career as a notorious spy. My father had just died, my mother dead four years earlier. My elder brother who inherited our father's title was off being heroic fighting Napoleon. Then I learned he had been killed in battle."

"I'm so sorry," she said. "That must have been hard, losing all those family members so close together."

He acknowledged her sympathy with a short nod, not wishing to dwell on his weak feelings of pain and abandonment. "I never wanted the title, never expected it would come to me. So, when I inherited, I ignored it. Went about drinking and gambling. Until I lost heavily one night. Wyndham found me the next morning at our club with an empty bottle at my elbow. When he tried to take me home, I swung at him. Instead of challenging me to a duel, he took his fist to my jaw, knocked me out cold, then drove me home and dumped me on my doorstep. The next day, he visited with the suggestion of becoming a privateer. It took me a year to find a ship and put together a crew."

"Did you know how to captain a ship?"

"I've been sailing since I could walk. The Wildford country estate is in Devonshire, on the coast." He smiled at the memories.

Her next question made him scowl.

"How did you meet Rosalind?"

His hand fisted on his thigh. "We had stopped in Malta to

take on water and supplies. I met her at a dinner at the Spanish embassy. She told me a sad story about how she had been traveling with her husband to Venice when their ship had run into a bad storm and had sought refuge in Malta with the British Envoy. While they waited out the weather, she said her husband's heart gave out and she was left a widow, stranded. We were together for a fortnight, then she was gone. I learned she had sailed on a ship bound for England. That was when I discovered the box was missing, so I went after her. The day we docked in London, soldiers boarded my ship and arrested me for pirating. I couldn't prove my innocence because my letters of marque had been stolen."

Grinding his teeth, he looked out the window. Rage at being so easily deceived surged through him. He had been stupid, gullible, swayed by a beautiful face and honeyed words. He would not make that mistake again. He would find Rosalind and get back his letters of marque, then make sure she got what she deserved.

"If she was at the ball tonight, you should be able to find her again," Miss Blake said, sounding quite determined.

Her resolve brought a grim smile to his face. Yes, he would find her.

The coach stopped before his house and he helped Miss Blake down. Kelwin stood at the top of the steps and held the front door open.

"An early evening, sir?" he asked.

"Rosalind," Simon spit out.

Kelwin muttered a dark curse beneath his breath.

Miss Blake glanced from Simon to his butler. "You know about Rosalind?" she asked.

"Aye, miss, ah, my lady," Kelwin said. "I was with the captain when he discovered—" He sent Simon a look of panic at his misstep.

"Miss Blake knows what I did, Kelwin," Simon said, then turned to her. "Kelwin was my first mate."

"Oh!" A teasing grin tugged at her lips as she turned to Kelwin, "Then you must be a scoundrel, too."

Her light-hearted taunt to his butler lifted Simon's angry pall as he watched Kelwin's face scrunch up in confusion.

Simon chuckled. "We were all scoundrels."

With a lovely smile, Miss Blake said, "Kelwin, one day, some woman will be delighted to hear that about you. Good night." His butler-first mate grinned as she turned toward the small sitting room and tossed over her shoulder at Simon, "I think I'll sit in here for a while. Why don't you join me?"

Her endearing smile drew him. He didn't want to lose her company yet, so he accepted her invitation and trailed after her. She stopped before the fireplace and stared down at the flames. As he came up beside her, she sent him a flirty, sideways glance from beneath her lashes.

"How much of a scoundrel are you?" she asked.

Charmed by her playfulness, he said, "Very much a scoundrel, I'm afraid. How much of a scoundrel are you?"

"Oh, not very much of a one." She shook her head. "I follow all the rules."

"All of them? I disagree." He indicated the Turner painting that had been returned to its proper place above the fireplace.

A blush graced her cheeks as she faced him. "That was an aberration. I didn't know you were a *good* pirate back then."

He barked a laugh. "Miss Blake, there is no such thing as a good pirate."

"I disagree." She placed her hand on his chest.

He swore he could sense that touch on his heart.

Looking into his eyes, she said, "I think you are very good. You took me in and fed me and clothed me. You even had tutors teach me how to dance and everything." That hand crept upward and cupped his cheek.

The gesture nearly had him reeling. When he looked down into her beautiful blue eyes, he thought he might be drowning. Her pouty lips parted. The overwhelming urge to taste them made him grab the mantel so he'd feel something solid that would ground him. And then, without warning, she stood on tiptoe and placed her mouth on his.

A tentative kiss, but so surprising that he froze. Her lips were soft. Their touch staggered him. When the tip of her tongue snuck out and tasted him, he was flattened. Without thinking, he wrapped her up in his arms and pulled her tight against him. She came willingly, pliantly, and her arms slipped beneath his coat around his waist. He could feel her curves crushed against him, the hills and valleys fitting snugly.

Their tongues dueled and swooped. She wriggled closer. His hand dipped down to cup her bottom and bind her to him. All his focus constricted down to this woman, her mouth, her body, and the deliciousness of her. He wanted the kiss to last for a very, very long time.

It didn't.

With a gasp, she leaned away. "Oh," she said. "Huh." She dragged in breath as if she had been underwater for long minutes. Her eyes, slightly unfocused, were wide as she stared up at him. "That was—" Her words trailed off as if she couldn't find the rest of them.

Simon's brain reeled as he gazed down at her. He was rather surprised at finding himself standing on his feet, because he imagined he had been floating in space. The woman in his arms was flushed, a bit befuddled, and entirely adorable. He wanted to do the most outrageous things with her.

"Well," she said, as she backed out of his embrace and repeated, "That was —"

"Incredible. Intoxicating," he finished.

"That was very nice, Mr. Marquis," she said with an impish smile.

An inkling of suspicion poked at a far corner of his brain. "Nice?"

"Yes, Mr. Marquis. Nice."

Her name for him grated. "My name," he said distinctly, "is Simon."

"Is it? I'm sorry. I forgot." Her gaze slipped away as she dipped an elaborate curtsey. "Thank you for a delightful evening. Good night, Mr. Marquis." Then she turned and sashayed out of the room.

Just before the door closed behind her, he called, "My name is Simon."

Her answer was a light laugh.

Simon's eyes narrowed. That inkling of suspicion blossomed into complete realization. *The duel.* He had just been seduced. Damnation. Point to Miss Maggie Blake. The intensity of their contest rose a notch. Next time, he wouldn't be so gullible. He was not going to allow Miss Maggie Blake to take advantage of him like Rosalind had. Except that kiss had been the most sensuous, the most mind-jumbling one he had ever experienced. Despite his resolve not to be duped, he looked forward eagerly to the next kiss. Because two could play this game.

He began to plot his next move.

Maggie barely held herself together until she reached her room, then she collapsed onto a chair. Her knees felt as if they had dissolved, no longer constructed of solid bone and muscle. Her heart raced. Her nipples were swollen. And every cell in her lady bits throbbed. What had that man done to her?

She had wanted to kiss him from the first time she saw him, just to see what it was like to kiss a man who looked like every woman's dream hero. Then she had learned what Rosalind had done to him, and that made her want to comfort him. And, of course, there was their duel of seduction. But she never expected— She touched her lips and shook her head in bewilderment.

The idea to invite him into the sitting room had popped into her head as she had teased Kelwin. When he had followed her, she had nearly pumped her fist in triumph, but, of course, a nineteenth-century lady would never have done that. She hadn't planned to up the ante in their duel of seduction. All she had wanted to do was discover more about him and tease and flirt a little.

Learning that he was a privateer intrigued her. Even though she knew that privateers and pirates were different, she had seen *Pirates of the Caribbean* and had watched all the old pirate films of the 1930s and 1940s. Her head was filled with renegade men who sailed the seas, forging their way in the world, and dashing heroes who saved ladies in distress. Pure fiction.

In reality, she knew pirates weren't like that. But since she had been transported back to the nineteenth century, she felt as if she were living in a fictional world. But a real-life priva-teer, sort of a pirate, had followed her into the sitting room and stood right next to her. She wanted to know what it would be like to kiss him.

As soon as her lips touched his, the fiction in her head seared away. This was a man of muscle and heat. Strong, but gentle. The feel of his mouth sent an electric charge through her. Like a magnet, his body drew her to him. She couldn't deny the pull of him.

While one teensy, tiny part of her brain watched in surprise at her reaction, the rest of it cheered, applauded, cartwheeled and surrendered with glee. She could have kissed him for hours, days, weeks. But that little part of her brain that observed gave her a huge nudge of self-preserva-tion. She couldn't let herself fall for a nineteenth-century man, no matter how devastatingly good his kisses were. So, despite disappointing her hormones, she backed away, aston-ished the kiss had felt so good, so right, so perfect.

She heard him enter his side of the suite. The urge to unlock the door between their rooms made her grip the arms of her chair to hold herself in place. Her thighs throbbed. Her breasts swelled. She was not going to give in. She couldn't. This wasn't her century. She didn't belong here. If she gave in, she'd hate herself in the morning. She was not going to become attached to him.

A light knock on her door made her panic. Had he come for more kisses? But the voice of the young maid who helped her dress asked if she could enter. Maggie needed her to untie her dress and unlace her stays. With relief, she rose to let her in.

Getting unlaced and undressed helped distract her. After removing dress and stays and chemise and stockings and putting on her nightgown, the girl finally left. Exhausted, still a bit aroused, Maggie crawled into bed. A strip of light peeked beneath the door connecting her bedroom to his.

Simon.

Like the first night she had slept in the bed, his shadow paced back and forth. So, he had been disturbed by the kiss as well. In a good way or bad? She didn't want to know.

Flopping over so her back was to the door, she closed her eyes. But she knew very well that sleep wasn't going to show up.

Nine

It was nearly noon, the next day when Maggie slowly made her way downstairs. She had remained in her room all morning like a coward because she didn't want to face the marquis. Simon. Whom she had kissed. And who had kissed her back. As if their lives depended on the melding of their lips.

When a knock came at her door that morning, she thought he had come looking for her. Instead, he had sent a maid with a breakfast tray, a thoughtful gesture, and a note, reminding her they were making a morning call. Another hurdle for her to cross in this century. She had dithered about what to wear. How did one dress when making a call? And what armor could she don when making a call with a man she had kissed the night before as if she wanted to swallow him up?

She finally pulled herself together, gave herself a good scolding, and put on a dress that might be appropriate if she were running her antique shop in the nineteenth century. It was a long-sleeved, yellow and white striped muslin, embroidered in green leaves around the hem, with a fichu tucked into the low neckline, and it covered her up. Except for the fact that she wore no underwear.

Learning that women in the early nineteenth century didn't wear panties had been a surprise. When she'd asked Madame Fanchon about underwear, the modiste had asked why a woman would need underwear when her skirts covered everything. Maggie supposed that made sense. Then the woman had held up a pair of pantaloons, all lace and embroidery, and declared they were the latest thing and very risqué. But when Maggie tried them on, she realized they had no crotch. They were merely two separate legs attached to a tie at the waist. Instead of wearing the pantaloons, she usually slipped on her panties or her shorts beneath her dresses. But the maid had collected both her panties and shorts the night before and they were being laundered. This morning, she was going commando, and she felt naked and vulnerable.

She found the marquis in the small dining room. He was reading a newspaper, but he rose to his feet when she entered.

"Good morning. Did you sleep well, Miss Blake?" he asked.

"Thank you," she said. "I slept very well." Liar. He had probably heard the creaking of the bed as she tossed and turned.

"I had the tray sent up because I thought you might be exhausted from the ball last night," he said with complete, courteous innocence.

Was he being serious, or was he referring to her sleepless, restless shuffling in bed? She decided to take his words at face value. "The tray was perfect." She stepped farther into the room, but not too far. Getting too close to him would be very dangerous. "I thought we were going to make a call this morning. I hope I didn't keep you waiting too long."

"Not at all. Morning calls are made in the afternoon." He gestured to a pile of newspapers at his feet. "I was reading the news. It seems you were the queen of the ball last evening. The gossips are wondering why we left so early."

"Oh." Her forehead crinkled. "Is that a bad thing?"

With a smile, he shook his head. "Not at all. It means that we accomplished what we had set out to do, that is, announce that we are in London." His smile turned sly. "Besides, I am rather glad we left early."

Maggie's cheeks burned. She was not going to fall into his trap and discuss the kiss. "When do you want to make that call?"

He carefully placed the newspaper on the table. "Are you sure you want to go calling?" The question sounded more like an invitation to debauchery than inquiring about her preference to stay or go.

She was definitely going to decline that invitation. "Oh, it's such a lovely day!" she exclaimed. "Let's go." One look out the window told her that the sun had gone behind clouds and rain might be coming.

With a glance outside and a wry twist to his lips, he said, "Of course. Whatever you wish."

"I'll just get my hat and shawl," Maggie said, and escaped.

She knew that he knew that she was being a coward. But she didn't care. If she experienced another one of his kisses, she might go crazy. Or things might progress beyond a mere kiss. Far, far beyond.

A half hour later, she was sitting next to him on the seat of his phaeton and riding through London. His proximity made her want to squirm, but she controlled herself. His warmth made her want to lean toward him, but she held herself straight. His thigh, only inches from hers, made her want to reach out and place her hand on that hard muscle, but instead she clenched the handle of her parasol, open despite the clouds.

"Who are we calling on?" she asked, wanting to distract herself from her thoughts.

"Mrs. Edwards." He maneuvered the horses around a corner.

"Isn't that the recluse lady?"

"Yes. She and my mother were close friends, and my

mother made me promise to look in on her from time to time."

Intrigued at the hint into his life, she asked, "Were you close to your mother?"

A smile of reminiscence crossed his face. "When I was young, she would take me to the beach below our country house and tell me stories about the exotic lands beyond the sea."

"It must have been horrible to lose most of your family."

"It was," he agreed with a nod. "But you lost your father not so long ago. A tragedy."

"Yes." She bowed her head in sorrow, the reminder of her loss bringing tears to her eyes. And now she was stuck in the past with no family.

He was silent for a moment, then said, "When my brother was killed in the war, I couldn't face the responsibilities of being the head of the family."

Impulsively, she placed her hand on his arm in sympathy. "Oh, Simon, I am so sorry."

He looked down at her hand, then his gaze cut to her. His interested, heated gaze.

Immediately, she realized her mistake. She had called him by his first name and touched him. An invitation. Snatching back her hand, she cleared her throat and stared straight ahead, as if she hadn't just stepped over some imaginary line. Or invited him to step over it.

Clearing his throat as well, he said, "It was difficult." He turned his attention back to the road. "Maggie." Her name was a whisper.

Had she heard him correctly? She wasn't sure, so she ignored it and pretended to study the shops and houses they passed. But awareness pulsed between them.

After several minutes of uncomfortable silence, they stopped before the front door of the widow's house. Relieved she had something to distract her, she studied the building. Two large trees bracketed the entrance, and ivy climbed the brick walls. Neither the trees nor the ivy had survived the centuries, for in the twenty-first century, the front of the building was bare.

An overwhelming sense of sadness seemed to emanate from the house. Maggie had an eerie sensation of dejà-vu, not from knowing the house existed in her own time, and not from driving past it before, but from some distant memory. She attributed it to the confusion from being in a different century.

"This is a very strange place," she said, looking at the single open window two stories up, on the same floor and location of her father's flat in the twenty-first century.

"Mrs. Edwards is an unusual woman," the marquis said as he helped her down from the phaeton.

When the marquis knocked, the door was opened by a very proper butler, who appeared to nearly crack a smile when he saw the marquis. "Welcome home, m'lord," he said. "It is good to see you back safely."

"Thank you, Hawes," the marquis said. "I'm glad to be back."

Hawes led them to a lovely drawing room that looked out over groomed gardens at the back of the house. "I'll tell Mrs. Edwards you are here," he said and left.

Maggie surveyed the room, decorated tastefully in pale yellow and ivory, everything in order and well-cared for. She had expected the inside of the house to be dusty and forlorn, but it was just the opposite. Comfortable chairs were grouped in one corner, while a sofa sat facing the hearth. Small tables were conveniently placed nearby. Pastoral paintings hung on the walls, and one of them, she was sure, was by Thomas Gainsborough. It was museum quality and would have sold for millions in her time. She wandered to the windows. Outside, a riot of flowers bloomed in beds edged by low boxwood bushes. Fruit trees ran along the high wall surrounding the garden, and a gate in the back wall led to the mews. Neither the flower beds nor the fruit tress had survived into the twenty-first century.

Footsteps approached, and then a woman appeared in the doorway. She was dressed all in gray and a heavy veil covered her face.

"Wildford!" she exclaimed. "Welcome home!" She stepped into the room and offered her hand.

The marquis smiled and bowed. "Thank you. I came to visit one of my favorite ladies."

Mrs. Edwards laughed. "You are such a charmer. Who is

this with you?" As she turned to Maggie, she seemed stunned for a moment, but recovered quickly.

"This is my new marchioness," the marquis said. "Maggie."

Maggie dipped a curtsey. "I'm very pleased to meet you, Mrs. Edwards."

The lady glanced to him. "Your new wife? Best wishes on your marriage, Wildford." Her gaze dropped to Maggie's hand. "But no wedding band?"

"I lost it," Maggie said.

"It's being resized," the marquis said at the same time.

Mrs. Edwards looked from the marquis to Maggie and back again. Even through the heavy veil, Maggie could sense the lady's shrewd gaze.

"What is this, Wildford?" As he hesitated, the lady indicated the group of chairs in front of the windows. "Perhaps you should sit and tell me what is going on here."

After they were seated, the marquis cleared his throat. "As you know, I was out of the country for a while. Miss Blake and I, ah, bumped into each other. Beneath an old oak tree. In Boston."

Mrs. Edwards turned to Maggie, but the lady said nothing. Even though Maggie couldn't see her face through the veil, something made her think the woman didn't believe their story. The woman's scrutiny made her shift. As she did, a shaft of sunlight caught her pendant and sprayed rainbows across the walls.

"That is a lovely piece," the woman said.

Maggie placed her hand over it and immediately, the rainbows blinked out. "Thank you. It belonged to my mother. She died when I was very little. I don't really remember her."

Mrs. Edwards murmured her condolences, then said, "And the key? An odd piece of jewelry."

"It is mine," the marquis said. "Miss Blake is holding it for me."

The lady sent him a sharp look. "You keep referring to your marchioness as *Miss* Blake. And no wedding band? Simon, I have known you since you were in nappies. Please tell me what is going on."

This time, beneath the woman's gaze, the marquis shifted in his seat.

Annoyed at his slip, Maggie also felt the need to help him out of the awkward situation. Besides, by admitting that they were not married, he implied that they were having an illicit relationship, and in the nineteenth century, that was very much frowned upon. At the same time, something about Mrs. Edwards made Maggie want to confide in her and assure the woman that her morals were intact.

"I'm not from here," she blurted.

"That is quite obvious from your accent, as well as what Wildford told me," Mrs. Edwards said.

Maggie took a breath. "What I mean is —" She halted, hesitant about revealing she was from another century, even though she felt the woman might understand.

Mrs. Edwards turned to the marquis. "You did not meet her in Boston. You met her in Hyde Park under the ancient oak. Am I correct?"

His mouth dropped open in shock. "Forgive me, but how did you know?"

"Did your mother never mention anything to you about my mysticism?" she asked.

The marquis nearly choked. "I beg your pardon?"

"Evidently, she did not." The lady turned to look out the window a moment as if gathering her thoughts, then returned her attention to the marquis. "I have knowledge of certain abilities. Unusual abilities." She turned to Maggie. "When are you from?"

"I really am from Boston," Maggie said, misunderstanding.

Mrs. Edwards shook her head. "No, my dear. I asked *when*."

Maggie sent a quick glance at Mr. Marquis. His response was a helpless shrug. So, no help from him. She had the feeling that Mrs. Edwards wouldn't relent with her questioning, and the marquis seemed to trust the lady.

In a small voice, she said, "The twenty-first century."

The lady stared and murmured something about "two." Then, sitting back in her chair, she said, "Now, tell me how this came about."

With a quick glance at Maggie, Mr. Marquis related how he had been pulled from his prison cell and landed on the grass in front of her. She continued the tale and ended by explaining how she found herself in the nineteenth century.

When they had finished, Mrs. Edwards said to Maggie, "You are a Traveler, and your pendant is a time key. It will transport a person through centuries, but it will only work if that person is close to the door into time."

Stunned, Maggie sat in silence. She had suspected the pendant had something to do with her landing in the nineteenth century, but had dismissed that idea when it didn't work to take her back to her own time. How had her mother gained such a piece? Why had she owned it? Her sisters each had their own pendant, all exactly the same. Did Emma's disappearance have anything to do with her own pendant? Would her younger sister Darcy also travel through time?

She could feel the marquis's gaze on her. Turning to look at him, she saw he was just as surprised as she was. But why had he traveled through time? He didn't own a sapphire and diamond pendant.

Before she could voice her question, Mrs. Edwards said, "I believe that you pulled Wildford into your time."

"How could I have done that?" Maggie asked. "I didn't even know he existed."

"Were you wearing his key like you are now?" the lady asked.

Maggie nodded and placed her hand over the two pieces on her chain. How could two such innocuous pieces have such power?

Mrs. Edwards turned to the marquis. "Did you touch the pendant?"

His brow crinkled, as if he were trying to remember. "I believe I did," he said with a glance at her.

Maggie remembered very well. How he strode to her and looked like a dangerous pirate, like the hottest man she had ever seen. And she knew he remembered exactly what happened. He had grabbed the pendant and key and demanded how she had possession of his property. Then they had fallen through space. And landed together on the ground in a tangled sprawl of limbs. Aware of each other, even though they had ignored it.

Forcing her thoughts away from that dangerous route, she asked, "Is the door into time at the ancient oak tree in Hyde Park?"

Mrs. Edwards nodded.

"But I tried to go back to my own time, and nothing happened," Maggie said.

Mr. Marquis let out a snort.

Mortified at the memory of trying to steal his painting, Maggie sent him a look full of daggers.

"Then something is keeping you here," the lady said.

"What would keep me here?" Maggie couldn't think of a single thing.

"I cannot say." Mrs. Edwards turned to look out the window, indicating she would say no more.

Maggie felt as though the woman knew something but

wouldn't reveal it. She glanced at Mr. Marquis, but he shrugged, looking as confused as she felt. Was he the reason she was stuck in the nineteenth century? To help him clear his name? Was he the tether that held her in this time? Or was there another reason?

Mr. Marquis stood. "I believe we have stayed long enough and should take our leave." He held out his hand to Maggie.

She placed her hand in his and stood. "Thank you for telling me about the pendant."

"It was my pleasure," Mrs. Edwards said. "You must come back for another visit."

Maggie felt that the invitation was sincere, and she wanted to discover more about time traveling — how it worked, where she might end up, if she could time travel whenever she wanted or had to wait for Fate to decide. But her thoughts were in such a jumble after what she had just learned that she needed to sort them out first. In a daze, she allowed the marquis to walk her out.

DUMBFOUNDED, SIMON GUIDED MAGGIE OUT OF THE HOUSE. What he had learned about his late mother's friend astonished him. Beside him, Maggie appeared just as stunned. As they crossed to his waiting phaeton, a man jostled them, seeming to appear out of thin air. Simon hadn't seen anyone nearby when he and Maggie had stepped from the house, otherwise, he would have steered her out of the way. He felt a strange pulse in the air and seemed to lose his grip on her for a moment. But in the next second, everything righted itself. Maggie staggered a step, and he steadied her with fleeting curiosity about why she should do so.

"Here now," he said to the man. "Watch where you are going."

Immediately, the man backed off, tipped his hat and bowed. "My apologies, my lord. Please, excuse me."

Simon narrowed his eyes as he recognized the man. "Bowker?"

Roger Bowker bowed again. "At your service, my lord."

Something about him besides his obsequious manner made Simon wary, even though the man seemed unassuming. Maggie looked as if she had seen a ghost and tightly clutched his arm. Bemused at her expression and wanting to protect her, he moved to place himself between her and Bowker.

Bowker went on, "May I extend felicitations to you and the lovely marchioness upon your recent nuptials?"

"Thank you." Simon gave a curt nod, aware of Maggie's fingers digging deeply into his arm, a sure sign of her agitation. "We must be going. We have other calls to make."

"Of course," Bowker said. "My apologies for keeping you.

But, may I say, I am very glad we met by chance." With a tip of his hat, he strolled away.

Simon turned Maggie toward his phaeton, and as he did, she seemed to wilt and leaned on his arm. "Are you unwell?"

"That man." She sucked air into her lungs as if she had been holding her breath. "When he bumped into me, I felt strange, as if he pulled me somewhere."

"Pulled you?" His concern for her ramped up.

She shook her head. "It must have been my imagination." Straightening her shoulders, she appeared to revive.

With Miss Blake's recovery, Simon wanted to accost Bowker to demand he desist from whatever devilry he was involved in, but glancing down the road, he saw Bowker had already disappeared. That seemed odd. Perhaps he had gone into one of the houses, but Simon doubted he would be welcomed into any of them. He certainly hadn't had time to get to the intersection and turn the corner.

More concerned with Maggie than his own curiosity, Simon helped her up to the seat of his phaeton, then climbed up himself. With a snap of the reins, he headed off. And decided he would investigate Bowker, because something about this coincidental meeting seemed a bit off, even though it appeared innocuous. Besides that, he would make sure that Maggie never went out alone. He didn't trust Bowker's obsequious manner.

THE FARTHER AWAY THEY TRAVELED FROM THE SPOT WHERE they had met Bowker, the more relieved Maggie became.

She blew out a breath. "That was very weird."

"If you ever meet Bowker again, do not speak to him," Mr. Marquis said.

"So, you think he's weird, too. Do you think he's dangerous?" The memory of that strange sensation when Bowker bumped into her made her uneasy.

"I believe he is. I do not think you should go anywhere alone. I will accompany you when you leave the house." His tone suggested the pronouncement was non-negotiable.

Although she bristled at his imperious tone, she appreciated his protection and his company. She certainly didn't want to meet up with Roger Bowker again because he gave her the creeps. But she wanted to go out and explore the sights of London and the shops before she returned to her own time.

She slanted him a look. "Are you sure you want to go shopping with me?"

"Shopping?" Panic flashed through his eyes. "Why would you go shopping? Do you not have everything you need?"

"You have been very generous, more than generous, but I would like to browse in the shops and look at the pretty things for sale." She glanced away casually, as if she hadn't just dropped a challenge in his lap.

"Browse," he mused. "I must say, I have never had the experience of browsing. That might be quite enjoyable. Yes," he said with a nod. "We will go browsing tomorrow."

Surprised he had agreed so quickly, she grinned. "Perfect! Maybe we should go to the hat shop first. I think I need a replacement for your sister's hat."

"Wonderful idea."

She was sure he was not thinking about hat shopping.

His next words proved her right. "I do not like the way Bowker seemed to suddenly appear, then act as if nothing out of the ordinary occurred." A muscle jumped in his jaw.

Maggie shivered as goosebumps rose on her arms. Maybe she did need his protective presence. Bowker's sudden appearance right in front of them did seem very strange, and that weird sensation of nothingness when he bumped into her frightened her. Needing to reassure herself, she placed her hand over her pendant and the key.

Her pendant was gone!

"Oh, no!" She glanced down. The key still hung from the chain around her neck, but no blue sapphire and bright diamonds winked back at her.

"What is it?" The marquis turned to her, concern on his face.

Maggie held up her chain, allowing the key to dangle.

"My pendant must have fallen off the chain when Bowker bumped into me. Please, we have to go back to look for it."

With a nod, he turned the horses around and headed back. As soon as they stopped in front of Mrs. Edwards's house, Maggie jumped down and looked around for her pendant. The marquis joined her. After a few moments of fruitless searching, Hawes came out of the house.

"Mrs. Edwards sent me to inquire if I may be of assistance, my lord," he said.

Maggie explained they were searching for her pendant.

Dawes joined them in their search. After several more minutes of examining every inch of ground between the front door of the house and the spot where the phaeton had been parked, the butler said, "I'm afraid the pendant is gone. Mrs. Edwards would like you to return inside."

Maggie reluctantly gave up. A great sense of loss sat heavily in her chest. Fighting back the tears, she followed Hawes back into the house with the marquis beside her. The marquis's guiding hand beneath her elbow was a warm comfort, but even his touch couldn't erase her sadness.

The pendant had been her only connection to her mother, and now it was gone. How had she lost it? The street was quiet, with no one walking or riding past the houses. She and the marquis had barely left the street behind when she'd noticed it was missing, so she didn't think anyone could have seen it lying on the ground and picked it up. Now with it gone, she had no way to return to her own time. How was she ever going to get home?

Mrs. Edwards was waiting for them in the same sitting room as before and was pouring tea into delicate china cups. She waved them to their chairs and handed a cup of tea to Maggie and one to the marquis.

"I understand you lost the pendant," the lady said.

With a sad sniff, Maggie nodded.

"Drink your tea, my dear," the lady said. "I find it helps to soothe."

Maggie took a sip and found that the warm liquid was comforting.

Mrs. Edwards sipped her own tea, then placed her cup down. "I saw a man bump into you just after you left. I hope you are unharmed."

Maggie nodded, but the loss of her pendant nearly had her in tears.

"He is Roger Bowker," the marquis said. "I have known him since Eton, but we were never friends. Something about the encounter seemed odd."

Mrs. Edwards nodded. "I know of him. He is a dangerous man. I believe he has your pendant."

"How could he have it?" Maggie asked in alarm. "The chain was around my neck when he bumped into me."

The lady thought for a moment. "Did you feel anything unusual when that happened?"

Maggie glanced at the marquis, remembering. "Yes, it felt like he was pulling at me."

"That explains it." Mrs. Edwards sighed. "He time-traveled with you long enough to take the pendant off the chain without your realizing it."

Maggie gasped, astonished he could do that. "But what can he do with it? If it won't let me travel back to my own time, then he can't time travel either."

"I'm not sure what he can do with it," the lady said. "He has developed his own means of time travel, a mechanical means, but I don't think it has enabled him to travel through centuries, only a short time forward or back. He is determined to conquer the ability to travel through time, but has failed thus far. I fear his intentions are not for the good. But now, if he has your missing pendant—" Her voice trailed off, but her reluctance to speak said more than her words could have.

A sense of doom fell over Maggie. If the man could travel forward in time and then return to the nineteenth century, what would he do with the knowledge he might gain from seeing the future? What chaos or destruction might he wreak by knowing what the future held? And where did that leave her? The answer to that was obvious — stuck in the nineteenth century.

"I have to get the pendant back," Maggie declared.

"*We* have to retrieve the pendant," the marquis corrected and speared Maggie with a look. "As I said, I'll not have you traipsing about London on your own. The man is dangerous."

"Wildford has the right of it," Mrs. Edwards said. "If Bowker can steal your pendant like he did, then he could cause you great harm."

Perplexed, Maggie's brow crinkled. "Why would he want to hurt me?"

The marquis and Mrs. Edwards exchanged a glance, then the lady said gently, "If he cannot make the pendant do as he wishes, then he might want your help."

"He may not ask politely," Mr. Marquis added. "Which is why you'll not go out alone."

"Proper ladies should always have someone with them when they leave their houses," Mrs. Edwards said, then took a sip of tea as if she hadn't just given Maggie a mild verbal rap on the knuckles.

Disgruntled at the reprimand, Maggie lapsed into silence. But that didn't mean she couldn't sneak out on her own to look for the man.

"Do you know where we might find him?" the marquis asked. "I have paid him little attention since school."

Mrs. Edwards shook her head. "I truly have no idea. But I do believe his father was a jeweler who also toyed with time travel."

"I never knew his father was in trade," Mr. Marquis said. "I wonder how he was able to send his son to Eton."

"I believe he had some legacy connection on his mother's

side." Mrs. Edwards took another sip of tea, as if she knew more but wouldn't reveal it. "You might try inquiring at the jeweler, Rundell and Bridge."

Hearing a name that might lead her to Bowker, Maggie perked up, but she was very careful not to appear too enthusiastic. She wasn't going to alert the marquis to her plans. He would no doubt try to stop her from investigating.

Mrs. Edwards had no more information to impart, and so they left soon after. Maggie held on to the possibility of finding Bowker and getting her pendant back, but the emptiness she felt whenever she placed her hand over the spot where it had hung against her chest matched the sense of loss in her heart.

Ten

Simon sensed Maggie's sadness and fear on the drive back to his house. Who wouldn't be apprehensive upon finding oneself flung centuries back in time with no way to return home? Besides that, the loss of her only connection to her mother must have been quite dispiriting. He knew about the grief associated with the deaths of loved ones, but he couldn't imagine the emptiness of never having known his mother.

When they stepped into his entry hall, he watched her shoulders droop. She pulled off her bonnet, and it dangled forlornly from her hand. He wanted to wipe away that sadness.

"Come into my library," he said.

Without a word, she walked into the room. He watched her look around, taking in the walls of books, the comfortable chairs, the many lamps, then she turned to him with those lovely lips set in a determined line. "I'm going to get my pendant back."

"Yes, I know." He took her hand. "I will help you, but we must be safe about it." He kissed her fingers.

She looked down at their hands. "I — It —" Her bottom lip quivered. "How will I ever get home?"

Without thinking, he pulled her to his chest and wrapped his arms around her. The delicious scent of her filled his nose. His hand cupped the nape of her neck, and he soothed her with small circles of his thumb.

Leaning against him, she released a sigh, as if she had found sanctuary. He wanted to protect her and find some way to retrieve her pendant. While finding it might mean she'd be gone from his life, making her happy would be enough. They stood together for a long moment, then she lifted her head.

"Are you trying to seduce me, Mr. Marquis?" Her eyes glinted in teasing suspicion.

The idea had occurred to him, but seeing her so despondent had made him change the direction of his thoughts. He had only wanted to comfort her. But now that she had brought up the subject, his mind immediately went to the memory of their kiss.

"Do you want me to stop?" he asked, hoping that wasn't what she wanted.

Maggie gazed up into those green eyes. The feel of his warm embrace consoled her, and the circling movement of his thumb made her melt. Did she want him to stop? If she allowed him to continue on, he would win this round in their duel of seduction. But more than that, she didn't want him to stop. The kiss they had shared before made her toes curl. It had rocked her world. She had never experienced a kiss like that.

"No. Don't stop."

Heat flared in his eyes. And then he lowered his head and placed his lips against hers, a gentle touch.

His mouth felt perfect, as if he had known from birth how to kiss her. And then he deepened the kiss. The sweep of his tongue across her lips begged for entrance, and she let him in. Sucking, stroking, she couldn't get enough. The world fell away, and all her focus centered on the man who was kissing her, his arms wrapped around her, his body pressed against her.

His hand slipped down her back and cupped her bottom. The bulge of his erection centered between her thighs in exactly the right spot. Helplessly, she rubbed against him and was grateful for her lack of panties — one less layer of clothing between them. He felt so good, huge and hard against the softness of her thighs. A low growl told her he liked it, too.

He abandoned her mouth, and she whimpered in disappointment, but he trailed kisses across her jaw and down her throat. Somehow, his clever hand had pulled the fichu from the neckline of her dress and freed her breast. He cradled it as if it were a fragile baby bird.

"Beautiful," he murmured.

His thumb stroked her nipple, sending tingles to her core, making her throb. Her gaze flew to his eyes, and she saw heat and desire, reflecting her own. Then he bent his head and took her nipple into his mouth, licking, sucking. She gasped and went boneless as shafts of pleasure coursed through her. If he had not been holding her, she might have crumpled to a lump at his feet.

Her lady bits wept, ready for him to touch, to taste, to invade. Pressing against his impressive erection, she saw the advantage to no panties. He could easily sweep up her skirt and be where she wanted him most. But his hands were busy elsewhere and hers clung to him for balance. For now, his attention to her breasts was enough. They had all afternoon.

SIMON COULDN'T GET ENOUGH OF HER. SHE WAS THE MOST perfect woman he had ever kissed. He felt as if every other kiss he'd shared with other women had been a dull gray, while Maggie's was all the colors of the rainbow. Her plump breast fit exactly in his hand and was topped by the most delicious tip. He wanted to explore her, to trace her hills and valleys, to taste her exotic flavor.

He was about to investigate her other breast when a rapping nudged at the edge of his consciousness. Someone knocked on the closed door. Biting back a curse, Simon raised his head. Maggie mewled her disappointment. Her gaze was unfocused. She looked thoroughly kissed and thoroughly aroused. Simon wanted more than anything to see how aroused he could get her, because she was the most beautiful woman he had ever seen.

The knock came again, this time with Kelwin's voice. "My lord?"

Annoyed at the interruption, he called, "Just a moment."

Maggie's gaze focused, and when Simon was sure she wouldn't collapse, he released her and backed away. Her eyes widened in dismay, and turning her back, she hurried to fix her dress. He waited until she had covered herself and had stepped to the window before he called for Kelwin to enter.

"The Duke of Wyndham is here and asks to speak with you, sir," his butler said.

Simon raised a curious brow. Kelwin shrugged, indicating he had no idea what the visit was about.

"Good grief, the duke," Maggie muttered, pushing a stray curl back into place and smoothing her skirt.

"Show him in," Simon said, after a quick glance told him Maggie had put herself together.

Wyndham had evidently been standing right behind Kelwin, because he breezed right past the butler.

As much as Simon liked the duke, he wasn't at all pleased to see him. Besides interrupting a splendid interlude with the glorious Maggie, Wyndham appeared quite serious. And that expression usually boded unfortunate news for Simon.

MAGGIE TOOK A DEEP BREATH AND TRIED TO ACT AS IF SHE hadn't been about to succumb to the most seductive, luscious man she had ever met. Simon. More than Mr. Marquis. He had certainly won that point in their duel. If they hadn't been interrupted, Maggie might have lost entirely. She would have to be more vigilant. Forcing her brain out of its aroused fog, she focused on their visitor, who greeted Simon then bowed to her.

"Miss Blake, how delightful to see you again."

Maggie waved a hand. "Hi. Thanks. Good to see you, too." She could barely get her words to make sense.

A smile hovered around the duke's lips. "Your American expressions are quite unusual, but charming."

Heat flushed her cheeks. She needed to escape so she could regain some composure. Ducking her head, she murmured, "I'll leave you gentlemen to chat."

"No, please, Miss Blake," Wyndham said. "I think what I have to say might interest you."

That was not what she wanted to hear as she sank to a chair. "Oh."

After the men sat, Wyndham said, "We have had some odd occurrences in some of the government offices. Documents have gone missing, and a man has been seen appearing suddenly and then disappearing. This began soon after Miss Blake arrived." His gaze landed on Maggie.

"Look here, Wyndham," Simon said heatedly. "Miss Blake knows nothing about missing documents. And she surely has been nowhere near any government office."

Maggie appreciated his defense, but the duke's statements caught her attention. "What do you mean he has appeared and then disappeared? Like — Poof! — he's there, and then — Poof! — he's gone?"

Wyndham chuckled. "Yes, quite like that."

Maggie exchanged a look with Simon. "It could be Roger Bowker," she said.

"Who is this Bowker?" the duke demanded. "How do you know him?"

Maggie hesitated. "He stole something from me. A

pendant." She held up her chain where only the tiny key dangled.

"I fail to see how a jewelry thief would have any interest in secret documents," the duke said.

Simon thoughtfully tapped his fingers on the arm of his chair. "Unless he has somehow associated with Rosalind."

"Yet, I do not see the connection between the two, and how he is able to appear and disappear." Wyndham shook his head. "I thought because of your — ah — former friend-ship with Rosalind Hornley and Miss Blake's unusual arrival in England, you might have an idea about what is going on here. Although I trust your patriotism, Wildford, Miss Blake is from America, and we are currently engaged in a war with that country."

Simon shot to his feet. "Are you implying Miss Blake is behind the disappearance of those documents? Are you impugning Miss Blake's honor? Our friendship goes back far, Wyndham, but this is an insult. Do you really wish to meet on the field at Hampstead Heath?"

The duke stared up at him with narrowed eyes. A tense silence gripped the air. Maggie glanced between the two men, who looked as if they might attack each other at any moment, and abruptly realized what Simon had asked his friend.

"A duel?!" She jumped up. "Did you just challenge him to a duel?"

Simon's gaze cut to her. His jaw was set, and a muscle pulsed.

"No." Her hand sliced through the air. "No duel. Mr. Duke has every right to question my allegiance."

"Mr. Duke?" Behind his hand, the duke made a noise somewhere between a cough and a laugh. "Please, Miss Blake, call me Wyndham."

Simon ignored his friend and continued to stare at her. Insulted anger rippled off him. Maggie released a tiny sigh. No one was going to duel on her account. She had to reveal the truth even though the Duke of Wyndham might think she was crazy.

Sitting again, she took a moment, carefully arranging her skirt. She had never dealt with an enraged marquis who thought her honor had been impugned. She certainly didn't know all the nuances of dueling and challenges and such, but she had dealt with angry customers who thought their antiques that she'd sold on consignment in her shop should have sold for much more than they had received.

She looked up at the marquis. "I don't want anyone dueling over me, and I think Wyndham has every right to be suspicious of where I come from. Don't you agree?" She placed significant emphasis on that last question.

Simon stared at her a moment. Then with a muttered curse, he strode to the far end of the room, where he glared out the window.

Maggie turned back to the duke. "I don't know what the marquis told you about how we met."

"Not very much, I'm afraid," Wyndham said. "I assumed he somehow smuggled you into the country."

"And about his release from prison?" she asked.

The duke's gaze turned calculating. "He wasn't released, was he? Did his crew help him escape?"

"No, I did."

"I beg your pardon?"

Maggie took a breath. "I helped him escape. With my pendant that was stolen."

Confusion wrinkled the duke's brow. "Your pendant? How on earth —?"

"He's not going to believe you," Simon grumbled from the far side of the room.

"My pendant is a key into time," she said. "I'm not from this century. I'm from the twenty-first century. The pendant pulled the Marquis of Wildford out of prison and sent him to my time, and then brought us both to this century."

Wyndham stared at her, then he laughed. "The twenty-first century? That is a very imaginative, intriguing story, Miss Blake."

Keeping his back turned, Simon said, "I did say he wouldn't believe you."

The duke looked from her to Simon and back again. Maggie watched the expression on his face change from mirth to forbidding ire.

"I will not be gulled, Wildford," he finally said, his tone frosty.

With a sigh, Simon turned to face him. "I am many things, Wyndham, but I am not a liar, and neither is Miss Blake."

The duke turned to Maggie, and she felt his appraising gaze like a chilly breeze.

Crossing his arms and raising his chin, Simon said, "Although I was in the twenty-first century for a very short time, I saw things that would astound you."

"Yes?" Wyndham said, looking unconvinced.

"I saw a boy wearing shoes with wheels," Simon declared, "and I heard the most infernal noise that sounded like the scream of a banshee."

"Only a police siren," she murmured, but no one paid any attention.

The duke glanced from Maggie to Simon and back again. "Is this the truth?" he finally asked.

"Yes," Maggie and Simon answered together.

Wyndham's expression turned stormy. "This is beyond belief."

"Do not call Miss Blake a liar," Simon snapped, looking as if he wanted to tear his friend's head from his body.

"We told you the truth," Maggie said, attempting to keep Mr. Marquis from violence. Wondering how she could convince the duke, she suddenly had an idea. "Excuse me for a moment. I'll be right back."

She hurried out of the room and up the stairs to her bedroom, where she grabbed her sneakers. Returning to the library, she held out the running shoes to the duke.

"I was wearing these when I landed in this century," she said. "I don't think you've ever seen anything like them."

The duke stared at the sneakers. Hesitantly, he took them. Surprise crossed his face as he examined them.

"These are extraordinary," he said, weighing one of them in his hand. "I expected them to be quite heavy." Staring at the shoes, he was quiet a moment. "From the twenty-first century, you say?"

"Yes." Maggie gave an emphatic single nod.

"Bloody hell," Wyndham murmured, then he handed the sneakers back to Maggie, rose and strode to the opposite end of the room from Simon.

Maggie looked from one man to the other. One was aggravated. The other was befuddled. Simon glared at the duke as if he wanted to punch him. Ignoring him, the duke stared out the window and ran a hand through his hair.

Finally, Wyndham turned. "This is like something from a fantastical tale that might entertain children. If what you say is true—" He paused, shook his head, then said to Maggie, "You have the ability to travel through time?"

"Sort of," Maggie hedged.

"Does this Bowker fellow have the same ability?" he asked.

"Well, his ability is different." Maggie looked to Simon for help, not sure how much to reveal.

"It seems that he can travel through short stretches of time," Simon said. "But Maggie pulled me through centuries."

"That is a very unique ability." The duke thought for a moment. "If Bowker can also travel through time, then he might use his ability for evil purposes." He turned back to stare out the window.

"But is there any proof that Bowker is the person who stole the documents?" Maggie asked. Despite her uneasy feelings when she was near the man, she didn't want to accuse him of a crime as serious as treason.

"Who else could it be?" Simon countered. "I doubt anyone else could manipulate time like he can. What do you think, Wyndham?"

The duke turned back to them, his expression solemn. "We all have lost something. I need to retrieve those documents. Wildford, you need to retrieve your letters of marque. Miss Blake, you need to retrieve your pendant. I believe all three of these incidents are connected to Bowker, who seems to have the ability to travel through time at will, and to Rosalind Hornby, whom we know to be a spy. This appears to be a conspiracy of considerable proportions. I must present this to the Foreign Minister."

"But will you tell him I traveled through time?" Maggie asked apprehensively. "He'll think I belong in Bedlam."

With a small smile, the duke said, "I believe I can keep your secret safe, Miss Blake. Please trust me on this."

"Wyndham has been in the spy game for quite a while," Simon said, "and I would trust him with my life."

Maggie trusted Simon, so she nodded her agreement to Wyndham. But as she sank to a chair, she wondered how she had wound up in the middle of a situation that sounded like it was the plot of a spy novel.

LATER THAT AFTERNOON, MAGGIE SAT BESIDE SIMON IN HIS phaeton as he drove to Ludgate Hill where the establishment of Rundell and Bridge, jewelers, was located. They were planning to ask about Bowker's father, who used to work there, in the hope of finding a lead to his son's whereabouts. The plan that the Duke of Wyndham had laid out was simple and elegant. But she wondered what would happen if it didn't work.

If she didn't get her pendant back, she'd be stuck in the nineteenth century. She didn't want to think about that possibility. The documents that were stolen from the government office would reveal secrets that the English didn't want the French to know. That would perhaps prolong the war. But what would happen to Simon if he couldn't get back his letters of marque? Would the English throw him back into prison? Would they hang him for piracy? Maggie certainly didn't want that to happen.

"Didn't the men who arrested you know that you were the Marquis of Wildford?" she asked.

He glanced at her in surprise at the sudden question, then his lips twisted wryly. "I'm afraid not. When I tried to tell them who I was, they didn't believe me, because I never used my title when I was at sea."

"So, you were just Captain Simon Herrington?"

He grinned. "I was Simon the Blade."

Of course he was. The sword that sliced through the waves, wreaking havoc on his enemies. The name fit.

Before she could question him further, they stopped before the shop of Rundell and Bridge. Simon helped her down from the phaeton, and escorted her inside. The shop was elegant and looked like a drawing room, with a soft carpet covering the floor, several chairs situated around small tables, and walls painted a light blue. A slight, older man dressed in neat, dark clothes came from a back room at the tinkle of the bell over the door.

"I am William Bridge," he said. "How may I be of service?"

"My wife needs a wedding band," Simon said, "to replace the one she lost."

Maggie nearly choked at his words. They had never discussed what excuse they would use for visiting the shop.

Obviously, Simon had given the problem some thought. As his pseudo-wife, she obviously needed a wedding band. But even though they only pretended to be married, the idea of wearing his ring made her uncomfortable.

"I wish something with diamonds and sapphires," he added.

"No, please," Maggie murmured. "That's too much."

"Nothing is too good for the Marchioness of Wildford," Simon said, as he smiled warmly.

Maggie blushed, then frowned. That smile was too wily. She suspected he was trying to gain points in their duel of seduction. But she couldn't argue with him because she was supposed to be his blushing bride.

Upon hearing that a marquis and marchioness were in his shop, Mr. Bridge straightened his shoulders, and in unctuous tones invited them to sit at one of the tables. After they were seated, the man measured Maggie's finger for a ring. After that, he excused himself for a moment to fetch some stones to show them.

When Maggie was sure she couldn't be heard, she whispered, "Why did you tell him we wanted such an expensive ring? We're just pretending to be married."

Simon's lips tipped up at one corner. "As the marchioness, you need to look the part. Why wouldn't I shower you with jewels as the future mother of my children?"

His question made Maggie's stomach clench. The idea of

having children scared her. What kind of mother would she be? She'd never had a mother to teach her. But this marriage was pretend, a farce to allow her to move through society. A farce to allow Simon to retrieve his stolen document. She didn't have to worry about children at this moment. But she knew in her secret heart that someday, she would like to have them. As Mr. Bridge returned with a tray draped in black velvet and covered in diamonds and sapphires, she forced a smile and obediently examined the stones.

Simon glanced at the stones and said casually, "I understand you had a watchmaker working with you. A Mr. Bowker?"

Bridge glanced up sharply. "I am terribly sorry. He does not work here any longer."

"A pity." Simon leaned back in his chair as if he were merely passing the time while he waited for Maggie to look over the gems. "My father had a watch made by him. It has stopped working and I wish to have it repaired."

Maggie was impressed at the ease with which he spun his tale.

"If I may be so bold, my lord, I might be able to repair the piece for you," Bridge said.

Simon nodded his thanks at the offer. "That is generous of you, Bridge, but it is quite a complicated bauble. I believe I should have him look at it. Do you know where I might find him?"

"I'm sorry, my lord, but he has passed." Bridge shook his

head sadly. "I believe his son has taken over his business. Unfortunately, he has let it decline."

"All the same," Simon said, "do you have an address?"

With a reluctant nod, the jeweler agreed to write it down. After choosing several gems for the ring, Maggie and Simon were soon out the door and riding away. Excitement gripped her.

"We have the address," she said with a smile. "Now I can go to him and get back my pendant."

Simon shook his head. "You won't be going."

"Why not?"

"Because this address is near the docks, not the place for the wife of a marquis." His mouth was set in a firm line.

Maggie was about to erupt into an argument, when she realized something else. "If we go to the docks, then I can see your ship!"

SIMON'S HANDS CLENCHED ON THE REINS AT MAGGIE'S exclamation. On the one hand, he would enjoy showing her his ship, watching the wind blow through her hair and pinken her cheeks. Then take her below to his cabin where he could play the pirate with her. On the other hand, if he showed his face anywhere near his ship, he would no doubt get thrown into irons once more. That was not an experience he wanted to repeat.

In response to her, he shook his head. "No. You will not see my ship."

"But—"

"No."

"You know, sometimes you can be a killjoy," she said.

He didn't know what a killjoy was, but he had a feeling it was not a good thing. Reaching for patience, he took a breath. "Miss Blake, the docks are frequented by varlets, scapegallows, cutthroats and thieves. It is dangerous, especially for a woman."

She lapsed into mulish silence.

For some reason, he had the feeling that the subject wasn't closed. He was sure she would bring it up again. Before that happened, he intended to visit the address on the bit of paper in his pocket and retrieve her pendant. Alone.

With relief, he saw his house come into view, where he could distract her. He should have known that a woman who attempted to steal his painting would want to explore dangerous places.

Eleven

Later that evening, Maggie unlocked the door connecting her bedroom with Simon's. He had gone to his club to reacquaint himself with his friends and gather news and gossip, so this was the perfect time to snoop. Her curiosity about his room poked at her every time she glanced at the locked door.

The sun had set, so the room was beginning to dim, but enough light came through the windows that she didn't have to light a lamp. As she stepped across the threshold, she felt as if she were entering the den of a wild animal, forbidden, scary, and dangerous. Her gaze landed on the huge tester bed with its canopy of red damask and edging of gold tassels. It was matched by the counterpane, embroidered with deer and game birds in gold thread. The two wing chairs that bracketed the fireplace were covered in plum velvet. A Chinese carpet in jewel tones covered the floor.

The furnishings were costly, but they were bulky, and the colors were dark. She had the itch to redecorate, at least to change the color palette. But those weren't her decisions to make. She wasn't his marchioness with the right to change anything she pleased. Besides, redecorating wasn't the reason why she had unlocked that connecting door. She was here to find the paper with the address for Bowker's shop.

Slowly, she turned in a circle as she wondered where Simon might have hidden it. Nothing in this room was out of place. In fact, the only indication that he inhabited it was a book on a small table next to one of the chairs — *Waverly* by Sir Walter Scott. She flipped through the pages and turned the book upside down, but no small note fell out. Flummoxed, she puffed out a breath.

Then her gaze fell on another door on the far side of the room. Opening it, she peeked in and discovered his dressing room. A commode was tucked into a corner, and two huge wardrobes faced each other from opposite walls. Next to a door that she assumed led out to the hallway was a shaving table with a mirror.

She went to one of the wardrobes, but it was empty. The other one held a few coats, a small pile of shirts and various other items of clothing and accessories that a gentleman might wear. She rummaged through the piles, but found no paper with the address.

Just as she was closing the wardrobe, the door to the hallway opened and a man stepped in. He was not very tall, thin, and dressed perfectly in very subdued clothes, except for an extravagantly large yellow and white striped cravat tied in an elaborate bow.

"Oh!" he said, blinking in surprise. Then his brow furrowed. "What are you doing in here?"

Maggie came up with the only excuse she could think of. "I — um — thought I'd straighten Simon's — Wildford's shirts."

The man straightened and sniffed. "That is my duty. And you are much too familiar with his lordship."

Maggie nearly rolled her eyes at that. She was very familiar with his lordship.

He ran his gaze over her. "Are you new here? I've never seen you before. Why aren't you below stairs with the others?"

Below stairs? Maggie abruptly realized he thought she was a maid, and the man's outlandishly large cravat made a connection in her brain with a comment Simon had made. This was Deems, his valet.

"I'm Maggie, Wildford's new marchioness."

Deems's cheeks paled to the point where she thought he might pass out. Then his whole face turned bright red.

"Oh, my lady! Forgive me!" He bowed so low she thought his nose might touch the floor. "I am Deems, his lordship's valet," he said to his knees. "I am so very distraught at my mistake."

"Deems, it's okay." Maggie tried to soothe him.

"Okay? I do not know that term, but I will never forgive myself for being such a dunderhead." He remained bowed in half.

"Deems, please straighten up." Maggie thought this might be the perfect opportunity to find out more about the marquis who had fallen into her life. When the valet stood straight, she realized he was much younger than she first thought. "Have you been with the marquis a long time?"

"Since I was just a lad," Deems said proudly.

He wasn't much more than a lad now, maybe eighteen or nineteen. She had thought of valets as being older men with more life experience. "Were you always his valet?"

His gaze slipped away. "Oh, yes. Always."

"Deems." She used his name to reprimand.

Shifting from foot to foot, he ducked his head. "No, yer ladyship." His accent had gone from proper English to sounding like he might be from the poorer part of London.

"What were you before?" She gentled her tone.

"I'm not s'posed t'say." With a combative tilt of his chin, he dared her to probe further.

"I know Wildford was a privateer."

Deems's eyes widened.

"And I know he was arrested," she added for good measure.

"I wuz cabinboy." His words were nearly a whisper. "Then 'e made me midshipman."

"How did you end up here?"

"Oh, the cap'n, just afore he wuz arrested, told his crew t' run, and he give sum of us jobs in his house." Deems's eyes gleamed with adoration.

So that was how this young man had become a valet and Kelwin ended up as the butler. Maggie wondered how many other crew members were hidden within the staff.

"That was very generous of him," she said. "But your accent when you first walked in was very different."

He grinned and his eyes twinkled. "Me mum and da are actors with a travelin' troupe. I used t' travel with 'em, and I learnt t' speak like a high-born gent." He threw back his shoulders, looked down his nose and pursed his lips as if he had just sniffed something distasteful. "Is there something else I can do for you, your ladyship?"

Maggie laughed. "That's wonderful."

Deems's smile was radiant.

She felt she had made an ally, and perhaps he could help her. "Deems, I wonder if you would know where the marquis might keep a bit of information that he wanted to remember, like an address."

The boy's smile turned to a look of horror. "I can't be giving out his secrets, yer ladyship, not even t' you."

Of course he couldn't. Deems was loyal to his captain. Maggie scrambled for an excuse for her request. "Oh, this isn't a secret. Well, it is sort of. You see, I want to hide a note that he would find later. Sort of a reminder."

Confusion scrunched up his face, then his expression cleared. "Oh! Like a love note!"

"Yes, exactly." Maggie pounced on his explanation. She glanced away as if embarrassed. "Can you help me?"

He thought for a moment. "Prob'ly in his liberry. I seen him sitting at his desk and writing."

"Of course, that's perfect. Thank you so much, Deems." She sent him a wide smile, then escaped back to her own room.

The library was the perfect place for Simon to leave the address for Bowker's shop. She remembered the large desk hulking in a corner of the room. Why hadn't she thought of that before? With a smile, she headed downstairs for some dinner, and then some exploration of the library. And she'd pick out something to read while she was there.

MUCH LATER, MAGGIE SAT READING IN THE LIBRARY. SHE HAD gathered several oil lamps and candles and placed them on a table at her elbow so she could see the page, because she wasn't used to reading in such dim light. Simon had an eclectic collection of books, both non-fiction and fiction, and she had found Jane Austen's *Sense and Sensibility* on one of the shelves.

After eating her solitary dinner, she'd stolen into the library and rummaged through his desk. It hadn't taken long to find the slip of paper with Bowker's address. Annoyed at his refusal to take her with him to Bowker's shop, she decided she would go there herself. Surely, the area couldn't be as bad as he'd said.

She went upstairs to undress, then stole back to the library to read in solitude. Being alone allowed her to mull over the unnerving and disrupting events of the past few days and sort out her thoughts. How and why had she ended up in the nineteenth century? And with the man who said he owned the key her father had given her. That man, a privateer, a *pirate*, disrupted her equilibrium. He was too charming, too handsome, too devilish. Too male. His touch was much too devastating, and his kisses were much too delicious. She squirmed in her chair. No, she wouldn't think about that. Peering down at her open book, she forced herself to focus on the story.

Much later, she heard voices in the entry hall — Simon arriving home and Kelwin greeting him. The door to the room opened and then Simon was standing over her. Darn. She had meant to be tucked away in her bed by the time he arrived home.

"I thought you'd be abed," he said.

He smelled of tobacco smoke, and brandy, and the night

air. And subtly, beneath all that, he smelled of him. Salted caramel.

"I couldn't sleep," she said. "I worried that you might be attacked by varlets, scapegallows, cutthroats or thieves." She teased by throwing his terms for criminals back at him.

"Ah." His eyes crinkled at the corners. "As you can see, I am perfectly unharmed." He held out his arms, showing her that he was intact.

She ran her gaze over him and took in his stunning form in his evening clothes. Just looking at him sparked tingles in her belly. Without realizing what she was doing, she ran her tongue over her lips. His eyes focused on her mouth. The attraction between them crackled.

Maggie was not going to succumb to his magnetic pull. She was merely in her shift, naked beneath, and wrapped in a blanket, while he was fully clothed. An unfair advantage. It would not take much for him to seduce her into slipping her shift over her head and baring herself to him. As much as she wanted it, she wasn't going to allow that to happen. Putting down her book, she pulled the blanket tighter around herself and stood.

"Now that I know you're home safe and sound, I'm going to bed," she announced.

His gaze dropped to her bare feet, and he swallowed. "Your concern is heart-warming, Miss Blake, but won't you stay up with me a while?" His low tone teased at her.

She looked up at him, the candlelight dancing over the

sharp angles and hollows of his face, his eyes shadowed. "How will we pass the time?" she asked.

The question on its own was innocent, but it could also be a flirty invitation. If he was continuing their duel of seduction, she was determined to win this round. She wanted to even the score.

He tucked a stray strand of hair behind her ear. The light brush of his fingers across her cheek made her swallow. Resolutely, she ignored the magnetic pull of his body and didn't sway into him.

A corner of his mouth tipped up. "We could start with conversation. After that—"

His unspoken suggestion created wild and naughty images in her head.

She smiled, tamping down those images without much success. "Are you trying to seduce me, Mr. Marquis?"

Amusement lit his eyes.

Before he could answer, she said, "Because I can seduce you first."

She let the blanket slip from her shoulder. His gaze fastened on what she had revealed, no more than what he would have seen if she had been wearing an evening gown. Then she allowed the blanket to slip from her other shoulder. His gaze followed. A muscle ticked in his jaw.

"You know, I think I will stay up a while longer," she said. "Could I have something to drink?"

Surprise flashed through his eyes before it dissolved into

a sly smile. "Of course." He sauntered to a side table where a couple of crystal decanters stood with several glasses.

While his back was turned, Maggie let the blanket slip to her waist. By the time he turned around with a glass in each hand, she pretended to struggle with the blanket. And then it slipped out of her fingers and fell to the floor. He froze.

Her shift was translucent, a filmy garment of thin linen, and it only reached her knees. It revealed more than it hid, especially because she stood in front of those lamps and candles. With the rest of the room in darkness, her shape was clearly visible. And she knew that. One part of her understood she was playing with fire. Dangerous. The other part didn't care.

"Oh drat," she said as she bent to scoop up the blanket. "I can't seem to keep this on."

"Allow me to help." He quickly put down the glasses, strode to her, and pulled the blanket over her shoulders. "You don't want to catch a chill." His fingers came to rest against her collar bone.

Far from chilled, she felt heat bloom in her middle. She placed her hand against his chest. "Don't you want to get more comfortable? The evening is over, and if we are going to chat—" Allowing her words to trail off, she ended with a suggestive little shrug of one shoulder, the one where his hand rested.

"I would enjoy a chat," he said, but he made no move to get more comfortable.

"What would you like to chat about?" She undid the top button of his waistcoat.

"Whatever you would like." His fingers at her collarbone trailed down, halted by the edge of the blanket.

Two more buttons slid out of their buttonholes. "I think we should discuss literature. Maybe Homer's *Iliad* or Dante's *Divine Comedy*." She let the blanket slip off one arm.

"Ah, literature. An engaging subject." His hand followed the blanket down her arm, then back up again. Tracing across her collarbone again, he explored the neckline of her shift.

Maggie shivered at his touch. But she had reached the last button of his waistcoat. Slipping her hand inside, she let her fingers glide over his warmth, then circle his male nipple through the thin linen of his shirt. His eyes darkened.

"Let's talk about Dante's *Inferno*," she suggested.

"One of my favorite parts of the *Divine Comedy*," he murmured as his hand cupped her breast.

She sucked in a breath. "Do you think there are as many levels of Hell as he describes?" Her voice wobbled, distracted as she was by the gentle pinch of his fingers on her nipple.

"Definitely. Nine levels, each one more wicked than the last." His other hand cupped her neck. "But I particularly enjoy his *Paradiso*. Paradise." He lowered his head and swiped his tongue across her lips.

Of course, she couldn't resist. Because his kisses were heavenly.

Simon, surprised at finding Maggie still up at the late hour, fell, unsuspecting, beneath her flirting and seduction. He didn't care if she won this round in their duel. Her clever enticement was much more enjoyable than the evening at his club where all he heard was gossip about Parliament and chatter about the two wars the country waged.

She was delicious. Her mouth was sweet. Her breast in his hand was even sweeter. As she pressed against him, her soft curves made his blood race.

Dropping his hand from her neck, he gripped her bottom and bound her hips to him. His fingers caressed her delectable curves, dipped between her thighs and crept close to her cleft, warm and damp. With a tiny mewl, signaling her need, she wriggled against him. His erection pulsed to escape from his breeches. But not yet. Not now. The tiny part of his brain still functioning knew that her seduction had limits. But what a delight to push at them.

Releasing her breast from her shift, he abandoned her mouth to fasten on her nipple. He wanted to taste her again without interruption. When he sucked, she moaned, the sound going straight to his cock. And then her hand gripped his buttocks, and she ground against him. God's tears, she was luscious. He wanted inside her, spread beneath him, wrapped around him, soft and yielding and aroused. But again, no. He growled his frustration.

With a sigh, she pulled back. Her eyes were dreamy. Her lips curved softly. She was every bit as aroused as he was. But instead of inviting him to further his explorations, she said, "That was an interesting discussion, Mr. Marquis. Maybe we can continue it some other time. But right now, I think I'll retire."

Her hand slipped away from him, and she stepped back. With a smile, she turned toward the door. Just before she left, the blanket dropped to pool around her.

"Good night, Mr. Marquis," she said. "Simon." Then she was out the door.

He heard the patter of her bare feet as she ran up the stairs.

Simon closed his eyes and clenched his teeth. Those feet with their delightful toes. Someday he would get to taste them. But for now, he dwelled on the delicious interlude he'd just had with Maggie Blake. And huffed his frustration.

She was a minx. A vixen. She had seduced him with a cleverness that surpassed anything he had ever experienced. It was stupendous. Brilliant. It made his head spin. She had won that point in their duel.

Next time, he decided the point would go to him. With a wicked smile, he headed up to his own room as he plotted his next move.

Twelve

B efore sunup the next morning, Maggie jogged through
Hyde Park. She'd put on her shorts, tee shirt and
sneakers, slipped a frock over everything so she would
appear presentable as she walked through the streets, and
snuck out of the house before anyone could see her because
she needed to be alone. She had left the frock behind a bush
so she could retrieve it before she headed back to the house.
And hoped she didn't meet anyone who might be out for a
pre-dawn stroll.

After leaving the marquis in his library and escaping to
her room, she had spent another night tossing and turning.
Her foray into their duel of seduction had backfired, leaving
her aroused and unsatisfied, despite finishing herself off after
climbing into bed. No other man had ever come close to

winding her up as he did. She was playing with fire, and she had to stop. Except she didn't want to.

Forcing her thoughts away from the Marquis of Wildford, she allowed the events of the day before to swirl through her head. She still mourned the theft of her pendant, but she focused on the prospect of getting it back. The visit of the Duke of Wyndham with his plan to retrieve everything that had been taken made her brain whirl with ideas. Jogging helped her think.

Despite her attempt to keep the marquis out of her head, he returned to her thoughts like a sexy phantom. She wanted him. Very much. She wanted to finish what she had started. At least her hormones did. Her brain, on the other hand, kept telling her it was a very bad idea. So, she needed to run off all that pent up arousal.

Before her, the dusky park was empty because of the early hour. Shadowy mist hung beneath the trees where the faint light of approaching dawn hadn't reached. Birds twittered and called above her head. She ran past the ancient oak that had helped bring her here, the night still hovering beneath its broad branches, but she didn't stop. She felt no pull, no sense of falling through space. The loss of her pendant brought a pang of sorrowful longing. How could she ever get back to her own time? Pushing away the worry, she focused on the path before her.

Up ahead, the rhythmic beat of horses' hooves

approached, the sound coming closer. A rider galloped around the curve and came towards her. She edged to the side of the path and hoped the path was wide enough for the horse and rider to pass. She forgot that she was wearing scandalous, twenty-first century clothes.

The horse and rider kept coming. The beast was enormous, looming larger as it approached. She could hear its breathing, sounding like a bellows as it galloped. The rider leaned low over the animal's neck. Maggie stepped off the path, tried to ignore them and pretended it was only a car that was going to pass her, not some creature that sounded like it breathed fire.

Just before they swept past, the rider hauled back on the reins so hard that the horse reared, towering over Maggie's head. She stumbled back, awed by the power of the animal. It landed hard on its fore hooves, snorted and shook its head angrily. In shock, Maggie's gaze went to the rider. Her stomach dropped when she saw it was the Honorable Agnes Cuthbert.

"You!" the girl snapped, her gaze landing on Maggie with icy distaste.

Maggie decided to be polite and then get away as soon as possible. "Hello, Agnes. Out for a morning ride?"

"What are you running from?" The girl looked beyond Maggie as if searching for something. "Are you running from your marriage?"

"Not in the least," Maggie said, hiding her amusement at Agnes's obvious dig.

The girl's eyes widened with shock as she registered Maggie's clothes. "What are you wearing?" Then her gaze narrowed. "Is that how you caught him? Playing the harlot? I should have known. Are you running to meet your lover?"

Maggie refused to be baited, and she started to step around the horse. "Enjoy your ride, Agnes."

The girl tugged on the reins and forced the horse to block Maggie's way. She leaned down and hissed, "Witch. I don't know how you convinced him to wed you, but I'm going to destroy you."

With a sigh of forbearance, Maggie said, "You can try, Agnes, but whatever you do won't have any impact on me." Because she would be back in her own century.

With a screech of frustrated rage, Agnes whipped her quirt through the air. It landed with an excruciating sting on Maggie's upper arm. With a cry, she clamped her hand over the injury. Blood oozed from the wound.

"Get away from me, you bitch," Maggie snapped. Beyond Agnes, farther down the path, she saw a footman struggling to control a horse as he approached. She assumed he was Agnes's escort. With a jerk of her chin, she said, "Your nanny is coming." Then she turned and ran back in the direction of the entrance to the park.

"Wildford is going to be mine," Agnes called after her.

Maggie didn't bother to respond as she sped away, and

hoped the girl wouldn't chase her, because she couldn't outrun Agnes's horse. All the way to the street, unease tickled between her shoulder blades. Retrieving her frock, she hurriedly threw it on, then ran through the deserted streets. She didn't feel comfortable until she stumbled through Simon's front door.

Maggie was dismayed to see Kelwin in the entry hall when she entered. She had meant to sneak back in, the same way she had snuck out before the house came awake. But a maid was already sweeping out the hearth in the small sitting room where the Turner painting hung, another was dusting the stairway banister, and she could hear kitchen noises coming from below stairs.

"Miss Blake! Ah — my lady! Is everything all right?" Kelwin hurried across the hall. "You're bleeding!"

"A small accident, Kelwin," she said, breathless from running, as she blinked back tears of relief at being safe. But when she glanced at her arm, she saw blood staining the sleeve of her frock. "Could I bother you for a bandage?"

"Of course." He turned to the maid on the staircase. "Fetch the marquis."

Maggie started to protest, but with an implacable expression that she had never seen before, Kelwin indicated the small sitting room. "Please have a seat and I'll bring something to clean your wound."

She was glad to comply. Her knees were shaky from her escape from Agnes and blood seeped down her arm. She pitied the poor horse that Agnes rode when she used that quirt.

She had barely sat when Simon, wearing a deep red, brocade robe, burst into the room. He looked like an avenging angel.

"What happened? Dear God, you're bleeding!" He went down on one knee beside her as he examined her arm. "How did you —?" His gaze took in her hair caught in a ponytail and the sheen of perspiration on her skin. "Were you out doing that jogging thing in Hyde Park?" A line appeared between his brows. "I did say that you shouldn't go out alone. Thieves and cutthroats roam those parts at night, looking for easy prey. They would have licked their chops at a woman alone."

The scolding made guilt twinge through her. Glancing away, she swallowed her sigh. She couldn't stay cooped up in his house and not be able to go out when she pleased. But he did have a point, and he didn't know that more dangerous characters than outlaws roamed Hyde Park in the pre-dawn.

The gentle touch of his fingers as he examined her wound distracted her, and she tried very hard to ignore his bare chest revealed by the deep vee of his robe. Evidently her jog hadn't done much to tamp down her simmering arousal.

"I needed to run," she said.

"Yes?" He raised his gaze, and because he rested on a knee, he was nearly at eye level with her. Those eyes were dark with concern. They were the color of pine trees, of forests, of the deep sea. She fell into them, just for a moment, before she remembered herself and glanced away.

"A strange diversion, jogging," he murmured, as he focused on her wound again. "How did you injure yourself?"

"I ran into a bush. A thorn bush. I was distracted. By a bird." She came up with the story while she talked, because she wasn't going to tell him about the Honorable Agnes and her hostility. That was between her and Agnes. Even though she wasn't married to Simon, she was not about to let Agnes get her claws into him.

Kelwin entered with a tray of bandages, a bowl of water, and a crystal decanter. As he placed it on the table beside her, he said, "A nasty scrape, sir. Looks like the first stripe of a whipping." Then he carefully averted his eyes and left.

Simon's gaze pierced her. "The truth, please."

She shrugged, then winced as he began to clean her wound. "Just a thorn bush and my clumsiness." But she wouldn't look at him.

"Hm. Did you perhaps meet up with someone? Bowker, perhaps?" His casual questions thrummed with anger running beneath his words.

"No." She stared at the Turner painting, the memory of trying to steal it compounding her lie. She really didn't want to tell him, because Agnes's antagonism was aimed at her, not Simon. But maybe he should know, because when she went back to her own time, she wanted him aware of the girl's true nature.

She sucked in a breath and gritted her teeth as he dabbed her wound with something that burned. The scent of brandy wafted up, and she realized he had used it as antiseptic.

"I don't believe you." With a finger beneath her chin, he turned her to face him. "Tell me. I won't leave it alone until you tell me."

Of course he wouldn't.

Giving in, she mumbled, "Agnes."

His hands halted their first aid. "Did I hear you correctly? Did you say the Honorable Agnes Cuthbert? Whyever would she attack you?"

Men could be so dense sometimes. "She thinks I have stolen you from her."

Annoyance narrowed his eyes. "That again. I have never given the slightest hint that I might be interested in making an offer for her. I will speak to her father."

"No, please don't. That will make things worse. As soon as I get back my pendant, I'll go back to my own time." Saying that aloud created an odd little hollow spot in her chest. Going back meant she'd never see him again. She swallowed against the sadness and looked away. Anywhere but at him.

His hands jerked at her words as he wrapped a bandage around her arm. She could feel his gaze like a nudge.

"Then you would leave me to the ludicrous and some-what malicious imaginings of the Honorable Agnes?" he challenged, his tone light, but something heavier hung just beneath.

Forcing a smile, she said, "I'm sure you can handle it. You'll probably find some lovely lady at a ball or somewhere and fall madly in love. Maybe you could find a nice young man for Agnes, too, someone who would take her away into the country where you'd never have to see her again."

He stared at her a moment, and she was on the verge of tipping into that green gaze again when he focused on the bandage.

"I see that all women must have fanciful imaginings," he said. "Although I do find yours quite entertaining."

"Don't you want to get married?" she asked. "Aren't you supposed to get married, to continue your family line or something?"

He concentrated on tying off the bandage. "Yes. I am supposed to sire an heir, but I have no wish to do so at present. I have found no woman whom I wish to marry. Those I've met are giggly and empty-headed, concerned only with the next dance or the latest fashion." Once again, his words were breezy.

Maggie heard a discordant note beneath the flippant statement. "Perhaps you're not looking in the right place." She looked down at his bowed head and fought the urge to run her fingers through his hair.

"Where would you propose I look?" A smile curved his lips as he glanced up at her.

With a shrug, she turned away from those lips and that green gaze. "I don't know. A bookstore maybe? A woman who reads must be interested in other stuff besides dancing and clothes."

He tipped his head. "That is a very good suggestion. I saw you with a book last evening, Miss Blake."

She laughed. "I have to read. My sister is an author, so I have to read all her books." A tug of loss made her smile fade.

"Ah, yes. The one who is missing. I am sorry." He smoothed the bandage and stood. "Would you accompany me on an outing to a bookstore sometime? Perhaps you might point out a prospective bride for me. Or at least a good book to read."

"Sure." His gentle teasing eased her sadness. Taking the hand he held out, she stood with him. "I'd be glad to help." She should have dropped his hand right away. But she didn't. His warm grip on her fingers felt perfect. Strong. Comforting. As if his hand should always be holding hers. Realizing she lingered too long, she pulled away. "I'll go change and then see you at breakfast."

"At breakfast then," he said. "We can make a plan about our visit to a bookstore."

"Great." With a fleeting smile, she escaped into the entry hall and up the stairs. What was she doing trying to play matchmaker for him? She knew nothing about what he wanted in a wife, and she knew even less about the eligible ladies who were looking for husbands. For some reason, the idea of finding him a husband made her very sad. She told herself that was because she didn't want their duel of seduction to end because it was fun. It had nothing to do with the fact that she was beginning to like him. A lot.

SIMON WATCHED HER GO WITH A FROWN. HER SUGGESTION about trying to find him a wife was absurd and a bit presumptuous. He didn't want a wife. He wanted to clear his name and get back to privateering. Besides that, hearing Maggie talk about finding him a wife made him uneasy. Sad. Because if she found him a wife, then she would be gone. Gone from his house, gone from this century, and he would never see her again. He was enjoying her presence too much for that to happen. And their duel of seduction was the most exciting thing he'd had in his life in a long time, even more exciting than privateering.

Before she disappeared to the future, he needed to clear his name. In order to do that, he required the key she wore on that chain around her neck. And he had to find Rosalind. All of which involved Miss Maggie Blake. So, she couldn't go back to her own time. Not yet. Besides, she didn't have the pendant that would take her back. And that lightened his mood tremendously.

Until they could retrieve the stolen piece, he could enjoy her delightful presence and her wily seduction a bit longer. And he could plan his next move in their duel. With a smile, he headed to his room to dress and looked forward to meeting her for breakfast.

Thirteen

That afternoon, Maggie strolled arm in arm with the Duchess of Wyndham as they window shopped on New Bond Street. Jessica chatted about the shops which sold the best fans, which shops sold the most beautiful shawls, and the draper with the most exquisite fabrics. She stopped at the window of Clarimonde's, where a selection of beautiful hats was displayed.

"Look at that lovely bonnet with the pink feather," Jessica said. "Isn't it adorable?" Then she murmured, "Rosalind Hornley is inside."

Maggie focused on the interior of the shop, and watched Rosalind, Simon's former mistress, sitting before a mirror and putting on one hat, then discarding it for another.

"I think you should try on the bonnet with the blue flowers," Maggie said to the duchess, and whispered, "While you're trying on the hat, I can strike up a conversation with Rosalind."

Jessica smiled her agreement, and they entered the shop.

The woman who had been helping Rosalind abandoned her as soon as she saw Jessica. "Your Grace! How lovely to see you again."

As Jessica greeted the woman and asked to see the hat with the blue flowers and the one with the pink feather, Maggie strolled around as if she were looking at the caps and bonnets on display. She stopped near Rosalind.

"We seem to have taken away your help," Maggie said.

Rosalind met her eyes in the mirror. "A duchess out-ranks a mere Mrs. every time. You are quite cozy with the duchess for just having arrived in London."

Maggie gave a nonchalant shrug. "Through my husband —" She let her words trail off as if she had no choice.

Rosalind's gaze narrowed on her, then she turned back to the mirror. "Do you not like his friends?"

Maggie sensed the question was more than a casual inquiry. "I find the society different than that in Boston."

"A bit high in the instep?" Rosalind asked.

Maggie wasn't sure what that meant, but she nodded agreement, because she wanted to befriend the woman.

With a condescending smile, Rosalind explained. "It means arrogant."

"Of course." Casually, she examined some bonnets on a shelf nearby.

"Why are you conversing with me, Marchioness?" Rosalind asked. "I used to be your husband's mistress, and I betrayed him."

Maggie turned back to her. "I'm finding my husband—inattentive, and I thought you might give me some advice, since you have known him longer."

Rosalind gave a light laugh. "Inattentive?" Then her eyes narrowed suspiciously. "I somehow do not believe that of Wildford. What do you truly want of me?"

Maggie glanced to where Jessica sat trying on hats and keeping the saleslady occupied. Then she leaned closer and whispered, "You know I am from America. I think we might have certain ideas and goals in common."

Rosalind stared at her. Turning back to the mirror, she placed a flowery confection of a hat on her head. "Meet me on the bridge in St. James Park tomorrow morning at nine o'clock. No one will be about, and we can converse then."

Forcing a smile, Maggie said, "Thank you. I think we'll both gain something." She turned away and strolled over to Jessica.

Jessica glanced at her, then said to the saleslady, "I'll take the one with the pink feather, please. Be so kind to deliver it to my friend, the Marchioness of Wildford."

"Oh, my goodness!" Maggie exclaimed, surprised at her generosity. "Thank you so much!"

Behind her, she heard a huff of contempt from Rosalind. Jessica heard it, too, because a tiny smile played around her lips. Jessica linked arms with Maggie, and they escaped the shop.

"Well?" Jessica demanded when they were on the street.

"I think she might trust me." Maggie grinned and related the details of their meeting.

"Bravo! We need to tell the men," Jessica said.

AS SOON AS THE MARCHIONESS AND THE DUCHESS LEFT, Rosalind hurried out of the shop. She made her way down to the river, then hired a boat man to row her across to South-wark. This area was far different from the area she had just left. The docks were located here, where sailors roamed, where taverns lined the streets, where lightskirts lured with their offerings.

She stopped before a small, shabby storefront that had little in its window that would entice anyone to buy — a few cheap pocket watches, a watch fob with a broken chain, a stick pin for a cravat with tiny red gemstones, several of which were missing, and various dusty necklaces sporting glass jewels. Ignoring the *Closed* sign on the door, she walked in. An off-key bell signaled her arrival.

"We are closed," a man's voice called from a back room.

"Can't you read?" Then in a mutter, he answered his own question. "I suppose not."

"Bowker," Rosalind said. "Come out of your rabbit hole."

Roger Bowker emerged from a back room into the small shop. "Mrs. Hornley, how lovely to see you," he said with a smarmy bow.

"Leave off your foolishness, Bowker." She brushed her gloved fingers together to rid them of any dirt from the door-knob. "Have you been able to open the box?" That box, which she had stolen from the *Sea Raven*, contained documents that she dearly needed to retrieve.

He shook his head sadly. "Alas, dear lady, I have not." Then he brightened. "But I was able to procure a valuable piece." Digging in a pocket, he pulled out a sapphire and diamond pendant in the shape of a flower bud and held it out.

Rosalind stared at it. She'd seen that piece somewhere before. Where—? Then she remembered. "You stole it from the American wench."

With a satisfied grin, Bowker nodded. "I did."

"And you did not bother to steal the key that was hanging on her chain next to it?" Rosalind kept her tone mild, but inside she was seething with frustration.

"The key?" He stared blankly at her.

"The key that opens the box, you fool!" Rosalind wanted to bash him about the head for his stupidity.

Bowker drew himself up. "If you remember, Mrs. Hornley, I had only just made your acquaintance when I informed you of my plan to gain this bauble, and I had not yet examined the box to ascertain how it opened."

"Then you were negligent. You should have examined the box before you purloined the little trinket." She released a great sigh of forbearance. "Must I do everything myself?"

"I assure you, dear lady, that had I known the little key belonged to the box, I would surely have procured it." He closed his fist around the pendant, as if swiping it from the chain a second time.

Rosalind pursed her lips. "She still wears the key. Perhaps you might bestir yourself from your fanciful inquiries long enough to obtain it."

Bowker looked down his nose. "I'll have you know, Mrs. Hornley, that those fanciful inquiries, as you put it, allowed me to gain this bauble." He held out the pendant. "It will help me travel through time, a helpful aid when you need to evade the authorities."

"I do not need your services to help me evade the authorities, Bowker," she sneered. "I am perfectly capable of evading them on my own. What I need you to do is *open the bloody box*." She took a deep breath. Despite despising this man, she needed him. And she needed what was inside that box. "Bowker, I am sure you enjoy my donations to your little project."

He sniffed. "It is not a little project, madam. If — when — I decipher the working of this pendant, I will be able to travel through centuries, a tremendous achievement. I will be hailed as the greatest scientist of all time."

Rosalind held onto her temper with difficulty. The man was more than annoying. "Of course you will, and I will be extremely happy for you. But if you do not get that key and open the box, I'm afraid my contributions to your experiments will cease and you'll have no more funds to continue your research."

He bowed. "Of course, I am grateful for your contributions, Mrs. Hornley. I will do my utmost to accomplish what you require."

Rosalind smiled. "That is all I ask, Bowker. You may expect another contribution as soon as I hear you have made some progress with the box. Good day."

"Good day, madam" he said with a bow.

Rosalind barely heard him as she turned with a swish of skirts and left the shop. She always felt as if she needed a change of clothes and a bath whenever she visited. Dodging two drunken sailors and ignoring the disparaging calls from the lightskirts, she made her way back to where she had left the boatman, having paid him handsomely to wait. When she arrived, she discovered he had taken her coin and promptly abandoned her.

Her temper was nearly at the breaking point. Not only did she have to placate and cajole Bowker, whom she despised, but she had to do it in this undesirable part of London. No other boatman was in sight. Forced to walk, she headed to the nearest bridge to cross the river. As she did so, her mood brightened. She was to meet the Marchioness of Wildford the next morning on the tiny bridge in St. James Park.

Perhaps, she did not need Bowker to obtain the key. Perhaps, she could do it herself. She was so cheered by the thought that she dropped a copper in the bowl of a beggar she passed.

Fourteen

The next morning, Maggie threaded her way through St. James Park to the small bridge that spanned the lake. A fine mist fell, making the day drear and chilly, so besides the unfashionable early hour, the weather ensured that there were no others strolling the paths. She hugged the woolen cloak, borrowed from Simon's sister's wardrobe, tighter around her and peered from beneath its hood.

The bridge came into view, but it was empty with no sign of Rosalind. Maybe the woman had tricked her and wasn't going to show. Maggie decided she'd wait a few minutes. She walked onto the bridge and stopped in the middle. From this vantage point, she could see Buckingham Palace through the trees at the far edge of the park. Ducks quacked and paddled about, the only creatures enjoying the weather. But no Rosalind.

Hidden in a thicket not far away, Simon waited. He had been adamant about coming with her, his mistrust of his former mistress turning him dictatorial and surly, similar to his attitude when she first met him under the oak. Now that she was in the deserted park, she appreciated his company, even though she couldn't see him.

The silence, broken only by the occasional distant clatter of a passing carriage or a birdcall, unnerved her. Being alone had never bothered her before, but this was a different time, and the circumstances seemed precarious. Privateers and spies weren't part of her twenty-first century world.

She heard the crunch of light footfalls approaching. Turning, she saw a figure, cloaked and hooded like herself, coming towards her. Not until the figure stepped on the bridge could she see it was Rosalind.

The woman nodded a greeting, then said, "I thought the weather might keep you away. Perhaps your dedication to your cause is greater than I thought."

"I know where my dedication lies," Maggie said. "I wonder where yours is. You're English. Shouldn't you be supporting your own country?"

Rosalind's mouth twisted in a wry smile. "Not everything is as it appears. Perhaps not even your marriage."

Maggie had a moment of panic. Had the woman figured out that her marriage to Simon was a ruse? Then she remembered she had implied that Simon was being unfaithful.

Playing the beleaguered wife, she glanced out over the

lake that stretched away into the mist. "My husband was quite attentive in Boston and on the voyage here, but since we landed in London, he has become distracted."

"You spin a delightful tale, Marchioness," Rosalind said. "I am not sure how or when you met Wildford, but it certainly was not in Boston. He was in Malta with me, and then he sailed to London where he was arrested for piracy."

With a jolt, Maggie realized she had just blundered badly. Of course, Rosalind knew she didn't meet Simon in Boston, because he'd been with Rosalind. He'd had no time to sail across the ocean to America and back again. This wasn't the twenty-first century with jets that allowed travel across an ocean in a matter of hours. Travel in the nineteenth century took days, weeks, sometimes months.

Maggie said nothing for a moment as she tried to decide how to react. Act the insulted new wife and play out the charade? Or pretend she was a spy for America? But then, how would she explain how she had connected with Simon?

Landing on an answer, she smiled. "We all have our secrets, don't we? But I think you understand that in order to do what we do, they have to remain hidden. If you keep my secret, I can help with yours."

Rosalind's gaze turned crafty. "Fair enough. But my price is a bit higher than just keeping your secret. I want the key you wear around your neck. And I want to know how it happens to be in your possession."

Apprehension swept through Maggie. She had a sudden

suspicion the box that the key opened held much more than Simon's letters of marque. Placing her hand over the key where it laid against her skin, she ducked her head. She couldn't give that up. Not only did it hold sentimental value, but it would save Simon from prison and the hangman's noose, as well as help England in its war with France.

Raising her chin, she said, "How I got the key is not your concern. I will need quite a bit more than your assurances of silence about my marriage in order to turn it over to you."

Rosalind's eyes narrowed. "Very well. I'll see if I might find something useful for you. I will send round a note if anything falls into my possession."

"That would be great — ah — satisfactory. I'll look forward to hearing from you." Maggie struggled not to jump up and down with glee. She had just conned Rosalind into revealing she was a spy and incriminating herself.

With a pursed mouth, the woman nodded abruptly, then turned on her heel and stalked back the way she had come.

Maggie waited until she had disappeared down the path before she left the bridge and went in search of Simon. Her elation at outwitting Rosalind was very short-lived as the implications of what she had done landed with a thud in her brain. She was dealing with spies. International espionage. Dangerous people who most likely had no compunctions about getting what they wanted. The only thing she had to give them was the key, and she wasn't going to give that up without a fight.

The misty park with its dripping leaves and occasional birdcall turned eerie and sinister. Even the ducks seemed unnaturally menacing. She was cold and very damp, for her cloak had absorbed the precipitation while she'd met with Rosalind. All she wanted at that moment was the reassurance of Simon's large, warm presence.

But beneath her apprehension was a tickle of excitement at what she would be able to tell him. She had done it. She had outwitted a spy.

WITH DIFFICULTY, SIMON REMAINED STILL, HIDDEN BY THE thick cover of bushes and trees as he watched the meeting between Maggie and Rosalind. He had learned the hard way not to trust his former mistress, and so before the appointed meeting, he had roamed through the area to ascertain they were alone in the park and to assure himself that Maggie would be safe.

As he watched the conversation unfold between the two women, he could sense Maggie's tension, even though she hid it well. In the short time she'd been living in his house, he had learned her moods and the gestures that revealed them. When she placed her hand over the key hanging around her neck, he stiffened.

Somehow, Rosalind had threatened her. He wanted to strangle the duplicitous jade who had stolen his box and his freedom. Despite the bravery that Maggie possessed, he wanted to protect her from the dangers of dealing with the tentacles of his chosen profession. The people in that world were calculating and desperate and often dishonorable. He never should have agreed to this meeting.

He watched Rosalind stalk off, and his jaw unclenched. Maggie was unharmed and she seemed to have ruffled Rosalind's feathers. With a grunt of satisfaction, he waited until Maggie turned in the opposite direction and headed back the way she had come, then he made his way to where his coach waited unobtrusively on a side street.

He watched for her to emerge from the park and didn't realize how anxious he'd been until she arrived a few minutes after he did. Only after she climbed into the coach and settled on the seat across from him did he take a complete breath. She brought in the scent of the misty, verdant park, like Persephone, Goddess of Spring. The dim interior of the coach seemed brighter with her in it.

Beaming, she said, "I did it. Rosalind is going to incriminate herself."

"Yes? How did you manage that?" His mild words didn't match the shot of anticipation that burrowed through him, nor the pleasure he took in watching the glow of achievement on Maggie's lovely face.

Her gaze slipped away. "Well, I sort of had to promise her something."

"What did you promise?" Uneasiness stirred in his gut.

"Um, the key? I implied that if she brought me information, then she might get the key."

"You cannot give her the key!" he thundered.

An angry line appeared between her brows. "Do you think I really would?"

Aggravation tightened his mouth and he lapsed into exacerbated silence. This clandestine game of trading secrets made him impatient and dissatisfied. He was a man of action, used to fighting his way onboard a ship and stealing outright what he wanted. He should have stolen the key when he first met her.

Miffed that he would think she would give up the key to Rosalind, she crossed her arms and stared out the window. After a moment, she muttered, "I had to promise her something, and it was the only thing I could think of. Besides, I don't intend to give it to her."

Relief at her admission and remorse at his harsh words twisted through him. Rosalind had always been able to get her way. She would not have been any different during her meeting with Maggie.

"Perhaps we can find something else to give her," he said.

At his conciliatory suggestion of a compromise, Maggie uncrossed her arms and turned to him. "She desperately wants to open your box."

"Of course she does." He was not going to tell Maggie what else was hidden in his box. The less she knew, the safer she'd be. A shiver ran through her, and her lips were pale from the chilly air. Spreading his arm wide, he said, "Come here and let me warm you."

Her gaze turned speculative. He could see the battle waging behind those blue eyes, and he suppressed a smile because he knew exactly what she was deciding. Should she forgive him for his hasty words, or not? Get warm next to him, where he might take advantage in their duel, or stay safe and chilled where she was? She finally slipped from her seat opposite to sit next to him. The reprieve loosened his muscles. As he snuggled her close, he could feel the shivers running through her.

"We'll get you into a hot bath when we get home," he said, relishing the press of her thigh against his and the soft curves squashed to his ribs.

As she made a wordless mumble, a vision of her, rising warm and rosy from her bath, erupted in his head. He wondered if that vision would ever become reality. Most likely not. She would be gone before they ever became intimate enough for her to allow that.

Swallowing his sigh of disappointment, he contented himself with the pliant snug of her against his side and distracted his wayward thoughts with the next step in the plan to retrieve his box.

LATER THAT DAY, WRAPPED IN A SHAWL, MAGGIE STARED OUT the front window of the house at the rain that had finally taken over from the mist. She'd chased away the chill with a bath and had come to the library to find something to read. But instead of perusing the books on the shelves, she had been drawn to the window where the rain ran in rivulets down the glass.

Her elation at the success of meeting with Rosalind had been clouded by the harsh words she had exchanged with Simon. His anger over the key highlighted that she wasn't in a fantasy. This wasn't one of her sister's romances. His freedom, his life hung in the balance. The discovery of their sham marriage could be dangerous to both of them. Why had Fate put her here?

She missed home and her sisters. She missed her safe life in her antique shop. She missed the twenty-first century where she knew the rules. How was she ever going to be able to get back to where she belonged? Without her pendant, she was stuck. But then, it had only worked once, bringing her to this century. Heaving a sigh, she pulled the shawl tighter.

She was grateful to Simon for sheltering her, but she couldn't live in his house forever. Somehow, she had to find her way back to her own time. Either that or find some way to support herself. The auction houses of Christie's and Sotheby's were already in existence, so perhaps she might be able to work for one of them. She wondered if Simon had some furniture or bric-a-brac in his attic that she could sell for him.

The door opened and he walked in, as if thinking his name had conjured him.

"Am I disturbing you?" he asked.

Maggie shook her head. "I'll just get my book and leave you to your work. You probably have privateering stuff to plan." She gestured to the desk across the room where several rolled-up maps and other papers lay scattered.

"Please, don't go."

He came up behind her and placed his hands on her shoulders. His thumbs rested against the nape of her neck. Why did that simple touch feel so good? Without realizing what she did, she dropped her chin, stretching the skin on her nape to give him access.

"I wanted to tell you what a marvelous thing you did this morning when you met with Rosalind," he said. "I was perhaps less than enthusiastic in the coach."

His praise warmed her better than any hot bath. His wry second statement made her smile. He had been an ass.

"I don't plan to give her the key," she said.

"I know." His thumbs stroked up and down.

Maggie nearly moaned at the sensation. Instead, she caught her bottom lip between her teeth and her eyes slid closed. If he was making the next move in their duel of seduction, she didn't care. She felt very alone and overwhelmed. Frightened at the prospect of living in a century that wasn't hers. Frightened at the danger that seemed to be creeping closer. The weight of his hands on her shoulders, the caress of his thumbs helped her forget all of that for a moment.

She felt the touch of his lips on her neck between his thumbs. Craving the need for a hug, she turned to face him. His eyes, the color of pine trees, watched her, waited. She slipped her arms beneath his coat and spread her fingers against his back. The firm muscles there reassured her. He was solid, a breakwater against the tides of uncertainty.

Wrapping her up in his strong arms, he tucked her beneath his chin. "What is it, countess?"

She smiled at his nickname for her but didn't answer, instead she rested her forehead against his chest. Just for a moment, she could pretend that everything was as it should be, that she wasn't caught in the past and involved in clandestine machinations. His hug comforted, but it also broke down her defenses. This wasn't the time to be vulnerable. If she let loose the words that clogged her throat, that bashed against the walls of her mind, she'd end up a blubbering mess. She wasn't going to release her fears and dump them on him. Keeping them closed off kept her safe.

Raising her head, she traced his mouth with a finger, the top lip sculpted in hard lines, the bottom lip softer.

"Kiss me," she whispered.

His gaze probed, as if asking if she really meant what she said. Tipping up her chin, he brushed his lips across her mouth, once, twice. She shivered, not from cold, but from anticipation. His kisses devoured, devastated, destroyed her. They wiped out everything else in her brain. She wanted that badly, to have everything blotted out except this man.

His hand slid up from her neck to cup her head, his fingers tangling in her hair. She watched his eyes darken until only a thin ring of green remained. Then he lowered his head and claimed her mouth.

As if he had waved a magic wand, her fears and uncertainty drained away. Nothing mattered except his mouth pressed against hers, his tongue probing, dancing with hers, as if an invisible orchestra played a sensuous, passionate tune. Tingles tripped through her, ending in a pulse of need between her thighs. She edged closer, flattening against him. His erection, a tantalizing bulge, pressed exactly where she wanted. Except layers of clothing separated them. With a whimper of frustration, she squirmed.

He jerked away. "No."

His rejection stabbed like a knife to her middle.

Shame and confusion made her step back.

Wrapping his fingers around her upper arms, he halted her flight.

"I'll not take advantage," he said with a shake of his head.

His thumb traced across her cheek, and he tucked a stray strand of hair behind her ear. "Something disturbs you."

She let go of her hurt in a sigh. He hadn't rejected her, only put their lovemaking on pause. She felt stronger now, strong enough to share a bit of what she felt.

"I don't know if I'll ever be able to get back home," she said.

Compassion softened his gaze. "I'm sorry you are stuck here with me."

"You're not so bad to be stuck with," she said with a smile, then sobered. "But I would like to be able to get home."

His jaw tightened with determination. "We will get your pendant back."

"And we'll get back your box," she added with a nod.

"Until then, would you care for a game of chess?" He gestured to a small table and two chairs set up in a corner of the room with a chess board.

"I never learned how to play."

A sly look entered his eyes. "Then I think it's time you learned, because dealing with Rosalind is like a game of chess."

Maggie laughed. "Then definitely, let's play."

Because playing a game with Simon was the next best thing to seducing him.

Fifteen

Very early the next day, Maggie and Simon hurried through Hyde Park on their way to watch a hot air balloon ascent. The rain had disappeared, and the day promised to be bright and sunny. All types of people streamed into the park from all directions, because watching someone fly into the air was a marvel. The Wright brothers' flight at Kitty Hawk wouldn't happen for nearly a hundred years. She wondered what these people would think if they ever saw a passenger jet take off and land or leave its white contrail through a blue sky. All around them, people chattered with excitement. Even Maggie was eager to see the balloon, because seeing one rise up was such a beautiful sight.

They finally reached a field where hundreds of people had gathered, leaving a large open area in the center. Several men scurried around a contraption that was connected by fat tubing to a partially inflated balloon. It was made of wide, red and blue vertical stripes with a wide band of yellow curlicues around its middle. A net of ropes covered the balloon and tied it to a basket beneath, shaped like a miniature ship. Other ropes anchored it to the ground as the balloon slowly filled.

Simon nodded to several acquaintances and then became caught up in conversation with one of them. As the two men chatted, Maggie absorbed the atmosphere. Around her, she heard people commenting on the huge size of the balloon, the stylish pelisse of Lady Such-and-Such, the extraordinary contraption being used to fill the balloon, the atrocious frock of Miss So-and-So, the favorite horse at the upcoming race at Ascot, and on and on. She took it all in, trying to remember everything for the time when she would return to the twenty-first century, so she could tell her younger sister, Darcy, and maybe, if she ever found Emma, she could tell her, too.

At a distance through the crowd, she caught sight of a woman wearing a lovely, wide-brimmed hat with a jaunty white plume. As she was admiring her style, the woman turned, providing Maggie with a view of her profile. Maggie's breath caught in her throat. The woman looked like Emma, Maggie's sister! Was it really her? Maggie couldn't be sure, because the hat covered part of her face. But her chin and part of her nose seemed very familiar.

As people jostled to get a closer view of the balloon,

Maggie lost sight of the woman. She stood on tiptoe and craned her neck, but the woman had turned away. Just as she was about to plunge into the crowd to find the woman, someone grabbed her arm. She spun around to tell the person to let go. And came face to face with Roger Bowker.

"You!" she gasped. "Let go of me."

"Not until you tell me how the pendant works," he hissed, pulling her closer. "I know you are from the future. The pendant brought you here, didn't it?"

The last thing she would give up was knowledge about the pendant. "I don't know what you're talking about." Frightened that he might whisk her into the strange nothingness that he had before, she struggled against his hold.

"How does it work? How did you get here?" He gave her arm a shake, as if he could rattle the answer out of her.

"By ship," she snapped.

"Not by ship." His pale brown eyes turned darker, as if he was trying to see into her head. "What future century did you come from?"

"The future?" She gave an incredulous little laugh. "Are you mad?"

"Not mad, marchioness, if that is your true title." His gaze narrowed. "But I can start a rumor that the new Marchioness of Wildford has some very strange ideas and is behaving in a most unusual manner. Rumors can do more damage than a weapon ever could."

Maggie didn't care about her own reputation, but if

rumors started about Simon, then he might be discovered and thrown back into prison. She couldn't let Bowker know she was afraid. "Maybe I'll start a rumor about you, and how you are deranged and attacked me. Now, let go of my arm or I'll scream." What she really wanted to do was punch him, but she suspected that wasn't proper behavior for a marchioness. She'd save that response for another time when she wasn't in public and could bring a number of gentlemen running to her aid with a scream.

Bowker's mouth thinned, and his pale cheeks bloomed with two bright splotches. "The other one pretended ignorance, too. Maybe the two of you work together. Maybe —"

"Hold there!" Simon called out with steel in his tone. "Release her at once!"

Bowker shot a venomous look in Simon's direction. "We are not finished, marchioness," he snarled, as Simon wrestled Maggie away from him.

Jumping away from Simon, Bowker pulled out a pocket watch, fiddled with the knob, and began to fade away. With a pop, he was gone.

Several people nearby had seen the exchange, and Maggie didn't want her secret revealed. Pretending distress, she cried out, "He stole it! My reticule! Oh, my goodness, he stole it!"

Those near her sent up a cry, "Thief! Thief! Find him! Which way did he go? Catch him!"

In the resulting confusion, Simon guided her away. "Are

you all right?" he asked with a comforting grip on her arm. "Did he hurt you?"

"No, I'm fine." She gazed back at where Bowker had been standing. His last words echoed in her head. "He said there's another one, that he thinks we're working together."

"Another one? What did he mean?" Simon's forehead crinkled.

Maggie turned to look at the spot where she had seen the woman with the lovely hat. "I think he meant my sister. I think I saw her in the crowd."

"Your sister?" he repeated, sounding thoroughly perplexed.

She continued to scan the crowd as she said, "My sister who disappeared. That's why I was in London, to see if I could find her. I think she's here, in this century, because I saw someone who looked a lot like her."

At that moment, the crowd gasped, "Oh!" and then, "Ah!" Out of the corner of her eye, she saw the balloon ascending into the sky. It was a beautiful sight, but instead of watching it, she scanned the crowd as she tried to catch a glimpse of the woman with the white plume.

"I have to find her," she said and plunged into the crowd.

"Maggie!" Simon called after her, but she ignored him.

She pushed her way between people, excusing herself again and again as complaints and aggravated looks were tossed her way. She finally arrived at the spot where she had seen her sister's lookalike, but only strangers surrounded her.

"Did you see a woman with a white plume on her hat?" she asked this one and that. "Dark hair, blue eyes?"

All she received were negative answers.

Simon strode out of the crowd. "Maggie! There you are!" He turned to those standing nearby. "Please excuse the disruption. Forgive us. The excitement of the flight, you know." He took Maggie by the hand and led her away. "What were you thinking to run off like that?" he demanded in a whisper. "Bowker might have popped in and taken you."

He was right. But she had thought she could find the woman. She went along with him quietly, disappointment making her feet heavy. When they reached the back edge of the crowd where only a few people stood scattered, she said, "I thought I saw her. I really did. But she wasn't there."

"I'm very sorry, Maggie."

His gentle tone salved the ache at losing her sister. The crowd surged toward them as everyone stared and pointed at the sky. Maggie looked up. And gasped. The balloon was sailing overhead. It was a beautiful sight. But that wasn't what riveted her attention. Just visible at the edge of the balloon gondola, she could see the edge of a hat with a white plume. The woman had taken a balloon ride!

Excitement surged through her. Surely, someone would know who the woman was. All she had to do was discover the name of the man who had sailed the balloon and ask him. With her spirits buoyed, she hooked her hand through Simon's arm and watched the craft glide noiselessly through the air, its colorful balloon bright against the sky. The plume on the woman's hat swayed in the breeze.

As Maggie followed the progress of the craft, wondering if that was truly Emma, she had the sense of eyes watching her. She scanned the crowd, but everyone was looking up, not at her, and Bowker had disappeared. She dismissed the sensation as merely left-over anxiety from being accosted by Bowker.

Watching the balloon drift away over the city, she felt some hope rise up in her chest. If the woman riding in the balloon was her sister, she had a sapphire and diamond pendant, exactly like the one that Bowker had stolen. So maybe she would be able to return to her own century. But Bowker would most likely covet that one, too.

A sense of urgency grabbed Maggie. She had to discover the woman's identity. If it was truly her sister, she had to warn her. Bowker was dangerous. Maybe even deranged.

"How can I find out whose balloon that is?" she asked Simon.

His eyes crinkled mischievously. "Would you like a ride as well? I could probably arrange it."

Of course he could, and the idea of a balloon ride with him tempted, but that wasn't why she had asked. "I think the woman in the balloon is my sister."

He glanced up at the craft, now sailing across the city.

When he turned back to her, his gaze was serious. "I'll have Kelwin make inquiries."

At his statement, Maggie felt a tiny lifting of the heaviness in her heart that she'd been carrying around since the death of her father. It had become heavier at the disappearance of Emma. But the sight of the woman with the white plume and Simon's offer gave her some hope.

"Thank you," she said, "but be careful." She glanced around and lowered her voice. "If it is my sister, Bowker might be after her, too."

His lips twisted wryly. "I think Kelwin and I can be discreet. We've been sneaking around the English Channel and the Mediterranean for a while."

Of course they had. They were privateers.

Feeling more optimistic, her steps were light as she accompanied Simon back to his house.

Simon had seen the woman wearing the plumed hat in the balloon gondola and wondered if Maggie had only imagined it might be her sister. But he would speak to Kelwin about making inquiries. In the meantime, he would enjoy the morning with Maggie on his arm. The weather was fine, and they could stroll through the streets and perhaps stop at Parmentier's confectioner's shop. He had a feeling she would be thrilled at the idea. He wanted to see the delight on her face.

When had he begun to want to please her? The vixen was a thorn in his side. She had his key and wouldn't return it. She'd tried to steal a painting off his wall. She was not always a perfect lady. She was from the future and would most likely return to her own time. But she was bright and sassy and beautiful. She was sensitive. She made his blood pound through his veins.

The night before, they'd had several interesting and intense games of chess. Once Maggie learned the moves of all the pieces, she had been a formidable opponent. Although he'd won all the games, she had nearly outwitted him in two of them. No other woman he'd known had been able to do that.

As they left Hyde Park, they passed a boy selling *The Ladies' Confidante*, a scandal sheet with all the latest gossip. Maggie took one, Simon paid the boy his pennies, and he and Maggie strolled on. She read as they walked.

"Someone named BW danced the waltz without permission at Almack's," she said.

"Shocking," he murmured.

"The Viscount L has been seen in the company of a young lady from Shropshire."

"I hope they have a long and happy life."

Her step faltered. When he glanced at her, he saw her cheeks had paled.

"What is it?" he asked. "Are you ill?"

She shook her head. "No." Her voice sounded strained. "The next bit is about you." She shoved the paper at him.

He thought the item might be about his sudden "marriage" to an American. But Maggie's distress seemed too severe for that. Skimming the first couple of paragraphs, he finally came to the third one and read:

What a shock we received when we learned that a certain marquis, who had been absent from our fair city for quite some time, arrived back on our shores with a new marchioness. We are sorry to disappoint those young ladies who might have yearned for an introduction, but that is not the scandalous news we have to impart. No, dear reader, for what we have learned is far more disgraceful. This reporter has learned through a very confidential source, that said marquis had already wed a Miss AC in a secret ceremony at an undisclosed location. We are indignant at the humiliating treatment of such a fine young lady and appalled at the dishonorable and contemptible actions of a gentleman who should no longer be considered such. We leave the decision of what should be done up to our loyal readers and the courts.

Simon's temper soared, and he crushed the paper in his fist. The Honorable Agnes had somehow learned who wrote such rubbish and fed them the lies. Not only had she besmirched his honor by accusing him of bigamy, but she had also made Maggie an object of ridicule. He should have visited Cuthbert and had him leash his daughter when Maggie had her first run-in with the chit.

A hand on his arm made him look down. It was a small, delicate hand. Maggie's hand. The red haze in his vision cleared.

"I'm sorry," she said. "This is my fault for landing in your time."

"It is not your fault," he growled, his temper still leaking from his control. "This is the fault of that conniving baggage who thinks she should be my wife."

She glanced back at the boy selling the sheets. "How many people do you think will see it?"

He followed her gaze, then abruptly turned them back the way they had come. When they reached the boy, he said, "How much for the lot?"

When the boy mentioned a figure, Simon said, "I'll pay you double for what you have, and double again if you collect all the others waiting at the printer's and bring them to me."

With a grin, the boy handed over his pile, took Simon's coins, and ran off.

"Do you think that will stop the gossip?" Maggie asked.

"Not completely." Simon hefted the pile higher in his arm. "Some people have already read it, but it should slow it down a bit."

She was quiet for a moment as they turned toward his

house, then she asked, "What are you going to do about Agnes?"

"Visit her father and force him to make her print a retraction."

He wasn't sure how that would go, since Cuthbert disliked him. On the other hand, gossip about the man's daughter getting secretly married at Gretna Green and then lying about it would turn her reputation from lily white to a dingy gray. They would no doubt have to leave the city and retire to their country manor. He wouldn't be sorry to see them go.

But he was sorry about the change in his plans for the morning. Instead of a pleasant stroll and a visit to the confectioner's, they were returning to his house. He needed to protect Maggie as much as possible from the nasty gossip that would circulate because of Agnes's evil poison. And he had to make a call on her father.

Disappointment mixed with his anger. A sense of urgency to get Maggie safely behind his door and away from curious stares made his jaw clench. Only when they stepped across his threshold and Kelwin greeted them did he draw a complete breath.

NOT LONG AFTER, SIMON REINED IN HIS HORSE IN FRONT OF the Baron Cuthbert's town house. It was a newer house, part of a terrace of attached houses that ran partway down the street, and more modest than his own, with only a single window on each side of the entrance. He should have arrived in his coach with the coat of arms emblazoned on the side in a show of power, but he was so infuriated that he would not wait for the horses to be hitched.

Dismounting, he tied off his horse and strode to the front door, where he let the knocker fall several times. A butler opened the door, and Simon handed him a calling card. The man barely glanced at it.

"I am sorry, my lord, but the Baron Cuthbert is not receiving," the butler said.

Simon wasn't in the mood to be polite. "Either let me in and announce me to Cuthbert, or I will bloody your nose."

The butler's eyes widened and he opened the door. Simon stepped through into a narrow hall and the butler led him to a small drawing room.

Before the servant disappeared, Simon told him, "If Cuthbert isn't here in two minutes, I will search the house for him."

With another widening of his eyes, the butler bowed. "Very good, my lord."

After the servant left, Simon prowled the room impatiently. Even though he and Cuthbert had always been cool toward each other because of their differing opinions in

Lords, he never thought he would be in the man's house and about to threaten murder. But here he was, and with each passing minute, his anger grew.

The door to the room opened and Cuthbert appeared in a banyan, obviously not expecting visitors at this hour of the morning. "What is the meaning of this intrusion, Wildford?" he demanded.

Without a word, Simon pulled one of the scandal sheets from his pocket and held it out. "This is what brings me."

"What is this?" Cuthbert snatched the sheet from Simon's fingers and looked at it. "A scandal sheet? What interest could I possibly have with gossip?"

"The third item might interest you."

As Simon watched, the man's expression went from indignant to apoplectic.

"How dare you?" Cuthbert snarled. "How dare you abscond with my daughter and then have the audacity to announce it to me with this!" He rattled the sheet in Simon's face.

Simon wanted to strangle the man along with his sneaky daughter. Instead, he tamped down his anger into icy rage. "I have not wed your daughter." He pointed to the sheet in Cuthbert's hands. "That is a lie. I have been out of the city, in fact out of the country, for quite some time. I'm sure you are aware of your daughter's comings and goings, and I doubt very much that she was out of your purview long enough for a trip to Gretna Green."

Cuthbert's nostrils flared. "You will do right by my daughter and divorce that American strumpet."

"Divorce?" Simon couldn't believe what he'd just heard. "I'll do no such thing. I am not wed to your daughter, furtively or otherwise. I should call you out for her maliciousness, but I do not relish killing you and depriving your family of its head. Rein in the girl and have her retract this slander."

Before Cuthbert could respond, a light tap came at the door. "Father?" a female voice ventured.

"Get in here," the baron snapped.

Agnes stepped into the room with her eyes downcast, looking very shy and demure. After bobbing a curtsey, she held out a parchment. "I'm sorry to disturb you, but I thought you might wish to see this."

With a narrow glare, he grabbed the sheet. After perusing it a moment, he offered it silently to Simon.

Feeling as if he was reaching into a viper's cage, Simon took the parchment with two fingers. When he saw what was on it, he wanted to throw something. It was a short note written in a nearly indecipherable hand that stated that the Honorable Agnes Cuthbert and Simon Herrington, Marquis of Wildford were wed before witnesses. Two unreadable names were scribbled at the bottom.

He was so incensed that he couldn't speak for a moment. And the whole idea of his stealing away to Gretna Green with Agnes was so absurd he wanted to laugh. Raising his head, he looked from Cuthbert to Agnes, who kept her gaze on the floor in front of her.

"This is complete rubbish," he said, forcing a level tone. "I have been nowhere near Gretna Green, with or without your daughter." He tossed the paper back at the baron, who fumbled with it before securing it in his hands. "Either have her retract this lie, or my solicitor will be paying you a visit."

Without another word, he pushed past the baron, walked around the Honorable Agnes, and stalked out the door. After mounting his horse, he decided he couldn't return home in such an irate state. Instead, he turned toward the outskirts of the city where the roads turned to country lanes, and he could gallop his horse across open fields until his rage subsided. Then he would return to his house, decide what he should do about the Honorable Agnes as well as her father, and distract Maggie from her fears and worries by another skirmish in their duel of seduction.

As soon as Wildford left, Cuthbert turned on his daughter. "You stupid chit," he yelled. "What were you thinking?"

"He was supposed to be mine!" she whined. "You promised!"

"I promised nothing! When I said I wanted him leg-shackled, I meant in iron shackles, not wed to you." He stalked across the room and back, pulling at his hair as he went. "You have ruined everything."

"I was only trying to help!" she wailed.

As Agnes broke down into tears, his wife entered the room. "Did I hear raised voices? Good heavens, Agnes stop that caterwauling."

Silently, the baron offered the scandal sheet to his wife. When she read it, she drew a great breath and her lips thinned. Her husband gave her the second sheet, which Agnes has given him.

The baroness read it, then stalked a threatening step toward her daughter. "You are ruined!" she screamed. "Go to your room, and do not show your face until your father and I decide what to do." After Agnes fled tearfully, she asked, "What are you going to do?"

"Send the girl to the country until the gossip dies," Cuthbert said. "Perhaps some country swell will wed her."

"I don't mean that," the baroness said. "I mean the other."

Cuthbert shook his head. "I don't know. Wildford has threatened me with his solicitor."

"His solicitor!" The baroness paced two steps one way, then two steps the other. "I thought you had gotten him out of the way."

"I had. He was in prison. Do you know what a shock it was to see him in Hyde Park? And with an American wife?"

His gaze turned crafty. "Something is out of kilter. I mean to fix it. I believe I will pay a visit to the Waterguard at the docks. Surely, there is some contraband that was left on his ship."

The baroness gave a satisfied nod. "Excellent. That will prevent him from taking his seat in Lords." Holding up the scandal sheet and the forged letter, she said, "At least Agnes did one thing for us. She besmirched his reputation by accusing him of bigamy. When he is arrested as an escaped pirate, everyone will agree he is a blackguard and not to be trusted."

"And then I will be appointed as a Deputy Leader of Lords," Cuthbert said with a gratified twist of his lips.

"Of course you will," the baroness agreed. "Haven't I always told you that you will rise, no matter what?"

Sixteen

After Simon left, Maggie moped about out in the gardens behind the house, but they had been neglected while he had been at sea and only the boxwood hedges edging the plots remained. The item in the scandal sheet had shaken her. Why would a girl like Agnes make such a foolish accusation? Surely, she didn't expect Simon to admit to such an outrageous claim. And Agnes couldn't have possibly known that Simon's marriage to her was a ruse.

Not finding answers or consolation in the garden, she returned to the house and went to the library where she hoped to find something to take her mind off the mounting problems. In her despair, she decided that the woman she had seen in the balloon gondola couldn't be her sister. When Kelwin made inquiries as Simon had asked, he'd discover that the woman was only someone who resembled her sister.

Fate, or the stars, or the Universe had obviously decided that the morning was going to be filled with disaster and disappointment.

While she was trying to make a selection from the many books, Kelwin rapped on the door and announced the Duchess of Wyndham.

Jessica breezed into the room right behind him. "Oh, my dear Maggie!" she exclaimed. "I've just seen a copy of *The Ladies' Confidante*. What an atrocious accusation! Wildford must be furious!"

"He's gone to confront the baron." Maggie was very glad to see Jessica, both because she liked her and her presence would be a distraction from wondering what was going on between Cuthbert and Simon.

Concern drew Jessica's brows together. "I hope he will keep his head and not challenge Cuthbert."

"Challenge him? To a duel?" Maggie hadn't considered that, and her anxiety rose as she remembered the scene with Jessica's husband when Simon had nearly challenged him. "Do you think he might?"

"I'm sure he won't." Jessica waved away her concern, but Maggie felt she was only placating her.

"If I hadn't come to this century, this never would have happened," she said. "But I can't return to my own time because I don't have my pendant."

"You mustn't think of that," Jessica said. "You are here now, so I have come to take you out to an exhibition at the

Royal Academy. You must be seen in public without a care."

The thought of her missing pendant and the suggestion of an outing gave Maggie an idea. Simon was out of the house. That little slip of paper where she had written down the address to Bowker's shop lay hidden in her room. It beckoned. Maybe she could convince Jessica to find the place with her, because she'd had no chance to slip away and discover it on her own. Besides, she hadn't felt safe going out alone with the possibility of Bowker popping out of nowhere and threatening her.

"I'd love to go to the Royal Academy with you, but I wonder if we could go someplace else first," Maggie said.

Not long after, they were in Jessica's dressing room and giggling like two schoolgirls. As soon as Maggie had explained what she wanted to do, Jessica had enthusiastically agreed and then whisked her off to her mansion not far away. She had explained to Maggie that the location of Bowker's shop was not far from the docks, and two elegantly dressed ladies would be fair game for cutpurses and randy sailors. They needed disguises. Her younger brother, she said, lived with her and the duke, but he was away at school, so they could raid his wardrobe and borrow some of the clothes he had left behind.

So, they dressed like two hobbledehoys, not quite men but not boys either. Then they snuck out of the house and wended their way to the river, where Jessica hailed a waterman who rowed them across the river to Shoreditch.

Maggie was amazed at the number of ships tied up at the docks and moored farther out in the river. Some ships were quiet, awaiting their next adventure at sea, and others were crawling with men unloading or loading barrels and crates and sacks. Busy taverns faced the wharves where sailors and merchants mingled, and trollops called out invitations. A bit intimidated by the hustle and bustle, Maggie stuck close to Jessica, who, after asking directions of a man who appeared to be a merchant, strode through the crowd with determination.

They headed away from the docks and into the warren of lanes where houses crowded and leaned together. Maggie was careful where she placed her feet, for unrecognizable filth lay in piles and puddles on the cobbles, and churned with dirt where there was no paving. She was very glad she hadn't attempted to find the shop on her own. They skirted pedestrians of all shapes and sizes, donkey carts, men hefting large bundles, stray dogs and feral cats. Finally, they turned down a quieter lane. The houses and shops that lined the way were a little better kept, but not by much. Jessica stopped at the edge of a display window that was filmed with dust and grime.

"This is it," she said, pointing at the door with flaking blue paint.

Maggie peered through the window. She could make out the shape of a man's head and shoulders as he worked at a small table at the back. It was Bowker.

"Do you want to go in?" Jessica asked.

Now that she was here, Maggie wasn't sure what she wanted to do. If she demanded her pendant, Bowker would no doubt laugh at her. But she really wanted to see inside.

She shook her head, then cast a wishful glance through the window. "He might recognize me, but I really want to see inside."

Jessica studied her a moment. "Have you ever played Commerce?"

"I don't know what that is."

"It's a card game where you create three of a kind, or a sequence, or other combinations, and then the person with the highest ranked hand wins and collects tokens from the person with the losing hand. At the gaming hells, the players use coins, and a player can walk away with a fortune or nothing at all. You must not let the other players know what sort of hand you have."

Maggie realized she was describing a game similar to poker.

Jessica went on. "This is very much like that game. You

are disguised, and Bowker will only see two young gentlemen enter his shop."

With a nod, Maggie agreed, and she followed Jessica through the door.

At their entrance, Bowker raised his head. "Good afternoon, young sirs. How may I be of assistance?"

"I am looking to purchase a watch," Jessica said, lowering the timbre of her voice.

Maggie glanced around and noticed that only watches were displayed. She remembered that the jeweler, Mr. Bridge, whom she had visited with Simon, had mentioned that he was a clockmaker. Jessica asked about some time pieces displayed on a side counter and drew him away from his worktable, so Maggie had a chance to wander the space, as if she were merely waiting for her friend.

The shop was small and a closed door at the back most likely led to a workshop. She dearly wanted to see what was behind the door, but a quick glance told her that Bowker had only to raise his head to see what she was doing. Instead, she strolled nearer his worktable to peek at what he had been focused on. It was a wooden box about the size of a large loaf of bread with the carving of a raven on top and breaking waves on the sides. Each of its corners was reinforced with ornate brass braces, and an intricate brass escutcheon surrounded the keyhole. With a start, she realized she was most likely looking at Simon's box with his letters of marque on the inside.

How did Bowker come to be in possession of it when Rosalind was the one who stole it? Had she sold it to him? It appeared that Bowker had been trying to open it without much success. If he couldn't open the box without the key, that meant Rosalind hadn't been able to open it, so Simon's papers were safe. Perhaps Rosalind had given it to Bowker to unlock. Could they be working together? That thought sent a chill down her back.

Maggie placed her hand over the key hanging on the chain beneath her borrowed shirt. She dearly wanted to push the key into the lock to see if it fit, but she didn't want to try to open the box in front of Bowker. Maybe she could steal it.

Peeking over her shoulder, she saw that Jessica was keeping the man occupied. But how would she sneak the box past him? She worried her bottom lip as she thought it over. The only option she could see was to grab it and run.

Just as she wrapped her hands around it, Bowker called out, "Here now! What are you doing?"

She spun around with the box in her hands.

"Put that down!" Then his eyes narrowed. "You! I know who you are!" Pulling a watch out of his pocket with one hand, he grabbed Jessica by the arm with the other. His demeanor turned menacing. "Unless you wish for your friend to be deposited in a less desirable place and time, marchioness, you would be wise to put down that box."

Maggie recognized the watch he held as the same

unusual one that he had used before to transport her that one frightening time when he stole her pendant. She couldn't allow him to take Jessica to some other place or time. He might leave her there, never to be seen again. But she had Simon's box with documents inside that would clear his name. How could she leave it in this villain's hands? How could she risk Jessica's life? Coming to her decision, carefully, she placed the box back on the worktable but kept her hand resting on its lid. Maybe, somehow, she could sneak it away.

"Let my friend go," she said.

"Not until you tell me how the pendant works," he said.

Maggie worked very hard not to react. So, he did have it and had no idea how to use it to take him through time. But she had no idea how it worked either. Jessica shook her head, indicating she shouldn't reveal anything.

Pretending indifference, Maggie said, "The pendant? That silly bauble? What makes you think it can do anything?"

Bowker's eyes narrowed. "You know it can. It brought you here."

As if greatly insulted, Maggie stood straight and tall and took a step forward, bringing her closer to the man. And to Jessica. "I brought myself here. The pendant is nothing." She inched closer. "In fact, I believe it's paste, not even real gems."

"You lie," he sneered.

"Do I?" With an indifferent shrug, she said, "Well, we each have our own opinions."

Maggie lunged forward, grabbed Jessica and yanked her away. At the same time, her friend gave Bowker a shove and sent him crashing into a display case. Grasping each other's hand, they sped out the door and away from the shop, down alleys and streets, dodging around pedestrians and wagons, splashing through muck and puddles, until gasping, they came to the river, where Jessica engaged a waterman.

As they were rowed across to the opposite bank, Maggie explained about Bowker and his unusual watch, and about her pendant and how she had traveled through time. Jessica listened intently, smiling like a Chesire cat at Maggie's description of her arrival in the nineteenth century, and exclaiming with condemnation at Bowker's brazen theft.

"Wyndham already explained how you appeared in London," Jessica said as they climbed from the small boat. "But hearing you tell it was much more entertaining. Wildford will keep you safe. But that Bowker is quite disagreeable. He is a horrid little man." She shivered delicately and linked arms with Maggie as they walked up to Wyndham House from the river landing. "You must put all that out of your mind, for we will have a very enjoyable afternoon at the Royal Academy."

Maggie tried to do as Jessica suggested, but she didn't feel safe until they were back in Jessica's dressing room and donning their own clothes to continue their afternoon. She pushed aside her frustration at losing Simon's box, for she never would have forgiven herself if anything had happened to Jessica. Somehow, she would find a way to get it back for him.

WHEN SIMON RETURNED HOME, HE WAS DISAPPOINTED TO learn that Maggie had gone out with the Duchess of Wyndham. Although his gallop through the countryside had released some of his hot anger, a cold determination had replaced it. The Baron Cuthbert and his sneaky daughter would not win, whatever underhanded game they were playing. He decided that while he waited for Maggie to return, he would write to his solicitor to apprise him of the situation with Cuthbert, as well as to his estate manager to let him know he was back in England.

His estate, Sea Watch, located in Devonshire, was situated on a cliff overlooking a sandy stretch of beach at the edge of the English Channel. He had intended to make a brief stop there on his way back to London, but Rosalind had disrupted that plan.

Just as he finished his second letter, he heard voices in the hall and then a light tap on the door to his study. Maggie peeked around the door.

"May I come in?" Without waiting for an answer, she stepped into the room.

Simon stood as she entered, a bubble of happiness popping in his chest at her appearance. The house had seemed empty without her in it, a sensation that made him wonder that he wasn't somehow adversely affected by being flung through time to her century and then back to his. He had never experienced such a thing. He certainly wasn't alone in the house, for Kelwin and Deems and the others he employed were present and attending to their duties. But they didn't fill the hole that Maggie did.

"I hope I'm not interrupting anything important," she said, as she stopped before his desk.

"I just finished." He replaced his quill in the inkpot and sanded his letter. "How was your outing?"

Her lips twisted wryly. "It was—interesting."

"Yes?" He wondered where she had gone that would warrant such a description.

"Jessica, um, rather, the Duchess of Wyndham and I visited the Royal Academy, where we saw some beautiful paintings."

"Ah. Did you try to steal any of them?"

Her eyes widened, then she sputtered a laugh. "Well, there was one portrait by William Beechey that caught my eye, but it was too big to fit in my reticule."

"A pity." He strolled around to the front of his desk to stand before her. "Being seen with the duchess will dampen the wagging tongues."

Her glance slipped away for a moment, then returned to

him. She merely nodded, indicating she had been subjected to nasty whispers and sly looks.

"I'm sorry you had to endure that."

"But that is just gossip." Concern drew her brows together. "What about you? Agnes has accused you of bigamy. Isn't that a crime?"

"She has done more damage to herself than to me," he said with a shrug. "My solicitor will deal with the baron and his daughter." He brushed a stray strand of hair from her cheek. "But it pains me to hear that you must endure foul whispers." As he trailed his fingers along her jaw, he was gratified to see her lips part.

She swallowed. "Yes, well, I ignored them."

"Excellent." He dropped into his own whisper. "Because the only whispers you hear should be pleasant."

MAGGIE STARED INTO HIS EYES AND WONDERED HOW A conversation about art and malicious whispers could make her breath hitch and her insides flutter. His touch on her jaw made her sway towards him, as if he held a string that tugged at her. Of course, she knew what he was doing. This was his next move in their duel of seduction. She didn't care. Because she wanted it. She needed it after the fright she'd experienced that afternoon, as well as that horrible accusation from the Honorable Agnes, and thinking she had seen Emma. Besides, two could play this game.

In the back of her mind, she debated whether she should tell him about the adventure she and Jessica had before they visited the Royal Academy. Obviously, the box she saw was important to Bowker or he wouldn't have threatened her. But was it actually Simon's?

If she told him about it and what she'd done, he would be furious because he had told her not to go to Bowker's shop. He didn't want her going alone. Well, she hadn't. Jessica had been with her.

His thumb landed at the corner of her lips, a question, an intention. Her decision about telling him or not could wait. Right now, she needed him, his warmth, his strength. With only a tiny turn of her head, she sucked that digit into her mouth and swirled her tongue around it. His gaze turned intense.

"What do you want, Maggie?" he murmured.

What she wanted, she shouldn't have. She'd promised herself she wouldn't fall for him. Her time here was temporary, but she could enjoy it while it lasted. Besides, she wasn't going to let him win the duel.

With a last swirl of her tongue, she released him. "A kiss," she said.

"Ah." He rubbed his wet thumb across her lips. "What sort of kiss?"

"What sort of kisses are you offering?"

Mischief crinkled his eyes. "I could name them, but demonstrating is much more enlightening."

"Show me."

"There is this—" He placed a chaste kiss on her cheek.

Shaking her head, she said, "No, not that one."

He nodded agreement. "You're right. Not that one. How about this one—?" He kissed the curve where her neck met her shoulder.

"Hm. That's very nice, but not quite right." Actually, it was very right, because it made her a bit melty, but she wanted to see what else he would do.

Sweeping his fingers across the spot he had just kissed as if brushing it away, he said, "Of course. That won't do. We'll save that for later." He thought for a moment. "I know just the thing." After touching his lips to one corner of her mouth, then the other, he asked, "Is that the type of kiss you wanted?"

She held back her smile. "Not exactly. I think I'm going to have to show you."

"Perhaps you should, for I seem to be getting it all wrong." He appeared flummoxed, but his lips twitched with humor.

She placed a hand on each of his cheeks. "You see, the type of kiss I want should make me all quivery on the inside."

"Quivery?"

"Yes, and hot."

"Hot. I see." His glance went to the open window behind her. "It is quite warm outside. But you mentioned hot on the inside?"

She nodded. "Allow me to demonstrate."

Drawing his head down, she placed her mouth against his and kissed him thoroughly. As she slid her tongue across the seam of his lips, his tongue met hers, tangling, sweeping, sucking. His arms wrapped around her, and he tugged her against his broad chest. The kiss seemed to last forever, and not long enough. By the time they took a breath, she was very quivery and very hot on the inside.

He touched his forehead to her. "I believe I understand now. I have other kisses in my repertoire. Would you allow me to demonstrate?"

"Of course. I am always eager to learn new things."

He trailed his fingers across her shoulder to the neckline of her dress. "While the kiss you demonstrated was quite delightful, I believe I can show you another that might fulfill your requirements of quivery and hot."

"Yes?"

He nodded. "Yes." His fingers traced around the neckline to the front of her dress where several buttons closed the neckline. First slipping the buttons loose, he then pulled at the ribbon holding her chemise closed. "A good kiss," he said, "an excellent kiss requires some preparation."

She widened her eyes innocently. "I didn't know that." The light brush of his fingers against her skin as he unbuttoned and untied was certainly preparing her. As she sipped in a breath, she felt her nipples tighten and dampness between her thighs. She knew where he was going, exactly where she wanted.

"An excellent kiss," he murmured as he kissed across her collarbone, "is quite satisfying, while at the same time creating the desire for more."

"Oh-h." The single word, meant as a response to his statement, came out more as a moan, as he released her breast from the stays and rubbed his thumb across its tip.

His tongue traced a line down across the top of her breast, but halted before he reached the nipple. She wriggled, trying to get him to take it into his mouth, but he annoyingly refused. Instead, he squeezed it between his thumb and finger, which felt very nice, wonderful in fact, but she wanted more.

He raised his head. "A kiss that qualifies as excellent requires the involvement of quite a bit more than one would expect."

Then he captured her mouth at the same time that he toyed with her nipple. His other hand cupped her bottom, pressing her against his erection. She whimpered with need. The touch of his fingers, the slide of his tongue, the sly seduction of his words combined to make her throb deep in her core. He dragged his mouth away from the kiss and licked his way down across her breast, where he finally—

finally! — sucked at her nipple. Her head fell back as a shot of pure desire streaked through her.

He turned her so she leaned back against his desk. With a gentle boost, he lifted her to sit on its edge. Her knees fell apart, but they were restricted by her skirts. Impatiently, she hiked them up and wrapped her ankles around his thighs.

"Greedy wench," he murmured as he reclaimed her mouth.

Despite the distraction of his kiss, she was very aware when his fingers circled her knee, then inched up above the top of her stocking. Then higher. The touch of his fingers on her bare thigh, the anticipation of where those fingers were going made her squirm. And then his thumb was there, resting on her bud.

"Is that what you want, Maggie?" he whispered against her mouth.

Was it? Yes, she decided. She did. Let him have his win this time in their duel, because she didn't care. She wanted his touch. She wanted this memory to hold close when she returned to her own time.

Opening her eyes, she rested her forehead against his. "Do me," she said.

"Do you," he repeated, his eyes crinkling with amusement. "A very succinct expression. Yes, I will."

His thumb ran up and down her lady bits and circled her bud. Sucking in a breath, she clung to his shoulders as her muscles clenched in exquisite arousal. Her breath released in a moan.

She heard a knock from somewhere. But his thumb was working magic.

The knock came again. She ignored it.

It sounded a third time, a bit louder and more insistent. This time, it was followed by Kelwin's voice. "Sir? Sir? Captain!"

Simon's head rose up, and his thumb halted its magic caress. "Yes?" he snapped. "What is it?"

Maggie wanted to scream in frustration.

"One of the crew is here, sir," Kelwin said. "I think you need to hear what he has to say."

Simon looked at her with sly mischief. "In a moment, Kelwin," he said. Then he slipped two fingers inside her.

Maggie's eyes slipped shut at the delicious sensation. Her muscles clenched around him, and she wouldn't have cared if His Majesty's whole army was outside the door. Simon made a series of deft moves, and she tipped over the edge, clenching her teeth so she wouldn't make a sound as waves of intense pleasure washed through her.

SIMON HELD HER CLOSE AS SHE FLOATED BACK TO EARTH, HER head resting against his shoulder. Kelwin sometimes had the most incredibly bad timing. But his tone was urgent, and so Simon needed to see to the unwanted problem, as soon as he dealt with the most delicious problem of an aroused Maggie.

As limp as a well-loved rag doll, Maggie slumped against him. The slight weight of her body felt delightful in his arms. The thought of telling Kelwin to deal with the emergency, whatever it was, flicked through his mind, but he squashed it immediately. He was still the captain of his ship, both literally and figuratively, and he needed to be responsible.

He brushed his lips across her temple. "Beautiful," he whispered, then reluctantly held her away. "Are you all right?"

Her eyes were dreamy and unfocused. She blinked, nodded, and straightened up. "Yes."

"I apologize. That's the second time we've been interrupted," he said with a smirk. "We'll have to find some place very private for the next time."

"If we're interrupted again, I might have to kill whoever butts in," she said.

Chuckling, Simon helped her stand, then he walked to the door. Just before he opened it, he glanced back at her to make sure she was decent. She had straightened her clothes and put herself back together. After smoothing her skirt, she sat in one of the chairs before the hearth.

He opened the door and Kelwin held out a folded bit of

foolscap. After reading it, he met Kelwin's troubled gaze with a questioning lift of his brow. His butler merely turned to indicate with a sweep of his arm one of his crew, standing uncomfortably in the middle of the hall and twisting his hat in his hands.

"We go," Simon said shortly. "Gather them." Then he stepped back into his library, carefully closed the door and turned to Maggie.

"I hope that had nothing to do with Baron Cuthbert and his nasty daughter," she said.

He glanced down at the foolscap and wondered the same thing. But Cuthbert wouldn't have the influence to arrange such a thing. Or would he? He would investigate that later.

Meeting Maggie's gaze, he said, "It appears that someone has accused the Marquis of Wildford of piracy. I am going to be arrested again tomorrow," he said.

MAGGIE JUMPED FROM HER CHAIR. "WHAT? HOW COULD THEY? You're not a pirate! You're a privateer! Don't they know you've been risking your life for your country?"

His lips twisted ironically. "I don't think everyone is aware of that. Or perhaps certain people might wish to ignore it."

"Certain people? Like Rosalind?"

"Perhaps." He shook his head. "But she's not working alone. Others are helping her."

Maggie thought of his box with its secret contents in Bowker's hands and wondered again how it came to be in his possession. The suspicion that the despicable man was somehow connected to Rosalind became a very strong possibility. If she told him that Bowker had possession of it, he would want to go after the man and take it back. But he couldn't. If he stepped foot outside this house, someone would see him and he would be arrested. Caught in the dilemma and concern for Simon's safety made her hand fist in her skirt. "What are you going to do?"

A wily grin spread across his face. "We're going to disappear. Would you like to go for a sail?"

Seventeen

ⓒ∾〇

Late that night, Maggie stood in the shadows of an alley that ran between two warehouses. In front of her, she could just make out the white of Simon's linen shirt. Behind her stood Kelwin and Deems, and across the narrow alley were several of Simon's crew. Peeking around his broad back, in the moonlight, she could see two guards standing at the bottom of a gangplank that led to the deck of a ship — Simon's ship, the *Sea Raven*.

They had come to the docks to steal it and escape his arrest. From taverns along the wharves, she could hear music, loud conversation, and raucous laughter. A scattering of ladies of the night slouched against the bricks of the warehouses and called out invitations to the sailors who ambled by, but they were few. The hour was late, and most revelers were already ensconced in their chairs with a tankard before them or tumbling with the harlot of their choice. The docks were nearly deserted.

A door opened to her right farther down the wharf and two drunken sailors staggered into sight. With their arms around each other's shoulders, they warbled an off-key sea shanty. They came abreast of the two guards, and one of them stumbled.

"Here now," the guard said, as he prodded the sailor with the butt of his rifle. "Move along there."

The sailor straightened, and weaving, saluted the guard. As he snapped his hand down, he knocked away the guard's rifle. The two sailors were suddenly stone sober, their movements efficient and deadly, as they attacked the two guards, knocked them unconscious, tied them up and gagged them. The whole incident took less than a minute. When the guards were incapacitated, the sailors dragged them into the alley and dumped them deep in the shadows. Simon murmured a few words to the sailors, and with a wave of his hand, he signaled everyone to move forward. Then he took Maggie's hand, led her across the wharf and up the gang-plank. His crew followed, hardly making a sound as they boarded the ship.

Maggie was amazed at the quick skillfulness that had everyone on board in a very short time and without raising an alarm. She watched crew members raise the gangplank, and others lowered a large rowboat into the water. Several sailors climbed down into it. A rope was attached at its back end, which was tied to the bow of the ship. Using the current of the river, the men in the rowboat pulled the ship away from the dock, and very slowly, the *Sea Raven* began to float down the river.

Maggie finally drew air into her lungs. She'd felt as if she'd been holding her breath ever since they had climbed into the coach at Simon's house. Even now, they weren't really safe. At any moment, someone could find the unconscious guards, and an alarm would be raised, or someone on shore could become suspicious at a ship floating away in the dead of night.

She had no idea how Simon had gathered his crew so quickly, as if a silent call had gone out to gather them. Watching the men as they duped the guards and then took them out of action was like being in the middle of a spy thriller. Dangerous, but exciting.

Standing at the rail of the *Sea Raven,* she watched the shadowy, black buildings of London slip by silently in the moonlight. After Simon had made the announcement about his impending arrest, they had shared a quick, cold meal of sliced beef, cheese, bread, and fruit, and then had parted to pack a few belongings. After dark, along with Kelwin and Deems, they had stolen out through the gardens behind the house, where a hired coach waited in the mews. Maggie had been happy to see that this one was cleaner than the one Simon had bundled her into when she'd arrived in the nineteenth century. He had left strict instructions with the staff that they should act as if he were still in residence, which would allow him time to steal away. So far, his plan seemed to be working. But how long before someone figured out where he had gone to hide and come after him?

Turning her head, she could make out the large rowboat attached to the bow of the *Sea Raven* by a sturdy rope, and the men pulling at the oars, which moved the ship silently down the Thames until Simon thought he could safely raise the sails. They were heading to his country estate, Sea Watch, in Devonshire, while he attempted to get the matter of his arrest resolved. He'd told her if the authorities came after him again, he could always put to sea.

She turned her head in the other direction. He stood at the helm and guided the ship along the river. Looking every inch the privateer, he had abandoned the superfine coats, the silk and brocade waistcoats, the intricately tied cravats of a gentleman of the ton and instead wore only a full-sleeved shirt, open at the neck, and buckskin breeches tucked into high boots. An old-fashioned tricorn hat sat low on his brow with a single raven feather tucked into a band around the crown. He looked like the pirate she thought he was when he first dropped into her life. Except this time, he wasn't disheveled and dirty from being in prison. And she now knew he was so much more than the grumpy, hunky guy who had landed on the grass in front of her in Hyde Park.

Turning back to the shore, she watched the jumble of warehouses and taverns along the docks slide away as they passed. Somewhere in that maze of streets was Bowker's shop and the box he had been trying to open. She should have told Simon about it after her outing with Jessica, but he had teased and seduced, and she had been thoroughly distracted. And she wasn't sure how he'd react to her going there without telling him. Then he had announced he was to be arrested. And that made everything fly from her head as they rushed to escape.

But she needed to tell him about the box. That was only fair, no matter how angry he got.

She glanced back at him again. This time, their gazes caught. A smile curved his lips, and something flipped over inside her chest. What was that? She sent him a shaky smile, then turned away as she examined the strange feeling. Fear? No, she felt perfectly safe with Simon on his ship. Anxiety? Perhaps a little uncertainty about his reaction to her visit to Bowker's shop, but not much. What was it then? Her thoughts skipped around and avoided the most logical reason for her unusual reaction to his smile.

The riverbank slid past and the congestion of the city began to give way to mansions, fields, cottages, and stretches of wooded areas. A low order snapped out, and sailors scurried up the rigging to drop the sails. Tipping her head back, she watched the white sheets unfurl. A beautiful sight in the moonlight. But she couldn't avoid the reason for that flip-flop in her chest at his smile. Gripping the rail with two hands until her knuckles turned white, she faced it head-on.

She loved him.

That was not supposed to happen. How could that have happened? She had specifically guarded her heart so she wouldn't fall for him. Her intention had been to return to her own time as soon as she was able. How could she do that if she loved this man? But how could she not return to her own time? Her younger sister was back in the twenty-first century. She couldn't abandon her. But what if her older sister was in this time? What should she do?

She put aside the dilemma for the moment, because she couldn't solve it. Bowker had her pendant, so she had to stay where she was, in the nineteenth century, and for now, on Simon's ship.

Behind her, she heard the sailors' footsteps as they jumped from the rigging back to the deck. The sails above her snapped, catching the wind. And a warm body stood next to her.

"I've given the helm to Kelwin," Simon said. "You should go below and get some rest."

Maggie wasn't the least bit sleepy. Too many thoughts were careening around in her head. But one thought stood front and center. She had to be truthful with him, at least about one thing.

"Can I talk to you for a minute?" she asked.

A dark brow shot up, and a corner of his mouth deepened with sly taunting. "Are you interested in continuing what we began this afternoon, marchioness?"

She puffed out an exasperated breath, although his question made her waver just the tiniest bit. "No. I need to tell you something."

"We can speak in my cabin."

He waved her toward a door under the quarterdeck. When she reached it, he pushed it open. She stepped into a cabin, lit only by moonlight, that encompassed the width of the ship and was surprisingly large. She realized this was the captain's cabin. Simon's quarters. A table with six chairs sat in the middle. A bed tucked into its own cabinet was in one corner, and against the opposite wall was a sideboard. Above it, a series of cubbyholes held rolls of paper. Maps and charts, she assumed. A window at the rear of the ship showed a view of the dark river disturbed by the wake of the ship and London receding into the distance. Below the window was a large chest with a padlock. The room was spare and utilitarian, but it suited him.

She turned to face him and came directly to the point. "What does your box look like, the one that Rosalind stole?"

Surprise lifted his eyebrows. "That was not what I was expecting," he said and went on to describe it. "It's about this big." He held his hands apart the length of a large loaf of bread. "A raven is carved on the top."

"I think I saw it." As soon as the words left her mouth, she let her gaze drift away, as if what she had just revealed meant little. She really didn't want to face his anger.

He stilled. "I beg your pardon. Did I just hear you correctly? You saw my box?"

"Um, yes?" She wasn't looking forward to the next revelation that he would demand.

"Where?"

And there it was. She had to tell him. She owed him that. Dropping her chin, she mumbled, "In Bowker's shop."

He remained silent, so she peeked at him from the corner of her eyes to judge his reaction. A muscle jigged in his jaw and his mouth was set in a straight line. He was definitely not happy.

"When?" he snapped. As she opened her mouth to reply, he guessed, "On your outing with the duchess."

Afraid to speak, she bobbed a nod.

He swung away, stalked across the cabin, stopped at the window, ran a hand through his hair, then turned back to her.

"Did I not tell you that area was too dangerous? What were you thinking? Bowker could have twiddled his watch and deposited you someplace foreign where you wouldn't be able to return." Then his eyes narrowed. "How did you know where his shop was? I had written the address on a slip of paper and left it—" His mouth clamped shut. "You didn't." He stalked a step towards her. "You invaded my desk." He came a step closer.

At his dark expression, Maggie fell back a step. But she wasn't going to allow him to scold her. "Yes, and I'm sorry for invading your space, but I wanted my pendant back, and you didn't seem to have time to go after it."

His brows snapped together. "I was trying not to get arrested, and keep you entertained and safe, and extricate myself from a horrid lie."

"Yes, I know you were very busy." She nodded in agreement, then sent him a bright smile. "But I found your box!"

He stared a moment, his mouth set in a line, before he let out a deep sigh. "I'm not sure whether to feel disturbed at the invasion of my privacy or kiss you for your bravery."

"I'd much prefer the kiss," she murmured.

He regarded her thoughtfully. "That would be rather more pleasant." He sighed again. "I suppose you didn't have much trouble convincing the duchess to go along with you."

With a grin, she said, "We dressed up as young gentlemen."

"Good God! And I suppose Wyndham knew nothing about any of this?"

"We never saw him, and I swore Jessica to secrecy."

He shook his head and his lips twisted with humor.

She laid a hand on his arm. "Please don't tell him," she said. "I don't want to get Jessica into trouble."

"You have my word," he said. "Now about my box—"

"I couldn't take it because Bowker was watching us." She wasn't going to tell him about the man's threat. "But now we know where it is, we can get it back. And maybe get back my pendant."

"Yes?" His question was more challenge than agreement. He sauntered closer, stopping only a step away. "*We* are not going to do anything. When we are able to return to London, *I* will deal with Bowker."

"But—"

"Hush. No more arguing." His voice dropped to a murmur. "Because I am going to kiss you."

Maggie wasn't going to argue with that.

SIMON COULDN'T BELIEVE HIS GOOD FORTUNE. HE DIDN'T HAVE to cajole, or tease, or seduce. Maggie came willingly, pliantly into his arms. She was luscious, an armful of soft curves topped by a wily mind. He was in awe. Her daring and bravery astonished him. Few ladies he knew would be so bold, certainly not the sweet girls who had made their come-out and were looking for husbands. Part of the reason he had agreed so quickly to Wyndham's proposal to privateer had come from wanting to escape them.

Now he had Maggie. At least for a little while. When his lips touched hers, he felt his whole body come alive. No other woman had done that to him. The other women he'd been with aroused him, but none of them intrigued him like Maggie Blake. He wanted to explore all of her, body and mind. She tasted delicious. Cupping the nape of her neck, he tangled his fingers in her hair, soft, like silk, so she would be in just the right position for him to—

A knock on the door to his cabin distracted him.

"Cap'n?" he heard. "Mr. Kelwin says to tell you we've reached the Strait of Dover, sir."

He held in a groan of annoyance. Reluctantly, he raised his head and drew away.

"Do you have to go?" she asked.

He wanted to stay with his arms wrapped around her, drinking in her sensuality. But he had to captain his ship. The waters they had to navigate were the narrowest that ran between England and France, and they could easily happen upon a French ship.

Drawing his fingers along her jaw, he nodded. "I'm sorry. These waters are dangerous. Stay here and rest. You won't be disturbed. I'll be on watch all night."

She cupped his cheeks and placed a gentle kiss on his lips. "I'll be right here waiting."

The gesture made him want to stay even more than before, but he couldn't. He took a step back, and another. Then turning, he strode out the door and desperately tried to push the vision of Maggie, lit by a shaft a moonlight, out of his mind.

BEMUSED, MAGGIE WATCHED HIM GO. THE LATCH ON THE DOOR clicked behind him, and he was gone. She was alone. With her thoughts and confused emotions.

The kiss they had just shared had been different than the others. Neither of them had tried to seduce. Somehow, their duel had been discarded and forgotten. Was it because of her confession and the discovery of his box? The tension of sneaking away from his arrest? Or was it because of something else?

She touched her fingers to her lips, still tingling from the feel of his mouth. The passion had been there, the hunger, but beneath that, she sensed a gentle possession, something that implied deeper feelings, as if he wanted to protect her from the world's hurts. Was that the reality, or had she imposed her own newly discovered feelings on something that, to him, was merely a light-hearted romp?

With a sigh, she turned away from the door and stared out the stern window. Whatever she felt didn't matter. Their relationship couldn't go anywhere because it wasn't meant to be. She would return to her own time, and he would wed some daughter of an earl or a duke. Maybe when she was back in the twenty-first century, she would do some research on him and his descendants, just to satisfy her curiosity. Just to make sure his life had been long and full, with many children and grandchildren and great-grandchildren.

The water beyond the window had widened and the rhythm of the ship changed. They were entering the Channel. He'd told her to rest, but she couldn't sleep. But she could make herself comfortable. She sat on the bed and tested it out. Not as comfy as the canopy bed she had at Simon's house, but better than sitting in a hard wooden chair all night.

Curling up, she watched the dark night through the window and tried not to think about the future, where she couldn't have Simon in her life, and he would have someone else in his.

Eighteen

Maggie awoke with a start. Blinking, she tried to figure out what had drawn her from sleep. The sky beyond the stern window had paled to pre-dawn pearl, so she must have slept for a couple of hours. She hadn't meant to fall asleep, but when they emerged from the mouth of the Thames, the motion of the ship on the sea had lulled her into dreamland. As she lay there, she realized that the pitch and roll of the ship had changed. It was more of a rocking sensation, as if they weren't sailing forward but had come about.

The bang of a cannon startled her. Were they in a battle with the French? Or had whoever wanted Simon arrested sent a ship after them?

She scrambled from the bed and hurried to the window to look out, but all she could see was water, no other ship, and they seemed to be drifting, as she suspected. What was happening? As she craned her neck to see, she realized no sound came from the deck, only the ring of the rigging and the slap of sails being blown by the wind. She felt as if the ship held its breath.

Quietly, she went to the door and opened it a crack. Deems, dressed in simple sailor garb of plain shirt and linen breeches, barefoot and without one of his extravagant cravats, crouched just beyond under the ladder to the quarterdeck. He turned, grinned and put a finger to his lips, indicating silence.

Keeping low, she scrambled to his side. "What's going on?" she whispered.

"We've come upon a Frenchie ship, a smuggler," Deems whispered back, his accent now one of the middle class of London. "It's the *Belle Annabelle*. We took 'er once before and brought 'er to port, but the Frenchies ransomed her. The cap'n knows the *Annabelle's* cap'n, an' so we're playin' dead to see what the *Annabelle* will do — run or fight."

Maggie glanced around the deck. The gun ports were open, and the guns run out. Each cannon had a crew crouched beside it, ready to spring into action. No one was visible above the rail. She twisted around and looked up. On the quarterdeck, Simon stood tall next to Kelwin, who had the helm. They were the only two men who would be visible from the other ship.

Anxiety clutched at her as she realized that if the other

ship came close enough, they might be shot by someone up in the rigging. She peeked over the rail and immediately Deems dragged her back down. But she had been able to see that the French ship was too far away for a marksman to take a shot. A bit of relief eased through her.

"Marchioness." Simon's voice came to her clearly, even though the timbre of his voice hadn't been loud. "Please return to my quarters."

Maggie resented his formal tone, especially after that last kiss, and wanted to argue. She nearly did, but as she twisted around to look up at him, those green eyes, hard with command, pinned her. With a mulish slant to her mouth, she turned back around and gazed across the deck of the ship. The tension of the men was palpable as they watched for orders to fire from their captain. Realizing she would only be in the way if a battle broke out, she ducked back into the cabin. But she left the door ajar a tiny bit so she could peek out and listen.

"Another warning shot, if you please, Mr. Harris," Simon said.

A large man, whom she hadn't noticed before standing beside one of the masts, called out. The men huddled around one of the cannons near the bow sprang into action. One of them touched a burning cord to the fuse of the gun, then they all scrambled away and covered their ears. Soon after, an ear-shattering boom erupted and then a moment later, she heard a large splash.

Someone called out, "They've struck their colors!" and a cheer went up from the crew.

Maggie opened the door wider so she could watch. The sailors jumped into action. Some still remained vigilant beside their cannon, but others pulled pistols from waistbands and cutlasses from scabbards. The ship turned and the wind caught the sails. After a few minutes, the two ships came side by side. Grappling hooks were tossed across and a gangplank connected the ships.

She stepped out of the cabin because she wanted to see what would happen next. It appeared that the French ship had surrendered and was about to be boarded. Kelwin ordered the sailors across to the other ship, then he followed. Looking up to the quarterdeck, she saw Simon, calm and confident, as he watched and waited. On the *Belle Annabelle*, the French sailors were lining up and the *Sea Raven's* sailors, with their weapons drawn, stood guard over them.

As Simon headed toward the ladder, a shot rang out. His step hesitated and he staggered. A bright red stain bloomed just below his collarbone on the white of his shirt. He'd been shot!

Racing up the ladder, she was just in time to support him as he collapsed to one knee. "Oh, my God! Simon!"

A line appeared between his brows. "You should be in my quarters, Maggie, where it's safe."

"You should be where it's safe," she said, as she felt his weight lean on her.

He shook his head and huffed. "I'm the captain. I'm not supposed to stay safe." Draping his good arm across her shoulders, he said, "If you wouldn't mind, could you help me stand, please?"

She debated whether to comply or not, because he really needed to be lying down. But she couldn't get him to his cabin on her own, and all of his crew were on the other ship, so she supported him as he regained his feet. From the *Belle Annabelle*, a cheer went up from his crew.

"You need a doctor," she said.

The look he gave her was tinged with humor. "This is a small ship. A privateer. We have no doctor. Kelwin sees to the wounded."

She glanced across to the other ship, where Kelwin stood, stoically watching, but he made no move to come help his captain. "Why isn't he coming to help?"

"Because he's otherwise engaged at the moment." He dropped his arm and stepped away.

"Where are you going?" she demanded.

Turning stiffly to her, he said, "To take possession of the ship we just captured."

The blood on his shirt had spread, and she could tell he was in a tremendous amount of pain. He kept his arm on his injured side close against his body.

Concern and exasperation made her exclaim, "But you've just been shot! You need to take care of that wound." Panic took her breath. He could bleed to death, or the wound could become infected. He might die. She pushed that thought away.

"Later." He started toward the ladder to the deck below.

"Wait." Desperate to help him, she bent and tore a strip from her petticoat, then wadded it up and handed it to him. "Put this over the wound and put pressure on it. It will help the bleeding."

Solemnly, he stuck the material inside his shirt. "Thank you. Wait for me here. I'll return presently." His fingers tangled with hers. "I'll be fine, Maggie." Then he turned and descended the ladder.

Maggie watched him go. He strode across the main deck, then stepped to the gangplank and crossed to the other ship. To anyone else, he appeared strong and unscathed, despite the blood on his shirt, but she could see his movements were stiff, as if he was in a great deal of pain. She wanted to go to him, to support him, to demand he allow someone to tend his wound. But she understood he had to appear strong, not weakened by an injury. So, she remained where she was.

The French captain offered his sword to Simon, and then a young sailor was dragged from among the French crew and forced to his knees before Simon. She surmised that was who had shot him. Simon said a few words and the man was taken below. After exchanging a few more words with the French captain, Simon returned to the *Sea Raven*.

Maggie rushed to meet him. His face was drawn, pale,

and covered with a sheen of perspiration. She slid beneath his good arm to support him, but Kelwin stopped her.

"I've got him, my lady," he said, and took Simon's weight.

Although Maggie regretted letting him go, she was glad for the help. Simon was heavy. She followed the two men to the captain's quarters, where Kelwin helped his captain onto the large table. Simon laid back, his face pinched with pain. Immediately, Kelwin went to work, ripping open the bloody shirt and applying pressure to the wound to staunch the blood.

"If you don't mind, my lady, please fetch the brandy from the chest there and my tools from that cabinet," he said.

Maggie did as he asked, placing the bottle of brandy on a chair beside him and the roll of tools in his hand. Simon's eyes were closed and he barely breathed. Fear fluttered in her chest. *Please don't die.*

A grizzled sailor knocked and entered, carrying a bucket of water, rolls of bandages and a handful of rags. "'Ere yer go, Mr. Kelwin."

With a nod of thanks to the sailor, he said to Maggie, "Higgins will help me. Please wait outside."

She wanted to argue, to stay near Simon, but Kelwin's tone discouraged that, and the sailor's disapproving expression made her hold her tongue. Instead, she silently left the cabin. She hoped Kelwin knew what he was doing, that he cleaned the wound thoroughly, that he used the brandy as a disinfectant and not just as an anesthesia or a bracing drink, that he removed the ball and sutured the wound. That he wouldn't let Simon die.

As she paced before the door to the cabin, Deems approached and paced beside her.

"Mr. Kelwin knows wounds," he said. "He was a barber-surgeon in his home in the West Indies."

While Deems meant that as encouragement and consolation, it didn't ease Maggie's apprehension. Medicine and surgery were still primitive in the nineteenth century in comparison to the twenty-first. But she nodded and continued pacing. Time stretched, and along with it, her nerves. She was vaguely aware of sailors moving back and forth across the gangplank connecting the two ships. Finally, after what seemed like days, Higgins, carrying the bucket with water that had turned bloody, emerged from the cabin.

"Mr. Kelwin says you can go in now, yer ladyship," the sailor said.

Maggie flew inside. Kelwin was wiping his hands on a rag. A small pile of cloths, dark with blood, lay at his feet. The scent of brandy hung heavy in the air. She found Simon, on the bed, unmoving, with his eyes closed and his bare chest and shoulder wrapped in bandages.

Her heart jumped into her throat. "Is he—?"

Kelwin shook his head. "I gave him laudanum. The shot did not hit anything vital, but it was deep. He'll recover." He gathered the pile of bloody rags. "If there's nothing else, my lady, I have duties."

Emma stepped aside to let him pass, but kept her gaze on Simon. He always appeared strong, nearly invincible. But the sight of him, injured and weak, disconcerted her. Her perception of him as a privateer had been fanciful, a romantic vision. But he was not a fanciful vision. He was real and he had put himself in danger to help his country. He could have been killed. The sudden realization made her knees weak, and she collapsed into a crouch so she wouldn't topple over.

"Maggie."

Her name, slurred by the laudanum, made her head snap up. His eyes were open, those lovely green eyes. Although he was still very pale, his lips curved up in a smile.

"I apologize for ruining our sail," he said.

She rose from her crouch and stepped to the bed. Wrapping her fingers around his hand, she said, "I'm glad you weren't killed."

He huffed a laugh. "I am as well." His brows drew together. "I should have let the *Belle Annabelle* pass. I shouldn't have taken her. I put you in danger."

"But you had to take her. That's your job."

Something passed through his eyes. Respect? Admiration? Whatever it was, it made her cheeks heat.

"Will you stay with me a while?" he asked.

"Of course."

She dragged over a chair that had been knocked away from the table when Kelwin had brought him in. After she sat, he held out his hand.

"Your touch comforts me," he said, his words beginning to slur once more, and his eyes grew heavy.

Maggie took his hand, glad that it was warm with life. His touch comforted her as well. What would she have done if he had died?

Not wanting to explore the answer to that, she watched him fall into a deep sleep.

"Have you learned how to use the sea-quadrant?"

Maggie's head jerked up at the question. Simon was awake and his eyes held mischief. She let *The Mariner's New Calendar*, one of the books she had found tucked into a cabinet, fall to her lap.

"I've discovered many useful facts," she said, pretending to lecture. "For instance, I learned that the next full moon should occur in seven days."

"Always useful if one is out and about at night," he murmured.

"Yes." She nodded solemnly. "I've also learned that high tide in Fishguard — wherever that is — will occur at 3:18 on September 27."

"A good fact to know," he agreed. "It's a town in Wales."

She met his gaze and all the anxiety she had felt abruptly bubbled up into tears.

"Maggie—" Her name held both regret and sympathy.

Dashing away the tears with her fingers, she said, "I'm sorry. I shouldn't be such a cry-baby."

"Come here." He held out his good arm, inviting her to snuggle.

Slipping from her chair, she knelt beside the bunk and laid her head on his chest. His uninjured arm came around her, and his fingers stroked her shoulder. His embrace calmed and comforted her. After a moment, when she had regained her composure, she raised her head.

"I should let you rest," she said.

"I've rested enough." He started to push himself up into a semi-reclining position, but fell back. "If you wouldn't mind helping me?"

"Of course." Maggie helped him sit up, then fluffed the pillow behind him.

He sat back, but couldn't seem to get comfortable.

"What's wrong?" she asked. "Should I get Kelwin or Deems or one of the men to help?"

"Kelwin is helming the *Belle Annabelle* to bring her to port." He glanced up at her, his eyes crinkled in speculation. "Perhaps you could get on the other side of me and help from there?"

Maggie thought that over. She would have to crawl over

him, and then would be caught between him and the wall. On his bed.

"Are you trying to seduce me, Mr. Marquis?" she asked.

In a completely innocent tone, he said, "Why ever would I do that, Miss Blake? I am injured and can barely set myself straight."

"Of course."

As she outwardly agreed with him, on the inside, the idea of being in the same bed with him made her lady bits weep. His kisses, his touches had been delicious, but she had either stopped them or they had been interrupted. What would making love with him be like? She wanted to be seduced by him, to fall under his spell, to hear his whispered words, to feel his breath against her skin.

Going along with his little game, she took off her shoes, hiked up her skirt and climbed across him. Crouching on his other side, she fluffed this and straightened that and fluffed some more, all the while trying to pretend that she didn't want to kiss across his bandaged chest, or lick up the side of his throat, or cup his cheeks and cover his mouth with hers. As she leaned across him, he caught the key dangling from her necklace and pulled her close.

"I find I am in some pain," he murmured, only inches from her lips.

"What can I do to help?" she whispered.

"This." He demonstrated by closing the inches between them and capturing her lips.

Maggie gave in. She had no resistance against his gentle onslaught. Besides, she had already decided that what she wanted most of all was to make love with him. She'd nearly lost him to a gunshot, and she had no idea how long she would be with him before she would whisk forward to her own time. More than anything, she wanted this one memory.

Bracing her hands against the wall of the cabinet behind him, she straddled his legs. Somehow, as they kissed, with one hand, he had unbuttoned the tiny buttons down the bodice of her dress and loosened the laces of her stays. He cradled one breast in his hand and stroked the nipple, bringing it to elated attention. Releasing her lips, his kissed her jaw, the hollow of her throat, her collarbone, finally covering the tight tip of her breast with his mouth, stroking with his tongue and sucking.

Maggie moaned as a frisson of pleasure shot straight to her core. She could feel his erection, hard and big, against her nub, and she rocked against it. But she wanted more. His fingers crept up beneath her skirt, brushing lightly, swirling across her skin.

"Touch me," she whispered, extremely glad that women in the nineteenth century wore no panties.

His obedient thumb did just that, circling, stroking. His fingers slipped inside her.

And she was gone, in a burst of sensation, a cascade of pleasure.

The climax took her by surprise at its swiftness and

intensity. But then, her last relationship had ended quite some time ago, and since her father's death, she'd had no time and no interest in pursuing another. Not until Simon. The man from the past. The man she loved.

When she could think again, she opened her eyes and saw him gazing at her with awe and a bit of male satisfaction. A tiny smile curved his lips. Her lips curved in response.

"That was—" she began.

"Delightful? Exceptional? Spectacular?" he finished.

She laughed. "Yes. All those. I want to do you."

An odd expression swept across his face, somewhere between surprise and desire. "You do not—That is, it's not—" He stopped for a moment and gazed at her. "Are you sure?"

"Yes." To prove her point, she slid back and began to unbutton the fall on his breeches. "Don't you want me to do you?" She stopped in the middle of slipping a button from its hole and sent him a look of wily innocence. "Because I can go sit in my chair and continue to read *The Mariner's New Calendar.*" She ran a hand down the bulge sitting between her thighs.

A choked groan came from his throat.

"So, you'd like me to keep going?" Coming to the last button, she rested the pad of her finger on it. "I can stop whenever you want." She gave that bulge beneath her hand a gentle squeeze.

"No," he croaked.

"Very well." She lifted her hands in surrender.

Those green eyes pinned her and he growled softly.

She smiled. "I guess that means you'd like me to continue."

Undoing the last button, she opened the fall of his breeches, and his erection sprang free. She wrapped her hand around it, silk over steel. A drop leaked from its tip, and she licked it off, then ran her tongue from its base up its length.

He groaned.

When she took it into her mouth, she heard him gasp. As she sucked and licked, he went completely silent and still for many moments.

"Maggie." Her name was a plea, an entreaty, a prayer.

Then he was all action. Somehow, despite his injury, he flipped her to her back and lay between her thighs, her dress hiked up around her waist. He propped himself up on his uninjured arm, the muscles in his shoulder becoming defined by the pressure. She was reminded again of how strong he was and admired the beauty of him.

"I want to be inside you." The tip of his erection gently pressed against her opening.

She met his gaze, intense, focused, penetrating, reflecting what he wanted to do.

"Will you allow me?" he asked.

"Yes." She needed no thought to answer.

And then he slipped inside, filling her, and she welcomed him, as if she had been waiting for him her whole life.

SIMON GROANED WITH SHEER PLEASURE AS HE SHEATHED himself inside her. She was slick and tight and perfect. Magnificent. He had never wanted a woman more. Her teasing, her touch, her boldness captured him. He was humbled by her gift.

As he rode her, he watched her eyes, their gazes locked, as if they were connected there as closely as they were below. He wanted this to last, to keep in his memory, for she would return to her own time and be gone. And he wanted this to be a memory that she might keep, to give her as much pleasure as he could.

So, he went slowly, sucking on first one breast, then the other, making her whimper, loving every gasp, every moan. He captured that moan in his mouth, answering with one of his own. And then he knew she was ready to erupt, and she did with a breathy scream, and he was ready, and he pulled out and came in a resplendent explosion.

Nineteen

Maggie listened to his breathing, slow and deep, indicating he had fallen asleep. He was sprawled across her, his body exhausted from his injury as well as the hot sex. She drew little circles on the bare skin of his back above the bandage, needing to touch him, wanting to soothe. Their lovemaking had been exquisite and intense, as if they had known instinctively what would arouse the other. Perhaps their duel of seduction had prepared them, but that was over now. It had been a draw, for they both had equally won and lost, each surrendering to the other.

"Shall we go again?"

His voice came muffled, his face turned away as he spoke into the bunched-up bodice of her dress.

She smiled. "Do you think you should with your wound?"

He flopped over on his back with a grimace and a hiss through his teeth. "Most likely not. I think the laudanum has worn off."

"Are you in much pain? Should I get you more?"

He shook his head. "Thank you, but no. I've seen too many people shackled to it. The wound isn't that serious."

Maggie thought the wound might be more serious and painful than he admitted, but she agreed with his refusal of pain medication. "What is going to happen to the boy who shot you?"

"He'll be kept in the brig until the ship reaches port. After that, I've ordered him released and treated like any other French smuggler. He was only doing what he thought he should."

Before Maggie had a chance to tell him that she thought he was being very fair, a quick rap sounded on the door and Deems burst in.

"God's teeth, Deems!" Simon yanked the cover over Maggie. "There's a lady on board."

From beneath the cover, Maggie watched Deems clap a hand over his eyes and straighten to attention. "Sorry, sir. We're coming up on Hastings, and Mr. Kelwin signaled that he's sailing ahead."

"Thank you, Deems," Simon said. "Tell Higgins I'll be on deck shortly."

As soon as Deems left, Maggie pushed off the cover and

sat up. "You can't go on deck. You were just shot. And how can Kelwin sail ahead? Isn't he on this ship?"

Simon pushed himself into a sitting position, but Maggie saw his clenched jaw and the grimace of pain he tried to hide. After he swung his feet to the deck, he said, "I have to go topside. Higgins has been manning the helm since we took the French smuggler, and he needs to be relieved. Kelwin, along with half my men, are on the *Belle Annabelle* as crew and guarding the French prisoners. We're going to stop at Hastings to procure some supplies, since we left London so quickly, and Kelwin is sailing the French smuggler on to Portsmouth where he'll turn her in."

He stood and staggered a step, catching himself against the side post of the bed.

Maggie scooted to the floor and steadied him. "How can you go topside if you can't stand?"

"I have to go." The look he sent her was a mild reprimand. "This is my ship, and my crew need to see me."

Maggie realized he had responsibilities and he was determined to shoulder them again. He would go up on deck to reassure his crew and take command because he cared about them. She had sensed this when she learned he had placed Kelwin and Deems and most likely others into his household to protect them when he was about to be arrested. He was considerate and kind. Wasn't that why she had fallen in love with him? Among other things, of course. Like his mind-wiping kisses and his dexterous fingers. And—

"Maggie, if you keep looking at me like that, I'm going to have to take you back to bed, and I can't do that at this moment."

She blinked and forced the thought of his mouth and his hands and his very substantial erection out of her head. Although the idea of being taken back to bed was very appealing. "Oh, sure." She blinked again. "Did you ask me something?"

"Would you be so kind as to get a shirt for me, please?" He indicated the trunk at the foot of the bed.

She did as he asked and restrained the urge to explore those exquisite muscles as she helped him put it on. When she was done, he slipped his hand around her nape and brushed his lips across her mouth.

"Thank you," he said, paused, and gazed down at her, as if trying to come to a decision.

Then he captured her mouth in a soul-searing kiss. When he was finished, she was the one who staggered.

"I wanted you to remember me," he said, his lips tipped up at the corners.

"Okay." She couldn't think of anything else to say, because he had wiped out every thought in her head.

Laughing softly, he strode across to the door and was gone.

Maggie stared at the closed door. Then giving herself a mental shake, she began to straighten her clothes and put herself back together. She would go up on deck and watch him to make sure he didn't collapse, as well as to watch him captain his ship. Because seeing him in command excited her nearly as much as his touch.

THEY MADE A BRIEF STOP IN HASTINGS, A SMALL VILLAGE, famously known as the landing point of William the Conqueror, where they took on water and supplies, and then sailed along the southern coast of England. Their trip was leisurely, and they saw only one sail for a short time before it dipped below the horizon. No other ship chased or threatened them.

When Simon wasn't at the helm of his ship, he was sleeping, in too much pain and too tired to do anything else. He had commandeered a wild cravat of purple with green stripes from Deems and used it as a sling for his arm. Maggie spent the time watching Simon, or the very distant shore slip past, or sitting in a bit of shade on deck and reading more of *The Mariner's New Calendar,* which she found fascinating.

Early in the evening of the third day, at twilight, they made anchor in a small cove. Beyond a small beach rose a cliff, and sitting atop the cliff was a stone tower that seemed to be attached to a building that stretched back from the edge. They were rowed to the beach where Simon led her to a path that zigzagged up the cliff. At the top, a stretch of lawn lay before her and the imposing front of a castle.

"Welcome to Sea Watch," Simon said.

The tower and the part of the building closest to the cliff looked like it had been built during the medieval period, when knights rode the land on their chargers and ladies waited behind stone walls for their return. Maggie surmised that one could see for miles out to sea from the top of the tower, which most likely gave the estate its name. Beyond that, at a right angle and facing the cliff, was the three-story main building, newer than the tower, with large, mullioned windows on its front face and multiple chimneys sprouting from its roof. A lower wing spread to one side and a circular drive curved before the porticoed entrance.

Maggie stared in astonishment at the size and grandeur of the house. "This is a castle!"

Simon appraised the mansion with a critical eye. "Yes, I suppose it is." He held out his hand. "Would you care to see the inside?"

She glanced at him and placed her hand in his. His face was drawn with pain.

"You should be in bed," she said.

A corner of his mouth tipped up. "Will you join me?"

How could she refuse? The prospect of making love with him in a large, comfortable bed sent a shiver of anticipation through her. But the sex could wait until after he slept.

Playing hard to get, she tipped up her nose. "We'll see."

"Vixen," he muttered.

They traversed the lawn and stopped before the massive, carved, wooden front door. Before he had a chance to knock, it was thrown open by a very proper butler.

"My lord! You're safe!" the man said, then cleared his throat and assumed a decorous mien. "Welcome home, my lord."

"Thank you, Akers," Simon said, then introduced Maggie. "This is my new marchioness, Lady Maggie." After Akers bowed and welcomed her, Simon explained, "Akers agreed to come to Sea Watch when Kelwin went to my London house."

Akers stepped back to allow them in, and Simon swept her into the house.

"We'll be retiring, Akers. Please send up a light supper when you have a chance," Simon said, as he guided her across the hall to the wide staircase leading up with its intricately carved bannisters.

Once again, she found herself craning her neck to look around the magnificent entrance hall. The floor was of ivory marble, and the walls were decorated with framed panels of trompe l'oeil depicting gardens and country scenes. In the middle of the vaulted ceiling hung a huge chandelier.

At the top of the stairs, Simon turned left and they headed down the hallway to the end, where a single door faced them. He opened the door and waved her through. Maggie found herself in a lovely sitting room with windows that looked out on a garden just coming into flower. Through an open door on the right side she could see the corner of a four-poster bed with a lacy blue canopy and matching coverlet. Another open door on the left gave her a glimpse of a room decorated in gold and green. The mistress's and master's bedrooms, connected by the sitting room.

"Both beds are equally comfortable," Simon said.

Maggie hid her smile as she said seriously, "I will have to decide that myself."

"Of course you will." He spoke from just behind her, so close that his breath brushed her ear. "Which one would you like to try first?"

His sly arrogance made her laugh. Turning to face him, she said, "You, sir, need some rest."

"I understand that," he said with a solemn nod. His hand cupped her neck, and with his lips nearly touching hers, he murmured, "I am only trying to ascertain where I should rest."

Caught in his gaze, her thighs clenching in anticipation, she whispered, "You decide."

"That is a difficult decision." He kissed along her jaw, then the pulse at her throat. "Akers will be sending up a tray soon. I find I am quite famished." He backed her up. "I need sustenance first. This is an important decision."

Maggie, focused on his kisses that landed everywhere but her mouth, paid no attention to where he was guiding her, so she was surprised when she felt the seat of a chair at the back of her knees. When his mouth finally captured hers and his tongue requested entrance, she forgot about the chair and gave herself up to the swirl of his tongue and the press of his body. Another surprise came when he gave her a little shove and she fell onto the seat of the chair.

"Oh!"

Before she could recover, he knelt before her and pulled his sling over his head.

"Should you take that off?" she asked innocently.

"Two hands are better than one." His eyes glinted mischievously as he ran his hands up her legs, then down again, stopping at the tops of her shoes. Glancing where his hands rested, he frowned. "These are not quite right."

Confused, Maggie's brow wrinkled. "What's wrong with them? They're the shoes you bought me at the cordwainer's."

He picked up her foot, cupping the heel in one hand. "I would imagine your feet would be much more comfortable without them." As he spoke, he untied and loosened the laces.

"Um, yeah, I guess so." Disappointed he hadn't continued his exploration up her thighs, she watched as he removed one shoe, then the other.

He carefully placed the shoes side by side next to the chair. Then he lifted her left foot. "You have the most delightful toes," he said.

Wiggling them, she enjoyed the freedom of no shoes, but still couldn't understand why he was focused on the wrong end of her leg. She itched to have him where she was wet and wanting. One of his hands slipped beneath her skirt, and she felt him untie her garter, then slowly strip it down her leg. With a flourish, he pulled it off and flung it away. His gaze turned sly.

"I have been waiting to do this for quite some time," he announced, then bowed his head over her toes and ran his tongue across their pads.

Maggie giggled at the tickling sensation, but at the same time melted. How could her toes be such a turn-on? When he took each one into his mouth and sucked, a surprised breath escaped her. This was the most subtle seduction she had ever experienced. And it was working wonderfully. She squirmed.

He glanced up at her, his gaze mischievous. "Would you like me to stop?"

"No," she whispered.

He proceeded to strip off her other shoe and stocking, and gave her right foot the same attention. Maggie squirmed again. Twice. After the second time, he gently placed her foot on the floor and traced up her calves, behind her knees, then higher, stopping with his hands spanning her thighs and his thumbs resting against her thatch.

Finally. Her knees fell open, because she knew what he could do with those thumbs. She met his gaze, a silent question asked and answered. Slowly, with one hand, leaving the other with promising delights to come, he lifted her skirt. And then he kissed her, there, between her thighs.

She gasped at the lovely sensation of his tongue. And then it was not only lovely, but much more. Exciting, thrilling, throbbing, breathtaking. She moaned and held onto the arms of the chair as if she might fly off into nothingness. Until the clench of her muscles released in a shower of shooting stars.

When she could finally think again, she opened her eyes and saw him smiling.

"That was a delightful repast," he said. "Did you enjoy it as well?"

Before she could comment, a knock sounded at the door.

"Ah," he said, standing. "Our supper."

As he went to let in the servant, Maggie pulled down her skirt, stuck her shoes and stockings beneath the chair, and tried to look like all of her faculties were working, which they were not. She felt as if her head was floating about six inches above her body, and her body was filled with cotton. The pirate had just boarded her and plundered her soul.

MAGGIE SPENT THE NEXT SEVERAL DAYS IN FOGGY BLISS. WHEN she and Simon weren't walking hand in hand around his estate or looking out at the English Channel from the tower or exploring the moors that ran across the top of the cliffs, they were trying out the beds in their rooms. Each one was as comfortable as the other, being equipped with feather mattresses, so Maggie declared, out of fairness, they would have to give each one equal time. Which they did, enthusiastically, many times.

On the fourth day, when no one came to arrest Simon, Maggie said at breakfast, "Maybe they have forgotten about you, or maybe the threat to arrest you wasn't real."

Simon smiled. "I rather doubt either of those. I believe something else is going on."

"Like what?" Maggie took a sip of tea.

"Like Rosalind is up to something." He chewed thoughtfully for a moment. "Or Cuthbert. Or both."

The sound of the doorknocker falling echoed through the house.

Alarmed, Maggie stared at Simon. "I hope talking about it hasn't brought someone to arrest you."

Simon shook his head, but the muscles around his eyes tightened.

A moment later, Akers entered, bearing a silver salver. "A message for you, my lord."

Simon thanked him, slipped the envelope from the tray and opened it. After reading, his face relaxed into a smile.

"The Earl of Cranleigh extends his greetings and would

like to visit with his new countess." He glanced up at her. "His country residence is on the other side of the village."

"How did he know you were here?" Maggie had a moment of panic. Maybe word had traveled to London and Simon's arrest was imminent.

"Not much happens here that people don't notice. It is a small village and people talk."

"Can you trust him?"

"Of course. He's a school mate and a good friend." After a pause he said, "He's had his own difficulties."

"We could invite them to dinner," Maggie said, extremely relieved that Simon wasn't about to be arrested.

Simon nodded. "I'll send round a note. Shall we say tomorrow? Akers can help you plan the meal."

As Maggie agreed, she wondered what sort of difficulties the earl might have had, and she looked forward to meeting another of Simon's friends.

Twenty

Maggie waited in nervous anticipation in the entrance hall for the arrival of the Earl and Countess of Cranleigh. Simon stood beside her, looking quite debonair, despite having his arm in a sling, and she could sense his amusement at her anxiety.

"I've never hosted an earl before," she explained, her tone exasperated.

"But you've been to a ball at the residence of a duke," he said with a curve of his lips.

"That's different," she huffed. "I could hide in the crowd."

"And a duke has visited us in London." An amused brow lifted.

"It was an unexpected call."

"And you've been bedded by a marquis," he murmured.

At the reminder, her cheeks flared with heat, which made her even more nervous.

She had planned the dinner menu with the cook and had dressed in the only decent frock she had brought with her. Since they had left London hastily, she'd only packed a couple of dresses. Through the front door which she'd left ajar, she watched the coach pull up, and one of Simon's footmen stepped forward to open the coach door. A lady stepped down.

Maggie gasped. She couldn't believe what she was seeing. It was Emma! Standing in the drive before Simon's mansion. Safe. Unharmed. Elegant, dressed in the latest fashion. And evidently wed to an earl.

"Emma!" she screamed and ran out to greet her.

Her sister froze for a moment, startled. Then joy crossed her face, and she opened her arms to welcome Maggie into them. They hugged and laughed and cried at seeing each other again. And then the questions started.

"How did you—?"

"When did you—?"

"Where have you—?"

"Are you really—?"

Maggie finally gained a bit of her composure, backed away and swiped at her wet eyes. "I can't believe you're here. I thought I saw you at the balloon launch in Hyde Park, but then I convinced myself it wasn't you."

"I was there," Emma said with eyes shining. "I even got to go up in the balloon."

"Then it was you! The lady with the white plume in her hat!" Maggie hugged her again.

She heard Simon discreetly clear his throat and realized she was forgetting her manners. She turned to the two men standing side by side, both handsome and broad-shouldered. Simon was a bit taller than his friend, but the earl would certainly stand out in a crowd with his nearly black, wavy hair and silvery eyes.

Simon introduced her, then said, "May I introduce Brandon Connaught, Earl of Cranleigh?"

Maggie offered her hand and as the earl bowed over it, she said, "I saw you in Hyde Park when I — ah — first arrived."

Cranleigh sent a speculative glance at Simon, then turned back to her with a wry twist to his lips. "Yes, but Wildford kept you well hidden behind a tree, and for good reason. If I had not just wed the most delightful, beautiful woman in London, I might have easily fallen madly in love with you."

With a laugh and a blush, Maggie ushered their guests inside.

After they were seated and the soup course was being served, Cranleigh indicated the sling holding Simon's arm and said, "Wildford, you have added an accessory to your haberdashery."

Simon met Maggie's gaze before he answered, "A slight mishap on the journey here."

Cranleigh nodded. "I noticed your ship anchored in the cove. Any success?"

"Quite a bit," Simon said, satisfaction warming his tone. "We came across a French smuggler and relieved her of her bounty."

"Bravo!" Cranleigh exclaimed. "But we were a bit concerned for you."

Emma added, "We thought you might be captured by the French."

Simon's brows rose. "What led you to believe I might be captured?"

Maggie saw a look exchanged between her sister and Cranleigh, and then the two of them launched into a story about discovering secret notes and codes and the treachery of Cranleigh's half-brother. The tale reminded her of the book Emma had been writing before she had disappeared from the twenty-first century. Maggie decided she would get the whole story at another time when she could quiz Emma.

The dinner was a complete success, and Maggie was thrilled to see her sister again. When she asked how Emma had landed in the nineteenth century, her sister confirmed that their mother's pendant and the ancient oak tree in Hyde Park had something to do with the time travel. Emma related how the man she had been dating in the twenty-first century,

Stephen Thrale, had been a descendant of her husband's half-brother.

Maggie reached across the table and grabbed her sister's hand. "I'm so glad you're not anywhere near that jerk."

Cranleigh related how Emma had helped him gain his rightful title from his slimy half-brother, Thrale's ancestor.

Maggie gasped as she realized why she hadn't been able to get in touch with Stephen Thrale, her contact in the antique business in England. "So, because your half-brother was disowned and killed trying to escape, his line disappeared and Stephen was never born!"

Emma and Maggie stared at each other as they shared a single thought. Maggie didn't dare say it aloud.

But Emma whispered, "Do you think it changed our history?"

Wide-eyed, Maggie shook her head. "Don't jinx it."

After dinner, Maggie and Emma left the table so they could catch up in more detail and to allow the men to chat. But they had silently agreed not to speak any more about the possibility of the future being changed because of what had happened in the nineteenth century.

As Maggie poured tea, Emma said, "There is a dangerous man in this time you must be careful of."

Maggie set down the teapot. "Bowker."

"You know of him?"

"He stole my pendant," Maggie said.

Emma gasped.

"But I don't think he knows how to use it," Maggie added.

Emma's forehead creased with worry. "What if he's able to figure it out and travels to our time? Darcy might be in danger."

Maggie's worry matched Emma's. Their youngest sister had no knowledge of the threat of the dangerous man living in the nineteenth century. "If I can get my pendant back, then I'll try to travel back to warn her."

The two men entered, and Simon suggested a game of Whist. But Maggie saw something flicker in his eyes, something grim, before he hid it and turned on the charm. Was his injury giving him pain? Or was it something else?

That concern was added to the worry over Darcy, and Simon's freedom, and Agnes's nastiness, and Bowker's deviousness. And if she returned to her own time, would she ever be able to get back to see Simon again?

Simon had overheard Maggie's last statement. She would go back to her own time. She would leave him. His heart clenched painfully in his chest.

Of course, he knew she didn't belong in his time, but he had buried that knowledge deep in his brain. Hearing her speak the words made him realize how much he had come to depend on her presence in his life. What would he do if she were no longer with him?

The farce of pretending she was his marchioness had somehow become more real than he realized. And their duel of seduction had turned into a joining of delight and deliciousness, of joy and caring.

He loved her.

His step faltered as the truth burst into his brain.

Cranleigh sent him a curious look, as if wondering about his stumble. Simon took himself in hand and gave his friend a quick smile.

"I must have that loose board repaired," he said.

But how could he repair his life if Maggie were gone? He could never tell her he loved her, for he would never make her choose between him and her younger sister, who lived centuries in the future. The choice had to come from her.

If she traveled back to her own time, he would head out to sea again, return to privateering, even if the war ended. There was always a war going on somewhere in the world, and he would lose himself in capturing ships and raiding their cargo.

With that decision made, he slapped a smile on his face and dealt out the cards for Whist.

SIMON STOOD NEXT TO MAGGIE AS SHE WAVED GOODBYE TO her sister and Cranleigh. Watching the sisters' reunion had warmed him, but the words Maggie had spoken just before he and Cranleigh entered the drawing room had chilled his soul. He had acted as if nothing were amiss, but the several games of Whist they had played had been torture to sit through. He wanted to bind Maggie to him, to make love to her, to make her see, without words, that she should remain in this century, to make her understand that she belonged to him.

He cupped the back of her neck, as the coach rode away and disappeared down the drive. "That was a very enjoyable evening."

"Yes, it was." She smiled up at him.

Her blue eyes gleamed with happiness, and he wanted to capture that look for himself. "I want to kiss you," he said, his tone husky. "I want to make you wet."

Her eyes widened at his provocative words. "That sounds—"

He cut off the rest of her words with his lips, unable to hold back any longer. Sweeping her along with his uninjured arm, he guided her up to his room, not giving her a chance to think. Stopping before his door, he plundered her sweet mouth again, then backed her through and kicked the bed chamber door closed with his foot. When they reached the middle of the room, he slowly released her. She blinked up at him, her eyes dazed.

"I'm going to undress you, Maggie," he said. "Slowly." He trailed his fingers along her jaw.

"Okay." She licked her lips.

Her slang made him smile. It was short and to the point and allowed him to carry on much quicker. A pulse jumped in her throat, and he bent to suck on it.

"Did I ever tell you that you smell like roses?" he murmured against her skin and pulled on the ribbon holding her frock closed.

She shook her head.

As he kissed his way across her shoulder, he found the ribbon at the neckline of her chemise and the ties for her stays and loosened them. Then he slipped his fingers inside and caressed her nipple.

She sucked in a breath.

He smiled and pushed the frock from her shoulders. Keeping his touch light, he brushed across the tops of her breasts. Her eyes were fastened on him, and her lips were parted. His plan was working.

He slipped his sling over his head because he would need two hands for what he had planned. He would deal with the pain. Turning her around, he gently pulled apart the back of her dress, revealing the smooth span of her back until it disappeared beneath her chemise. He kissed down the length of her spine.

She released a sigh.

With quick movements, he untied the ribbon on her

petticoat and pushed her clothing down to her ankles. She stepped out of the pile and turned to face him. All she wore were her stockings and shoes, and the thin chain with his key dangling between her breasts. He felt himself strain against his pantaloons.

"You are the most beautiful woman I have ever seen," he said.

She blushed. "I find that hard to believe. There must be other women much more beautiful than me."

"None that I can recall," he said, meaning every word.

Her lips parted as if to rebuff his statement, then closed. After a moment, she said, "I want to undress you."

Surprised and pleased at that declaration, he smiled. "Are we dueling again?" he said, challenging with a raised brow.

She ran her gaze over him, then met his eyes with a quirk of her lips. "Yes. To the death."

The thought of having her undress him made his blood run hot. The fact that she wanted to do that made him hope his plan was working. He would gladly lose the duel if it would bind her closer to him.

Spreading his arms in surrender, he said, "Then by all means, do your worst."

MAGGIE RAN HER GAZE UP AND DOWN HIM, FROM HIS HEAD TO his feet and back again, as if she were contemplating a complicated problem. In reality, she wanted him to experience the same teasing touch he had bestowed on her. Despite experiencing only his kisses and his light touch, she was wet and aroused. He was a master duelist.

She started by unbuttoning his waistcoat, slowly, keeping her gaze on his eyes, and watched that incredible green color darken. Next, she untied his cravat, but before she eased it from around his neck, she wrapped each end around a hand. Using the cravat, she dragged him down to her level, licked across his lips and finished with a light kiss that suggested there was more to come. When she pulled away, he followed, as if wanting more. But she smiled slyly and placed a hand against his chest to refuse him. Next, she undid his shirt and ran her finger lightly down his chest, across his bandage, until she reached the waistband of his pantaloons.

"These will have to go," she murmured.

He took in a breath.

Tipping her head thoughtfully, she said, "But not yet."

She spiraled her finger back up his chest and let it rest at the hollow of his throat. "What else? Ah, yes." She licked his chest following the same route her finger had taken.

His breathing quickened.

"I think you are wearing too many clothes, my lord," she said, hiding her smile.

She pushed his coat, waistcoat, and shirt from his shoulders, careful not to hurt his wound. With a rumble, he impatiently slipped his arms from the sleeves.

Primly, she said, "Patience is a virtue, my lord."

"Patience is going to kill me," he growled.

She snorted a laugh. When he started to reach for her, she twitched away with a tsk.

"I'm not finished yet," she scolded.

With a heavy, resigned sigh, he dropped his hands to his side.

"Now, where was I? Oh, yes." She curved her lips in a wily smile.

Reaching out, she unbuttoned the fall of his pantaloons, one slow button at a time. When she was done, his erection sprang forward.

"Dear me," she said, "that does look like it needs tending."

At that, she dropped to her knees and took him into her mouth.

He hissed through his teeth.

She ignored it. He was silk over steel, smooth and hard. The tip wept, and she swirled her tongue around it, then licked up the length, and down, before she sucked him into her mouth again.

"Bloody hell, woman!"

Grabbing her by the shoulders, he dragged her to her feet and took her mouth, invading, possessing, wiping everything else from her mind except for him. Drawing away, he shoved her back onto the bed. She watched as he stripped off his boots and pantaloons, then crawled onto the bed and straddled her.

"I've decided I'm going to win this duel," he murmured, as he bent over her and licked the contours of her ear and down her throat to the crevice between her breasts, where his tiny key rested. Taking it into his mouth, he met her gaze, silently reminding her that the key was his, and eventually he would have it. For a moment, Maggie thought this seduction was about the struggle for the key, and she considered handing it over to him. But he let it drop and his gaze focused instead on her breasts.

"Prepare to moan, vixen." Then his mouth fastened around her nipple.

A ribbon of desire slipped through her and curled into her core. When his fingers tugged and rolled her other nipple, she bit her bottom lip. She refused to moan for him. She would win this duel. But then he kissed his way down across her abdomen, swirling around her belly button, then lower, to where she was wet and wanting. His mouth fastened on her nub, swirled and sucked.

She moaned.

He lifted his head and grinned. "Do you yield?"

She looked into his eyes, dark with passion and something else, something gentler, softer, but she couldn't decide what that was. She didn't care. She wanted him. She wanted this memory to take with her back to the twenty-first century.

"I yield," she whispered.

His eyelids lowered, as if he were relishing the most delicious taste, and he slid into her, filling her up, making her whole.

She wrapped her legs around his hips, holding him tightly to her, as if he was the other half of her and she couldn't live without him.

Because he was.

Twenty-One

The next morning as they lay cuddled together, half-awake, a knock came at the door. Maggie groaned into Simon's chest beneath her cheek.

"It's not time to get up yet," she grumbled.

Simon kissed the top of her head and gently lifted her off him. "I have to see about this," he said. "No one would disturb us if it weren't urgent."

He slid from the bed, threw on his banyan, and strode to the door.

Maggie heard low words exchanged, and then the door closed. The mattress dipped with his weight.

"Maggie, I have to go to Portsmouth," he said, leaning over her with one knee on the bed. "Kelwin has sent word that there's a problem with the division of the spoils from the

French smuggler. It seems the customs officer is a bit greedy."

Her lovely drowsiness dropped away. "But you might be arrested!"

"I don't think the order has gone out from London. If it has, I'll let Kelwin handle everything and stay out of sight," he said with nonchalance.

Concern creased her forehead.

He kissed the line between her brows. "Don't worry. I'll only be gone a day or two."

"Can't I go with you?"

With a shake of his head, he said, "I'll be busy watching the customs officer tally up figures and examine cargo."

"Oh." She tried not to pout, but the idea of his leaving made her feel lonely, even before he was gone. Also, the thought that he might be thrown back into jail troubled her. What would she do if he were arrested?

With a swift kiss, he backed off the bed and disappeared into his dressing room, calling for Deems as he went.

The bed was cold and empty now, so she got up, wrapped a sheet around herself, gathered her clothes, and went to her own room to dress.

And tried not to worry.

MAGGIE STRODE ACROSS THE LAWN AND HEADED TOWARD THE house. She had gone for a walk in the woods that she and Simon had wandered through a few days earlier. He hadn't returned last night, nor this morning. The afternoon was half gone, and she was worried. Where was he? Had he been arrested again?

Fretting over his absence had done nothing except drive her crazy. She needed to do something besides sit and read, which was what she'd done to occupy herself since he had left. His library was extensive, and if she hadn't been so concerned, she would probably have happily spent days perusing the books.

She felt better after her walk, but she still worried. He had said he might be gone a couple of days, so she would be patient and wait. But the waiting grated. Women always had to wait.

Entering the house through a set of French doors into a drawing room, she nodded a greeting to Akers who was overseeing two footmen rearranging some furniture. Then she headed up to her room to freshen up in case Simon came home.

She was pinning up a stray strand when she felt a change in the air, and then heard a faint pop. Swinging around, she gasped. Roger Bowker stood in the middle of the room.

"What do you want?" she demanded. "Get out!"

He shook his head, and a malicious smile curved his lips. "No, I don't believe I will."

"How did you get in here?" she snapped.

A smug smile squirmed across his face, and he held out his unusual watch. "I merely went forward in time to discover where you would be today. And I discovered that the marquis would very conveniently be absent." Stepping forward, he grabbed her arm. "You are coming with me."

Maggie tried to wrench away. "I'm not going anywhere with you."

His grip tightened, and he fiddled with his watch. Without warning, the room faded and she was swept into an infinite nothingness. It was cold, colder than anything she had ever experienced. Everything around her was black, even Bowker disappeared from her sight, but she could still feel his tight hold on her arm. After a moment, she popped into a room with Bowker still holding her. Staggering as she found her footing, she saw the dusty display cases, the colorless walls, the shabbiness of his shop. They had time traveled, but to what day and time?

"Why am I here?" she demanded, as she tried to twist from his hold, but his fingers dug deeper into her skin.

"My dear marchioness, if that is truly your title," he said with a condescending lift of his brow, "I merely want you to show me how your pendant works."

"Never."

"I thought you might be resistant," he said. "Come. I wish to give you some incentive."

He dragged her into the back room, crowded with broken

clocks on several tables and scattered on the floor. But that wasn't all that was there. Sitting in the middle of the floor, tied to a chair and gagged, was her sister, Emma. Maggie stumbled, horrified. Her sister's eyes widened, then narrowed, and she shook her head, as if trying to tell Maggie something.

"This is your sister, I believe." Bowker said, as he pulled Maggie to a chair and forced her to sit. When she tried to twist away, he pressed her back and showed her a thick string that led to a device attached to Emma's chest. "If you try to run, I will pull this string, which is tied to an ingenious device I invented. It will send your sister to a place and time where she will have a very difficult time returning to the here and now."

Maggie met Emma's terrified eyes. Her own eyes probably looked just as frightened. That strange void she had just experienced was a horrible place, an emptiness, a nothingness. If he sent Emma there, her sister might never be able to return. She would die.

As Bowker tied Maggie's hands behind the chair and tied her feet to the legs, she said, "You have my pendant. Let my sister go, and I'll tell you how it works."

Bowker stood before her. "No, I'm afraid not."

He turned away for a moment and swept up something from one of the worktables. Turning back to Maggie, he held out his hand. On his palm lay her pendant. Then he showed her his other hand that held Emma's bracelet with her pendant. When he brought the two pendants together, they glowed for a moment, sparked, and then returned to normal. The pendants had never done that before.

Maggie's gaze cut to Emma. Did her sister know that would happen? But Emma shook her head and shrugged helplessly.

"You and your sister will show me how they work, or I will send one of you into the void," he said.

Maggie looked into Bowker's eyes and saw they were as cold and empty as the void he'd just dragged her through. The man was insane. Somehow, she and Emma had to escape, because she had no idea how the pendants worked, and she had a feeling that Emma didn't either. Even if she did, she wouldn't reveal that to the crazy man standing before her. Mrs. Edwards had warned her about him. Who knew what he might do if he could travel through time?

She met Emma's gaze. An idea started to take shape. If she could bluff long enough, Simon might return from Portsmouth and figure out what had happened. Perhaps he would be able to find them. With a quick glance at Emma, she tried to communicate to her sister to go along with her. Then she looked up at Bowker.

"If I tell you how they work, will you let us go?" she asked.

"Perhaps, if you tell me the truth," Bowker said.

Maggie didn't have the truth, but she needed to buy time

to figure a way out. In the meantime, she could make Emma more comfortable.

"I need my sister's help," she said. "You'll have to remove her gag."

Bowker narrowed his eyes suspiciously a moment, then he turned and untied the cloth covering Emma's mouth. Her sister blew out a relieved breath and sent Maggie a tiny nod.

Maggie returned the nod. "The pendants are magic," she said to Bowker. "In order to make them work, we have to perform a very long ritual. It requires many unusual ingredients." She glanced around the workroom. "I don't think you have them here."

"I will get whatever is needed." Bowker sat at one of the tables, pulled a sheet of paper before him and took up a pencil. "Tell me what I need."

Maggie tipped her head as if she were thinking. "First, you will need the toe of a frog."

Emma coughed, obviously covering a laugh.

Maggie waited as he wrote down the ingredient and hoped she could make the list of ridiculous items long enough for her to figure out a way to escape or give Simon time for a rescue. Provided he could find her.

THE SUN WAS A FIERY BALL SINKING INTO THE SEA WHEN SIMON reined up in front of his house, dismounted from his horse, handed the reins to the stableboy, then headed up the front steps to the door. He'd been gone for two days and was very glad to be back. The time in Portsmouth had been filled by haggling with customs officials and smuggling the French smugglers out of England. The French captain, an honorable man despite his profession, had become a friend of sorts, having been captured by Simon more than once. Simon had decided that losing his cargo had been enough punishment for the Frenchman. Besides that, he was worried that the order for his own arrest might arrive at any moment and he would be thrown back into prison. But he was home now.

He was looking forward to seeing Maggie and having a bath and perhaps having Maggie in the bath with him. He would wash each of her pretty, pink toes and then suck on each one. He'd been saving that treat like a delicious dessert, hoarding it like a miser. And then he'd lick up one of her lovely legs until he reached—

"My lord," Akers said, looking very solemn as he stood stiffly in the middle of the entrance hall.

Simon blinked, his fantasy dissolving. "Good evening, Akers." He began to stride toward the stairs.

Akers cleared his throat and did not move. "My lord, the Earl of Cranleigh is here. He is waiting for you in the drawing room."

His butler's manner seemed more serious than usual, but

Simon dismissed it. "Yes? Tell him I'll be with him presently." Anxious to see Maggie, he continued toward the stairs.

"My lord." Akers coughed into his hand and then stiffened even more. "The marchioness is missing."

Simon halted in mid-step and swung toward the man. "Missing? What do you mean *missing?*" His heart stopped beating.

"This afternoon, the lady came back from a walk, went to her room, and hasn't been seen since." Akers shifted. "The Earl of Cranleigh seemed quite disturbed when he arrived and asked after the marchioness. That was when we discovered the lady was gone, and the earl became even more distraught. He—"

Simon held up his hand to stop him. Unable to listen to any more explanation, he could only think of one thing: Maggie was gone. But where? Back to her own time? They were miles from London and the ancient oak that brought her here. Did the pendant work by itself? But she had lost it, stolen by that villain Bowker. A hollow opened in his chest.

He glanced at the door to the drawing room and wondered at Cranleigh's arrival. While one part of him wanted to race up the stairs, to see for himself that Maggie was gone and send out a search party, another part of him, the part that would coolly captain his ship to out-maneuver the enemy, decided that he should speak to Cranleigh and discover why he was here and what disturbed him. His gut told him that Maggie's disappearance and the earl's distraught arrival were somehow connected. Striding to the door, he pushed it open and entered.

Cranleigh turned at his entrance. He had been pacing. His cravat was coming unraveled, and it appeared he had been running his hands through his hair, for it stuck out awkwardly in several places. He held a glass with the dregs of Simon's rum in the bottom.

"Thank God, you're back," Cranleigh said. "Emma's gone, and I understand Maggie is as well."

Simon halted as the implications of both women disappearing hit him. Clearing his throat, he pushed out hoarse words. "Do you think they traveled back to their own time?" The thought that Maggie would leave without some sort of farewell made his heart clench painfully.

Cranleigh stared at him, devastation crossing his face. "They couldn't have. Emma wouldn't—" He shook his head. "She loves me."

Simon stalked to the small table where his decanter of rum stood. After pouring himself a good amount, he held out the bottle to his friend. Cranleigh took it and splashed some into his glass, then took a large gulp. Simon did the same, the liquor burning its way down to his stomach, but it didn't burn away the terrible feeling that was churning there.

Cranleigh turned and paced away, then stopped in the middle of the room and swung to Simon. "There was a strange man who was stalking Emma. He was in school with us."

"Bowker," Simon supplied. "He stole Maggie's pendant."

They stared at each other as the terrible possibility dawned on them.

"He's taken both women," Simon finally said.

"But to where?" Despair filled Cranleigh's eyes.

Simon's brain flailed for a moment as he thought of all the possible hiding places in London, then it settled. "He has a shop near the docks. I would wager he's taken them there."

"Then let's go after them." Cranleigh slammed his glass down, his mouth set in a determined line.

Happy to have a plan, Simon rang for Akers. When his butler appeared, he said, "Cranleigh and I are going to London. Have our horses saddled and ask cook to put together some food. We'll be leaving presently."

Akers nearly smiled as he bowed. "Very good, my lord."

Simon turned back to his friend. "We'll find them and bring them back."

He wouldn't even consider failure.

MAGGIE TWISTED IN HER BONDS, THE ROUGH ROPE CHAFING HER wrists. Across the small room, Emma did the same. Bowker had left some time ago to collect the long list of ridiculous items they had given him to make the "magic" of their pendants work.

After a few minutes, Maggie sighed. "Any luck?"

Emma shook her head, looking despondent and frustrated.

"How did Bowker find you?" Maggie asked.

Emma's lips twisted wryly. "Brandon and I had squabbled about redecorating one of the rooms." She ducked her head as if embarrassed. When she looked at Maggie again, her eyes shone. "The nursery," she whispered.

Maggie took a moment, then squealed in delight. "You're pregnant! That's awesome! Congratulations!"

"Thanks." Emma beamed. "Anyway, we had fought about how we were going to redecorate it. Brandon was positive we would have a boy, so he wanted the room to reflect that. I wanted something more neutral." She shook her head, then took a breath and continued. "I took a walk in the woods to cool off, and that's when Bowker popped in, and then brought me here." She glanced around. "What is this place?"

"It's his workshop," Maggie said. "He's a clockmaker."

As Emma was about to comment, the bell over the door tinkled.

"Hello! Help!" Maggie yelled, and Emma joined in.

Footsteps approached, and Rosalind Hornley entered.

Surprise crossed her face, then a crafty smile curved her lips. "Marchioness," she purred. "Bowker promised me a surprise, and I see he was correct. What a delight seeing you here. And all wrapped up like a delightful gift."

"I don't suppose you'd consider untying me," Maggie said.

"Oh, no, I wouldn't presume to ruin Bowker's fun." She looked at Emma. "And who is this enchanting creature?"

"She is the Countess of Cranleigh," Maggie said.

"Oh, my, two exalted ladies! I am honored to make your acquaintance, countess." Rosalind gave an exaggerated curtsey.

Emma's mouth twisted as if she had sucked on a lime.

To regain Rosalind's attention, Maggie said, "If you release us, I'm sure both Cranleigh and Wildford will reward you generously."

"Well, now, that is quite tempting," the woman said. After thinking for a moment, she shook her head. "No, I don't think so. I see a much better prize." Her gaze fastened on the key hanging around Maggie's neck.

Helpless, all Maggie could do was plead. "Please don't take Wildford's letters of marque again. He doesn't deserve to be in prison."

Rosalind gave an ironic laugh. "His letters of marque? Why ever would I want that?"

She disappeared into the front of the shop and then returned carrying Simon's box. The wooden raven on the top gleamed, and each of the waves on the sides looked as if they were just about to crash on the shore. After placing it on the table where Bowker had written down his list, she slipped the chain with the key over Maggie's head.

Maggie could do nothing to stop her. Helplessly, she watched as Rosalind inserted the key into the keyhole in the middle of the brass filigree escutcheon on the front of the box and turned it.

A click, and one of the waves on the side of the box popped out. Rosalind tried to push it in, but it wouldn't stay. Thoughtfully, she studied the box, then ran her hand over it. Stepping back, she studied the box again.

Despite her dismay, Maggie was intrigued. The box obviously contained a puzzle that needed to be solved before it would reveal its contents. From where she sat, tied up, she could see the key had only turned a quarter turn, not a complete half-circle that usually opened a lock. She wondered about that.

Rosalind stepped up to the box again and returned the key to its upright position. The wave that had popped out slipped back into its original position. She turned the key again, and once more, the wave popped out, but she kept turning. A wave popped out on the other side of the box.

"Ah," she whispered. "Very clever, Wildford."

With a third turn of the key, Maggie heard another pop, and she assumed something had opened in the back of the box. With a fourth turn of the key, the raven rose up from the top. But when Rosalind tried to open the box, it still wouldn't reveal its contents.

"Hell and damnation," Rosalind muttered. She turned to Maggie. "I don't suppose you know how to open the bloody thing." At Maggie's shrug, she turned back to the box. "Of course not. And you wouldn't tell me even if you did."

Rosalind stepped back from the box again and studied it some more. Then, in frustration, she banged her hand down on top of it. Nothing happened, except the raven had twisted a bit. Hesitantly, she gave the raven a little twist. When it moved, she twisted harder.

The top popped up.

"Hurrah!" Rosalind cheered. "Wildford, you cunning boots."

She scooped up the rolled papers inside and glanced through them. Then she tossed one onto Maggie's lap.

Maggie glanced down at the rolled sheet on her lap. It was open enough that she could read some of the very large words at the top written in a lovely cursive hand. She took a moment to digest what she was seeing. Then the words made sense. What Rosalind left her was Simon's letters of marque. But what were the chances she'd be able to give it to him, tied up as she was and Bowker's prisoner?

Rosalind rolled up the other papers she had taken and slipped them down the front of her dress. With an ironic smile, she said, "Thank you for the key. Tell Wildford, if you ever see him again, that I wish him no ill will."

"I don't think he wishes you the same," Maggie grumbled.

Rosalind sighed. "What a pity. Good day, ladies." She headed toward the door.

"Wait!" Maggie cried. "Untie us!"

"Please!" Emma added.

"Terribly sorry. Can't do that." With an airy wave of her hand, she stepped through the door. A moment later, the tinkle of the bell announced her departure.

Maggie and Emma looked at each other, disappointment, frustration and anger mirrored on their faces.

"Who was that?" Emma asked.

"It's a long story," Maggie said with a sigh.

In a dry tone, Emma said, "I think we've got time."

Reluctantly, Maggie agreed. Besides, Emma was always right.

Twenty-Two

Just before sundown, Simon and Brandon dismounted in front of Simon's London townhouse. Having been riding nearly non-stop for two days, only pausing to eat and change horses at every opportunity, they both staggered from exhaustion as their feet hit the ground. When they entered the house, Mrs. Alsop hurried to meet them. Kelwin was still making his way back from Portsmouth.

"My lord!" she exclaimed. "We were not expecting you."

"I apologize for not sending ahead," Simon said. "We have a bit of an emergency. Could you ask Cook to put together a small repast, please?"

Mrs. Alsop bobbed a curtsey. "Of course, my lord." She looked beyond Simon to the open door behind him. "Will the marchioness be joining you?"

Simon shook his head. "No, I'm afraid not. She's been kidnapped."

The woman's hand flew to her mouth in shock. "Oh, my! The poor lady!"

Simon was somewhat surprised at his housekeeper's reaction. He had thought the woman disapproved of Maggie. But his pseudo-marchioness had evidently charmed the woman. Of course. Maggie could charm anyone.

"Yes, quite," Simon agreed. "I need someone to deliver a message to the Duke of Wyndham. And please have the coach brought around. Cranleigh and I will be in the library."

As Mrs. Alsop bobbed another curtsey, Simon led Brandon into the room. He motioned to the table holding his brandy in a crystal decanter and several glasses.

"Help yourself," he said, as he sat at his desk to write his message to Wyndham.

Brandon poured two glasses and placed one on the corner of the desk. After taking a sip, he said, "Why are we waiting for Wyndham? We need to go after the ladies now."

Simon didn't bother to look up as he answered, "Bowker has a box that belongs to me. It contains French secrets that Wyndham will want, and he might know Bowker's whereabouts. He's had men watching him. Besides, we need to eat."

A footman tapped on the door as he finished the note and folded it. Simon gave it to him and instructed him to put it directly into the duke's hand. Another footman entered bearing a large tray with cheese, bread, and slices of cold beef. Simon and Brandon set upon the food, and before they had finished, the doorknocker echoed through the house.

A moment later, Wyndham strode into the room, not waiting to be announced. "What is the emergency? Why are you risking arrest in London? Cranleigh, what are you doing here?"

Simon explained about the disappearance of Maggie and Emma and the suspicion that Bowker had abducted them.

"Good God! I had no idea." Wyndham thought for a moment. "My men have observed Bowker frequently going in and out of his shop. He seemed to be collecting some very odd items."

"Odd items?" Simon asked.

"Yes, like a branch of witch hazel, and a container of rainwater," Wyndham said. "One of my men watched him try to bag a black cat."

"Sounds like items for a witch's potion," Brandon observed.

"That's the thing!" Simon exclaimed. "Bowker wanted the ladies' pendants so he could use them to time travel into the future. The pendants are magical. He must be collecting items that he believes will help him."

Brandon's brow crinkled in confusion. "But the ladies didn't need witch hazel or rainwater to come to this century."

Simon turned to him. "Don't you see? They're making Bowker collect those items to give us time to rescue them."

"Then let us do that," Brandon announced. "Where is your stash of weapons?"

As Simon strode to a cabinet tucked into the end of the wall of shelves, Wyndham blocked him. "I know you wish to rescue your—the ladies, but this could be a trap to throw you back into chains. To take you out of the game."

Rage at the duke's interference made him growl, "Get out of my way." He didn't care if he were arrested again if he could save Maggie.

After a moment, with a nod, Wyndham stepped aside. Skirting him, Simon threw open the cabinet. The inside bristled with swords, knives and guns. Each of the men armed themselves with a sword and pistol and tucked a knife into a boot. Then they exited the house.

After Simon gave the direction to the coachman, he climbed into the vehicle with the other two men. He hoped they would find both women unharmed and still in this century. Since realizing that Maggie had been taken, he felt as if a part of him was missing. The sensation was similar to the emptiness he felt upon learning of the deaths of his family, but added to that was a growing sense of fear. What if Bowker had taken the women somewhere that he and his friends couldn't reach? What if the villain left them there, unable to return? Pushing aside those thoughts, he focused on the positive. They would find both women. They had to.

Because he would only feel whole again with Maggie back in his arms.

MAGGIE AND EMMA SAT IN THE DARK, IN A CELLAR HOLE beneath Bowker's shop. Shivering in the cold damp, they clutched hands, the contact giving them comfort. He had put them in the loathsome place after he had brought back a frog and cut off its toe. Emma had squealed in horror and then thrown up all over Bowker's boots. Alongside Maggie's sympathy for her sister was a bubble of delight at the twist of disgust on the man's face.

Bowker had become angry, and Maggie feared he might pull on that string attached to the device on Emma's chest. Instead, he had pushed aside one of the worktables and heaved open a trap door in the floor. Then he had forced them down a ladder into the pitch-black hole.

The cellar had a dirt floor that was wet and muddy in spots and stone walls covered in moss that oozed moisture. Damp from the nearby river permeated the space. Before Bowker closed the trapdoor, shutting out the light, Maggie had just enough time to see the cellar was littered with parts of old clocks and other unrecognizable junk. When they heard him leave, Maggie climbed the ladder and tried to open the trapdoor, but it was either locked, or something heavy was holding it down.

Maggie sat on the bottom rung of the ladder that led up

to the workshop, and Emma huddled next to her on an overturned bucket. A black cat that Bowker had thrown down lay sleeping, curled up on Emma's lap. They had been kept prisoner for hours in near total darkness. The only dim light came from a crack where the trapdoor didn't fit tightly against the floor.

Emma screeched and kicked out with her foot. "Another rat. I hate rats." The cat jumped off her lap to chase it.

"I don't know why rats find this place so attractive," Maggie said. "There's nothing down here to eat."

"Except us, and the crumbs of that disgusting stuff Bowker gives us to eat," Emma added. After a beat of silence, she said, "Do you really think Simon will find us? Brandon must be frantic with worry."

"Of course, he'll find us." Maggie spoke with assurance, despite the swell of fear that wouldn't go away. "He'll figure out what happened, and he knows where Bowker's shop is."

"I hope he gets here before Bowker finds everything on the list of 'magical' stuff," Emma said. "What if he finds everything and then wants us to make the pendants work?"

"We'll figure out something," Maggie soothed. "Besides, you're a writer. You make stuff up all the time."

"I've never had to make stuff up to save our lives," Emma grouched. "How long do you think we've been down here?"

"Maybe a couple of days." Maggie glanced up at the thin strip of light, beginning to darken, that came through the gap between the trapdoor and the floor. "It looks like the sun's going down."

"Wonderful. Bowker will come back, and we'll get more stale bread and moldy cheese." Emma threw something against a wall.

"Sh," Maggie warned. "I think he's back." She heard a footstep and the scrape of a boot. Then she heard another set of footsteps and the low murmur of voices. They weren't right above her in the workroom, but out in the shop itself. "There are people here," she whispered in excitement.

"Should we call for help?" Emma asked. "What if they're Bowker's friends?"

"Do you think he has any?"

Emma snorted a laugh at her sister's snide comment. "Probably not."

"It's worth a try to call out, right?" Maggie tried to sound positive, tried to keep the fear at bay. The footsteps sounded like they were moving away.

"Okay." Emma's agreement didn't sound like she completely agreed.

Maggie was going to try anyway. Taking a breath, she cried, "Help! Help!"

Emma took up the cry.

The footsteps seemed to come closer. Maggie heard male voices.

"Down here!" she yelled.

"We're trapped!" Emma added.

"Help!" they yelled together.

Something heavy scraped across the floor, and then the trapdoor opened. Looking down at her was the most wonderful sight she had ever seen.

Simon's face.

"Maggie! Thank God!" He held out a hand.

Brandon's face appeared beside him, and Emma released a squeal of joy.

And next to both of them was the Duke of Wyndham.

Relief curled together with elation in Maggie's chest as she helped Emma scramble up the ladder, then followed behind. She didn't see what happened next, because she was wrapped in Simon's arms with her face pressed into his shoulder, the best place in the world. But she could hear their murmurs and Emma's happy tears.

"Are you unharmed?" Simon asked. "Did he hurt you?"

"No, we're just hungry and tired and dirty." Maggie raised her head and looked into those beautiful green eyes. "You found us."

"Of course." He brushed a strand of hair off her cheek. "I couldn't let you travel back to your own time without saying goodbye."

The thought of leaving him hurt her heart, but he spoke as if it meant little to him. She forced a smile. "I'm glad you did."

Wyndham cleared his throat. "I regret breaking up this happy reunion, but Bowker may be coming back soon. We should search for any diabolical time travel devices he may have and destroy them." He looked around at the many clocks, whole and in pieces, scattered around the room. "I'm not sure I'd know one if I saw it."

"There's one in the cellar," Emma said with a repugnant twist to her lips. "Bowker tied it to me to force us to do what he wanted. Maggie figured out how to get it off."

Brandon muttered some nasty words as he strode to the ladder and climbed down. He reappeared after a moment holding the clock-like device. Throwing it to the floor, he stomped on it until it was only a mangled mass of metal.

"And there's this." Maggie walked to the worktable where Simon's box sat, still open, the tiny key still in the lock. "Rosalind figured out how to open it."

Dismay crossed Simon's face. "She took all the documents, the French battle plans for the Mediterranean, everything."

Wyndham's brow creased in disappointment. "That is a blow."

"Well, she didn't take everything." Maggie reached into the box and pulled out Simon's letters of marque. Holding out the parchment, she said, "Rosalind left this."

Simon took the parchment, glanced at it, then handed it to Wyndham.

A small smile curved the duke's lips. "You are vindicated, my friend."

"I am still curious who alerted the admiralty court about me and my ship," Simon said. "There's another layer to this."

With a nod, Wyndham said, "We will find the culprit."

Out in the shop, the bell over the door tinkled.

The duke put a finger to his lips, signaling silence, and motioned everyone into separate corners. Maggie and Simon huddled closest to the door. She heard Bowker's footsteps crossing the shop, then, carrying a large stalk of deadly nightshade, he stepped into the room where they waited. He stopped just inside the workshop when he saw Brandon and Emma, then Wyndham. Maggie and Simon eased behind him, putting themselves between him and the doorway, and blocked his escape.

Wyndham stepped forward, leveling his sword at Bowker's chest. "You are under arrest for thievery, abducting two ladies against their will, and any other crimes I may be inclined to charge you. Surrender peacefully."

Bowker turned in a full circle, his bland expression turning ugly when he saw Maggie and Simon behind him. Facing the duke again, he bowed humbly.

"My lord," he said, his tone unctuous. "I was merely performing a few experiments, a harmless pastime of mine. The ladies were helping me."

"You stole my sister's pendant," Emma said. "Stealing is a hanging crime."

Surprised at Emma's knowledge, Maggie's gaze flew to

her sister. She surmised Emma must have done some research for one of her books.

A corner of the duke's mouth deepened. "The countess is correct."

"But the baubles are there." Bowker gestured to the worktable, where both pendants gleamed next to an odd assortment of things he had collected.

As everyone glanced to where he pointed, Maggie saw him slipping his hand into his pocket. Before she registered what he was doing, he began to fade.

"He's time traveling!" she yelled. "Stop him!"

Simon reached for him, but his hand passed through a misty form.

With a pop, Bowker disappeared.

And when they looked at the worktable, one of the pendants was gone!

THE COACH STOPPED BEFORE SIMON'S HOUSE AND HE HELPED Maggie down. He couldn't wait to get her inside and reassure himself that she was safe. Besides, he wanted her all to himself. The ride through the city had seemed endless with Wyndham, Cranleigh and his countess squeezed inside the carriage. His fingers itched to travel over Maggie's skin, to kiss the bruises around her wrists and ease her aches.

After a fruitless search of Bowker's shop for other time travel devices, Wyndham had pronounced defeat, so they left, the ladies in a hurry to wash off the grime of the cellar. The duke, along with Cranleigh and his wife, who had claimed the cat, had been dropped at their respective houses, each of them glad the ordeal was over, at least for now. Wyndham had vowed Bowker would be caught and justice served. But that was for later. Because at that moment, Simon was anxious to get Maggie up to his room to determine that every inch of her was unharmed.

After stepping down from the coach, she reached back inside and grabbed his box. "We don't want to forget this," she said with a smile.

Taking it from her, he tucked it under his arm. "I'm not sure I'll ever use it again to hide documents."

"I think it's a perfect place to hide important stuff," she said. "Just don't tell your mistresses about it."

His mistresses. He would never have another mistress, not after losing his heart to the woman beside him.

They entered the house and Mrs. Alsop hurried to greet them. Kelwin strode up behind the housekeeper.

Surprise at seeing his first mate halted Simon's steps. "I thought you were in Portsmouth."

"When I heard what happened, I sailed back to London

in the *Sea Raven*," Kelwin said. "Couldn't let my captain fight battles alone."

Simon nodded his thanks, asked Mrs. Alsop for a tray of food, then hurried Maggie up the stairs and into his bed chamber. After setting down his box, he turned to her. Now that he had her to himself, he was unsure how to approach. She gazed back at him, those lovely blue eyes wide, but her expression unreadable.

He cleared his throat. "You found your pendant."

"Yes." Maggie placed her hand over the piece, now back on its chain around her neck. Emma had allowed Maggie to take the one Bowker had left behind, because she was staying in the nineteenth century with her husband, the Earl of Cranleigh.

"And you found your sister."

"Yes. She seems very happy. And she told me she's going to have a child."

"That is wonderful. I'll have to send my felicitations." Disconcerted at the jumble of emotions he was feeling, his gaze slid away from her. "I suppose you'll try to get back to your own time again."

She was silent for a long moment, then, "Simon."

Despite his apprehension at what she was about to say, he looked at her.

"Simon," she repeated, her lips curved in a smile. "I think I need some funny business." She paused. "That is, if you don't mind a couple of days of dirt."

"Oh, Maggie." Two long steps brought him before her. Gently cupping her face in his hands, he said, "I would commit funny business with you through a year's worth of dirt and grime." Then he kissed her.

To Maggie, the touch of his lips felt like coming home. Wrapping her arms around him, she gave herself up to his kiss, his touch, his possession. Because she needed this night with him. Although he had rescued her, although he wanted to make love to her, she knew she didn't belong here. He didn't love her, so she wouldn't stay. Tomorrow, she would have him drive her to the ancient oak tree in Hyde Park. Hopefully, her pendant would work this time and send her back to the twenty-first century where she belonged.

But for this night, she would pretend she was his, and he was hers. Forever and always.

Twenty-Three

V ery early the next morning, Maggie and Simon were
seated across from each other in his coach on their
way to Hyde Park. Somehow, without speaking, they had
situated themselves apart, as if they were already in different
centuries. She didn't think she could have borne having him
next to her, his thigh brushing against hers, knowing that she
would never see him again. She had to be stoic and brave,
not reveal how she felt. She was not going to burst into tears.
He didn't love her, so she was leaving. If her pendant and the
oak tree let her. Besides, she had to think of her sister Darcy.

They entered Hyde Park and soon approached the
ancient oak. Simon rapped on the roof of the coach to signal
the driver to stop.

"We're here," he said, making the unnecessary
announcement.

"Yes."

She glanced out the window. Fog swirled beneath the branches of the tree. Like in a fairytale or myth, she could walk into the fog and disappear forever. And then what? She wasn't heading into a magical kingdom. She was going to head into another century with its traffic and cell phones and reality TV shows. Without Simon, her pirate.

Simon exited the coach, then helped her down. The air was chilly and damp, so she pulled the woolen cloak she had borrowed again from his sister tighter around her. Beneath it, she wore her shorts and tee shirt. On her feet were her sneakers. She had decided that if she were going back to the twenty-first century, she should be dressed for it.

Simon reached back into the coach and pulled out a package, wrapped in canvas, about the size of a looseleaf binder. "I want you to have this," he said, handing it to her. "It might be worth something in your time."

Beneath the wrapping, she could feel a carved picture frame.

He smiled. "It's a small Turner painting. I thought it might be easier to carry than the one above the fireplace."

She huffed a laugh, still embarrassed by her attempt at thievery. Ducking her head, she ran her hand over the canvas covering. Tears stung her eyes. "Thank you." Standing on tiptoe, she kissed his cheek. "You are a good man, Mr. Marquis."

He captured her chin between his thumb and finger, his

eyes serious and very green, and brushed her lips with his mouth. "Have a good life, Maggie Blake," he whispered.

With a shaky smile and a nod, she turned and walked into the fog. The urge to turn back, to look at him one more time was overwhelming. Instead, she gripped her pendant in her fist. And kept walking. Where was the hole that would take her back to the twenty-first century? She needed it. Now. Before she lost her nerve. Before she became a blubbering mess.

Stopping beneath the ancient oak tree, she looked up into its branches, filmed with fog. Or maybe the film was caused by the tears in her eyes. She took one more step. Her pendant sparked with heat. Another step and she fell into that hole.

And landed with a thud in bright sunshine in the middle of a group of teenage girls.

THREE DAYS LATER, MAGGIE TURNED THE LOCK ON THE antique shop on Newbury St. in Boston and stepped inside. It was past midnight, so the store was dark and only a dim security light and ambient light from the streetlights lit the space. But it was enough to see as she wended her way through Victorian-era cabinets, authentic Chippendale chairs, an Edwardian dressing table, a valuable Louis Quinze settee, and various other antiques, some priceless, others not so much. Her assistant had left everything in its place. She noticed a Georgian sterling silver centerpiece was gone, no doubt bought by some multi-billionaire, the only ones who could afford such elaborate, useless articles. But its sale had boosted her bank account.

Her gaze landed finally on the display case where she had first seen the tiny gold key. That spot wasn't dusty anymore, and a pair of art deco earrings lay where the key had been. Simon had the key now. Her hand went to her necklace where her pendant hung. It felt strange without the key hanging next to it.

Dropping her hand, she tugged the strap of her tote bag higher on her shoulder. Inside was the painting from Simon. After completing tons of paperwork that took several days, she'd finally been able to get it through Customs. The flight from London to Boston had been long, made even longer by her need to get away from England. She wanted to put her interlude in the nineteenth century behind her, because thinking about it was too painful. She felt as if she had an open wound in her chest.

Dragging her carry-on across the floor, she stopped before a door in the side wall of the shop. She unlocked it and headed up the stairs to the condo above where she lived. Her focus was on her bed and sleep, maybe for a year or two, until she could think about Simon, the Marquis of Wildford, with fond memories, instead of the sharp knife of pain that stabbed her heart. He didn't love her, didn't even ask if she would stay. But she wouldn't think about that.

After texting Darcy to let her know that she was home, she undressed and crawled into bed. But she couldn't sleep. Opening her laptop, she surfed the web for a while, watching silly cat videos and catching up on news.

Her phone pinged with a text from Darcy. *Have you heard from Emma? Did you find her? My internship with a MAJOR designer is great. Can't tell you who she is. Will be super busy. Will text again when I have a minute. XO*

Frustrated, she blew out a breath. She needed to tell Darcy about Emma, and Simon, and the nineteenth century, and the ancient oak tree in Hyde Park, and the sapphire and diamond pendant, just like the ones that Maggie and Emma had, that Darcy wore as an earring. But that was too much and too important to put in a text or email. Tossing her phone on the nightstand, shutting down her computer, she rolled over and finally went to sleep. And dreamed.

A woman, dressed in a dark blue frock in Regency style, walked toward her across a lawn. About middle-age, she somehow looked familiar, but Maggie couldn't remember ever meeting her before. Her mahogany-colored hair was piled on top of her head in a mass of curls. Stopping before Maggie, she smiled.

"My darling girl," she said. "Sometimes, you have to step back in order to see things clearly before you step forward."

"What do you mean?" Maggie asked. "Who are you?"

With another enigmatic smile, the woman turned and walked back across the lawn, her form fading into nothing. Maggie wanted to run after her, to demand that she explain, but she couldn't get her feet to move.

And then she woke up.

EARLY THE NEXT MORNING, BLEARY-EYED, MAGGIE PLODDED into the antique shop. After the strange dream, she hadn't been able to get back to sleep. The woman's familiar appearance, as well as her puzzling words, had kept Maggie awake, so she got up, dressed, and went to work.

She sat at her desk, but couldn't focus. Resting her chin in her hand, she let her gaze travel around the shop. Everything before her had been new at some point in time. She remembered Simon's insulted tone when she referred to his furniture as antiques. A tiny smile curved her lips until the pain of never seeing him again destroyed it.

Determined not to think about him, she opened her computer to work. But instead of looking at auction sites for the next lovely antique she could acquire, she did a search for the Marquis of Wildford. That took some time, for it evidently wasn't one of the more prominent titles. When she finally found an entry, it was quite short. The title had died out in the 1860s because the eighth Marquis of Wildford had had no children. In fact, he had never married. How terribly sad. Unable to cope with any more sadness, Maggie closed her laptop, got up, and wandered to the display window that looked out on Newbury St. Since the hour was still very early, the street was relatively quiet. But she didn't see the few parked cars or the occasional pedestrian hurrying to work. Her mind was focused on the eighth Marquis of Wildford, born in 1786. She did the math. And gasped. The eighth Marquis of Wildford was Simon! And he had never married and never had children. Why not?

She had thought Simon would have found a lovely young lady to wed, and he would have had a gaggle of children. Why hadn't he married? Had he gone back to privateering? Had he been so caught up in chasing enemy ships that he hadn't found time to get married and raise a family? The idea of him alone, wandering through that huge, empty Sea Watch, made her heart ache.

She mulled that over for a bit. The words of the woman in her dream came back to her. She had to step back to go forward. And Maggie abruptly knew what she had to do.

Two days later, Maggie raced through Hyde Park. She dodged around a couple of power walkers, a mother pushing a stroller, and a few suits striding to their offices. This time, she wore a long skirt and a long-sleeved blouse, not exactly running clothes, but better for where she was going. The ancient oak tree finally came into sight. Slowing to a walk, she approached cautiously. Would her pendant work?

She glanced around. The area was deserted. Stopping beneath the tree's wide branches, she looked up into the dense, green foliage, and took a deep breath. Was she doing the right thing? She was leaving everything behind. She was leaving Darcy behind. All the calls to her sister had gone to voicemail. So, she had texted her sister with an urgent plea to come to London and had left her a letter in their father's flat, telling her to read Emma's latest book, and instructed her to find the ancient oak tree. Because her sister had to travel to the past. She just had to. She hoped Darcy would believe her.

Wrapping her fingers around her pendant, she stepped closer to the tree. All she had to do was find that hole. This had to work.

The last time she had traveled through time, coming forward into the twenty-first century, her heart had been a raw, bruised thing, and she had found the hole quickly. The chaos she had created by falling into the middle of a group of teenage girls hadn't helped her shaky emotional state. Mumbling an apology amidst their cries of surprise and complaints of disturbing them, she had raced off, the tears streaming from her eyes. This time, although her heart still ached, hope was a bandage over the wound.

She walked around the huge trunk, but nothing happened. She reversed her steps and walked around in the other direction. What was wrong? The only warmth in her pendant came from her own fingers. Twice more, she circled the trunk, each time remaining solidly in the twenty-first century.

With a despondent sigh, she stepped onto the path, approximately the same spot where she and Simon had landed in a tangle of limbs after they had been transported to the nineteenth century. Looking out over the park, she whispered, "Oh, Simon, I tried."

The leaves above her head rustled, as if they were disturbed. Or angry. Suddenly, the pendant pulsed hot, once, twice, each time gaining more heat. The ground beneath her feet shifted. And she fell into the hole.

MAGGIE STOOD BEFORE SIMON'S IMPOSING BLACK DOOR AND let the doorknocker fall three times. As she waited, her apprehension about what she had done expanded in her head to block out everything else. Had she done the right thing? The *what ifs* and *what abouts* rattled around in her brain, making her fidget. If he rejected her, what would she do? Returning to the nineteenth century, standing in front of his door was a huge risk. She had convinced herself that he didn't want her. But was she wrong?

Finally, footsteps approached from the other side of the door, and it swung open to reveal Kelwin.

"The marquis isn't receiving—" His words halted when he saw who stood on the doorstep, then a smile creased his cheeks. "Miss Blake." Stepping back, he opened the door wide. "You'll find the cap'n in the library."

"Thanks, Kelwin," she said, relieved at his friendly welcome. One hurdle passed.

"Ah, he's not—that is—he's a bit off his game." Concern creased his brow.

"Off his game?" she asked, as she walked into the entry hall.

"Just be careful." Kelwin jerked his chin in the direction of the library.

Only silence came from the room. Maggie wasn't sure if that was a good thing or a bad thing.

"Okay," she said both to Kelwin and herself, bolstering her courage, then she approached the library door and knocked.

"I said I do not wish to be disturbed." Simon's tone was clipped and chilly.

Ignoring him, she opened the door and walked in. He was sitting before the cold hearth, his back to the door. One hand, draped across the arm of the chair, held a glass with dark liquid in the bottom. He'd been drinking.

"Did you not hear me?" he snapped. "Get out!"

"Only if you ask nicely," she said.

There was a beat of silence, as if every bit of furniture, all the books, even the molecules of air held their breath.

Then, very quietly, he said, "Stop torturing me, ghost of Maggie Blake."

So he was in pain, too. She smiled. "But torturing you is so much fun. I think I'll steal a painting."

Another beat of silence. Then he catapulted from his seat and faced her. "Maggie?"

His appearance contrasted sharply with his cold, precise words. He looked terrible. His eyes were bloodshot, his skin was pale, his hair stood on end in several places, his cravat was coming undone, and his waistcoat was buttoned wrong. But he was the most beautiful thing she had ever seen.

"I wondered if you still needed a pseudo marchioness," she said with a wry twist to her lips.

"Oh, Maggie." He took two steps toward her and halted, suspicion showing in his eyes. "Is that truly you?" He reached out as if he were going to touch her, then dropped his hand.

"Yes. It's really me."

"But you went back to your own time." Suspicion clouded his eyes.

She nodded. "I did."

"And you came back to my time." A line of confusion appeared between his brows.

"I did that, too."

"But, why?"

Pain zinged through her. He didn't want her. She had given up everything for nothing. Then his appearance registered. He was a mess, not at all his normally sophisticated, put-together self. She could only think of one reason for that. He was wallowing in his own stupidity. And that eased the pain, because she knew he wanted her, even if he wouldn't admit it. Yet.

Annoyance narrowed her eyes. "Why do you think?"

He blinked, looking befuddled. "Ah—"

"It wasn't easy," she said, using explanation to give him time to think. "I had to travel back to London and then go to the oak tree in Hyde Park to find the hole through time again. I wasn't sure the pendant would work. And I don't think the tree was happy with me."

"Oh, Maggie," he said again, understanding clearing his eyes, and closed the distance between them. "I am very happy you went to all that trouble." He cupped her face. "I love you, Maggie Blake."

Her eyes widened. "You do?" She needed reassurance.

"Yes. Shall I show you?" A tiny smile tugged at his lips.

"Yes, please."

He captured her mouth and demonstrated thoroughly.

When he finally lifted his head, she blinked up at him, her brain cells jumbled and the rest of her tingling.

"That was very convincing," she said solemnly. "I needed to know that."

"Yes?"

"Yes." She nodded. "Because, you see, I love you, too."

His eyes crinkled at the corners. "A good thing to know. Especially with what I need to ask you."

"Yes?"

He went down on one knee, "Will you marry me, Maggie Blake?"

She didn't have to think that over. "Yes!" With a laugh, she flung her arms around his neck and kissed him.

Epilogue

T wo weeks later, Maggie stood in the doorway of the village church not far from the Sea Watch. At the other end of the aisle, standing before the altar, Simon waited for her. This wedding was a secret, since she and Simon were supposedly already wed. She was reminded of the accusation of the Honorable Agnes, that Simon had absconded with her to Gretna Green and wed her secretly. The irony made her smile.

Agnes and her family had slunk out of London after the Duke of Wyndham, through his spies, had discovered that her father, the Baron Cuthbert, had paid bribes to have Simon arrested for piracy. Evidently, Cuthbert also had some connection to Rosalind, but she had disappeared as well. The woman was like a spider, weaving a wide web of alliances.

Maggie was distracted from her thoughts when Emma gave the skirt of her pale violet silk frock one last twitch.

"Stop fussing over me," Maggie complained in a whisper.

"You look beautiful," Emma said, smiling, then handed her a bouquet of pink roses and purple sweet peas. After kissing Maggie on the cheek, she headed down the aisle to sit next to her husband.

Despite the secrecy of the wedding, a handful of people sat in the pews. Besides the Earl and Countess of Cranleigh, Maggie saw the Duke and Duchess of Wyndham, Kelwin, and Deems. Mrs. Edwards had slipped into a back pew at the last minute. She wondered how the lady had known about the wedding, but was glad she had emerged from her solitude to attend.

Maggie's gaze landed on Simon, appearing a bit tight around the jaw. He was elegantly and properly attired in a dark gray superfine coat, black pantaloons, pale blue satin waistcoat and intricately tied cravat held in place by an emerald stickpin that matched his eyes. Those eyes beckoned. With a smile, she started down the aisle.

When she reached him, he held out his hand.

She gazed up at him, her pirate. "Do you yield, Mr. Marquis?" she whispered with a mischievous twist to her lips.

He grinned. "With all my heart, Marchioness."

"Then I do, too." Maggie smiled, placed her hand in his,

and together, they turned to face the vicar, ready to make their pseudo marriage into a real one.

THE END

I hope you enjoyed reading
MISCHIEF WITH THE MARQUIS
Rogues Out of Time Series ~ Book 2
Please consider leaving a review or a rating
on Amazon by clicking or scanning
the following QR Code:

Keep reading for a Free Preview of
DALLYING WITH THE DUKE
Rogues Out of Time Series ~ Book 3

Sincerely,
Patricia

Dallying with the Duke

with the Duke

ROGUES OUT OF TIME BOOK 3

PATRICIA BARLETTA

DALLYING WITH THE DUKE
ROGUES OUT OF TIME, BOOK 3

LONDON, PRESENT DAY

Darcy Blake stood in the middle of the living room of her father's flat in London and looked around. She had just arrived from Milan, where she'd abruptly left a highly prized apprenticeship with a famous clothing designer because her middle sister, Maggie, had begged her to come. A family emergency, she'd said. Their oldest sister, Emma, had disappeared and Maggie had been frantic. So, Darcy had dropped everything and flown to England. She could always get another internship, but not another sister.

Darcy had expected Maggie to be in the flat when she arrived, but she wasn't there. Nor had she answered any of the texts Darcy had sent after she'd landed. So where was she?

Frustrated and annoyed, she rolled her suitcase into the bedroom she and Maggie usually shared and left it in the corner. She wouldn't start worrying. Not yet. A pair of her sister's jeans, about five years out of style, lay across the bed. Shaking her head at Maggie's lack of fashion sense, she walked back out to the living room.

She stopped in the middle of the space, turned in a slow circle and took in the silence of the flat. Her dad had used it when he came to London on buying trips for his antique shop on Newbury St. in Boston. But he was gone now, missing and presumed drowned since his small plane had crashed into Cape Cod Bay six months ago. Her grief was a dull ache that never quite went away. Being in the flat where she and her two sisters had spent many school vacations with her dad made her drag in a breath to combat the pain of his loss. She slowly let it out and concentrated on why she was here: to help Maggie discover Emma's whereabouts. She decided Maggie had probably just gone to the store and would be back soon.

Nothing had changed since the last time she had been here, except instead of pristine order, her sisters' things lay scattered about. Emma's laptop sat open on her desk. Papers lay strewn beside it in a messy pile, topped by the antique paperweight their father had given Emma on the publication of her first book. A pen and a highlighter sat on an open notebook, as if her oldest sister had just gotten up from her chair to take a break from writing her latest historical romance. Maggie's sweater was draped over the back of a leather armchair, a pair of shoes was left carelessly in the middle of the floor, and a half-full glass of water sat on a side table. The place looked like her sisters had just gone out for a meal or a jog and would step through the door any moment. But something about the stillness gave Darcy a bad feeling.

An antique book on the seat of the sofa caught her eye. Curious, she flipped it open and discovered it was a journal, written by a woman named Emma. Weird coincidence. Goosebumps popped on her arms. On the first page was an inscription: 30 June 1814. To my sisters, whom I miss greatly. Even though we are separated, know that I hold you in my heart.

For some reason, the dedication brought tears to her eyes. She swiped them away and let the journal fall back to the sofa. The words sounded too much like something Emma might write in one of her novels. But Emma couldn't have written them. The date was over two hundred years ago. So the similarity was just a coincidence. Only a coincidence, she reassured herself. But her chest muscles tightened anyway. Anxiety had gripped her ever since she'd seen the first text from Maggie about Emma having gone missing. Now it welled up, threatening to turn her into a non-functioning, quivering mass. She couldn't let it take her over.

Emma couldn't possibly have written something two hundred years old. And Maggie had just gone for a jog, or to a nearby pub for a bite. Darcy returned to the bedroom to change her clothes. She'd go for a run and maybe Maggie would be back by then, wondering why Darcy was so worried. She wasn't going to panic.

Because she didn't want to think about both of her sisters going missing.

DARCY SAT CROSS-LEGGED ON THE GRASS IN HYDE PARK, HER brain whirling with questions and doubts. Where had Emma gone? And why hadn't Maggie answered her texts? The empty wound of loss opened wider in her chest. Guilt assailed her. When she was in Milan, she should have answered Maggie's texts and phone calls, right away, but her internship had absorbed all of her time and all of her energy because the designer was preparing to show her winter collection in another week. With both of her sisters missing, and grieving over their father's death six months ago, she felt very, very alone.

Heaving a deep sigh, she gazed around Hyde Park from beneath the huge oak tree where she sat. The lawn spread out before her, dotted with decorative gardens in full bloom and shaded by tall trees. From her perch, the park seemed deserted, but she knew that other people walked or jogged or lounged among the trees. The tree that shaded her looked ancient with a huge trunk and branches that spread wide. Glancing up into the mat of leaves overhead, she wondered how old it was.

Idly, she twisted the antique signet ring she wore on her thumb, a habit she had when she was bored or nervous or worried, like she was now. Even though it was obviously a man's ring, her father had gifted it to her when she had been accepted to Parsons School of Design. From the time she had been tall enough to barely be able to see into the display case in her dad's antique shop, she had been intrigued by the intricate coat of arms engraved on its face.

As she watched the leaves above her dance in the breeze, the sapphire and diamond pendant she wore as an earring brushed her neck. It was a keepsake from her mother who died when Darcy was too young to remember her. The pendant felt very hot, burning against her skin. With a hiss, she brushed it away. As she did, she felt her ring grow warm, then very hot. Yanking it off, she dropped it on the grass, then checked her thumb for a burn. Her skin appeared unharmed, no burn mark, not even any redness. She peered down at the ring. It didn't look any different than before. Why would it get so hot? And why had her pendant felt hot? It must have been her imagination. Or a streak of sunlight through the branches of the tree.

Gingerly, she touched her pendant. It was back to a normal temperature. Then she poked at her ring. That had cooled, too. She slipped it back on her thumb. As soon as she did, it grew warm again, then hotter and hotter.

Just as she was about to pull it off her thumb, a thud sounded behind her, then she heard a groan. Peeking over her shoulder, she saw a man lying face down on the grass. He hadn't been there a moment ago. Where had he come from? Had he fallen and hurt himself? Was he drunk? He groaned again.

Scrambling to her feet, she glanced around, searching to see if anyone else was in the area, but this part of the park was still deserted. She inched a bit closer to the stranger.

"Are you all right?" she called.

He flopped over onto his back and hissed in pain. When he turned his head to look at her, she saw blood from a wound on his temple smeared down one side of his face and an eye swollen shut.

"Oh my gosh! You're hurt!" She rushed over to him and went down on one knee. That was when she realized he was dressed very strangely, in breeches and boots and vest. The white, intricately tied cravat he wore was dotted with his blood.

"Where did you come from?" he demanded, his words a bit slurred from a split and swollen lip. He looked beyond her, up into the tree and around at the park. "Where am I?" His questions were breathless, as if he had trouble breathing.

"You're in Hyde Park," she said. "I was sitting over there when you um fell."

"Hyde Park? In London?" A frown creased his forehead. "Impossible. I was on the road to Bath."

Maybe he had amnesia from the blow to his head. Or maybe he was delusional. She indicated the park around them. "No, you're in Hyde Park. In London."

After another doubtful look at the surroundings, he started to sit up, gasped, and fell back. She noticed a wet stain on his side, darker than the dark blue of his brocade vest, that had a long slice through the material.

Darcy gasped. "Oh my gosh! What happened to you?"

His exasperated gaze landed on her. "I've been stabbed. Help me up." He held out an imperious hand.

Ignoring his dictatorial tone, she shook her head. "I don't think you should move. Let me get someone to help. You should probably go to the hospital." She pulled her cell phone out of her pocket, but realized she didn't know the emergency number for London. Glancing around, she searched to see if anyone was nearby, but the park was still deserted.

His hand nudged closer. "You're here. You can help. Give me your hand," he commanded.

Darcy narrowed her eyes at the snapped order, but with a stab wound in his side, he was probably in a lot of pain and grouchy. And if he didn't want to go to the emergency room, that was on him. Cutting him some slack, she stood, clasped his hand and helped him to his feet. Pain blanched his face when he finally gained his balance. He was tall, with the top of her head only reaching his nose, despite his slouch to favor his wound, and the side of his face that was uninjured was rather attractive — strong jaw, now clenched in pain, good cheekbones, and hazel eyes below a shock of dark brown hair.

He looked down at their hands, still clasped. "Where did you get that?"

She blinked, surprised and unsure what he was asking. His large hand enveloped her much smaller one, and only her thumb was visible with its antique signet ring. "What?"

"That ring. How did you get it?" His eyes accused suspiciously.

She tried to pull out of his grasp, but his fingers tightened, refusing to let her go.

"My father gave it to me," she said.

"Impossible."

Alarmed, she backed away a step, but her hand remained firmly in his grasp.

"It is not," she huffed. "It was in his antique shop and he gave it to me." She left out the part about her dad's comment that it might have belonged to her knight in shining armor.

He grabbed her other wrist. "How did he get it? Did he steal it? Or is he a fence? Does he deal in stolen goods?" Anger darkened his face.

"Absolutely not!" She tried to twist away from him. "Let go of me!"

"Not until you tell me the truth." He dragged her closer. "The ring is mine. Take it off and give it back."

"I will not!" Frightened at his strength despite his injuries, she struggled against his tight hold. "Let me go or I'll scream."

"Scream all you wish, but I'll have my ring whether you give it up or I take it from you." He grabbed the ring in his long fingers and began to twist it off her thumb.

She felt heat radiating from her pendant earring, and the ring blazed around her thumb. "Ow! Ooh! Hot!"

Her shocked gaze met his as the ground seemed to disappear beneath her feet, as if she had fallen into a sudden gaping hole. A really, really deep hole that seemed to have no bottom. She felt as if she was falling forever. And the aggravating man, who was still gripping her hand, was falling with her. Then the earth slammed into her feet. She staggered, barely remaining upright, and the stranger careened into her. His arm dropped heavily on her shoulders as he tried to keep his balance. That arm tightened around her like a vise, holding her still, not allowing her any escape. She was clamped against him, as firmly together as if they had just exchanged a soul-searing kiss.

"Don't move." His words came out strained and breathless. "Please."

That first bit of courtesy made her halt, despite the urge to dance away. Against her, his steely muscles were tight and taut, as if he were afraid to move. He seemed to be holding his breath.

"Please, if you don't mind, just give me a moment." His tone was thin and strained.

Again, his polite phrases gave her pause. She inched away her bottom half, attempting to put some space between them, while she let him lean into her. The warmth radiating off him and his scent of mossy cedar were much too intimate. But she couldn't help drawing in another breath of him. He smelled really, really good.

After a moment, he took a shaky breath. "Right. Hyde Park, you said?" He shook his head. "I'm not sure how I got here."

She remained absolutely still, uncomfortably awkward, but she couldn't ignore the hard muscles crushed against her. "Maybe you spaced out after you were attacked, came here, and then passed out."

"Spaced out?" He stared at her. "I know those words, but not the way you use them. Please explain yourself."

Darcy stared back. How could he not know common slang? Maybe he'd been in a very remote part of the world for a very long time. Patiently, because he was wounded, she rephrased. "Maybe you weren't really aware of what you were doing after you were wounded, then lost consciousness."

"I don't believe I did." The chilly look he sent her contrasted sharply with the warmth of his arm draped around her shoulders. "I believe you had something to do with the attack."

"What?! No! I've never seen you before in my life!" Her attempt to wriggle away ended when he clutched her tighter against him.

His eyes narrowed and his lips thinned, at least the part that wasn't swollen. "Perhaps not. Or perhaps you remained in the shadows while your henchmen did your dirty work for you."

"I—"

"Do not say a word," he interrupted, shutting off her protest. "You will come with me, and we will straighten this out later."

"I'm not going anywhere with you." Something hard pressed into her side.

"I have a pistol," he rasped. "Surely, you wouldn't want me to use it."

Darcy lapsed into frightened silence. Where had he hidden a pistol?

"I'll take your silence as agreement to my request," he said. "Wise decision." His hand circled her upper arm like a manacle, and dragging her along, he headed toward one of the gates into the park.

Darcy had no choice, so she went with him, but she watched for any chance to escape. Had this happened to Emma and Maggie? Had they been kidnapped as well, never to be seen again? But why would anyone want to hurt them?

And why would this stranger who'd appeared out of nowhere, beaten and stabbed, think that the antique ring on her thumb might be his?

The questions tumbled around in her head, but no answers tumbled with them.

ADAM BARRETT, DUKE OF THORNHILL, FOUGHT THE PAIN AND dizziness from his wounds. He just needed to get somewhere safe, someplace where he could reason out the events of the past hour. At this moment, everything that had occurred was a fuzzy jumble of scenes in his head. The coach ride with his sister, Clare. The fight with one of the highwaymen who stopped them. The slash across his ribs, the blow to his head. And the worst: the sight of his sister being thrown onto a horse with one of the brigands and screaming as they rode away.

His head hurt. The slice across his side hurt. He was desperate to go after the outlaws who had kidnapped his sister. But all that had faded away when he had seen the ring on the woman's thumb. His ring. How in damnation could it be in her possession? He'd had it on his finger when he'd first become aware that they were being attacked by high-waymen. He'd had it on when the outlaws had flung open both doors of his coach, pointed pistols at him and Clare, and ordered them out. He'd had it on when he was jumped from behind and nearly stabbed. Which was only minutes ago. So how had the woman come into possession of the ring?

He slowly became aware of the arm beneath his hand. It was bare, firm, and the skin was soft and silky. When they had fallen into that nearly bottomless hole—where had that come from?—he remembered the feel of her against him. She was lithe, with curves and hollows in all the right places. If he hadn't been in so much pain, he certainly would have taken more notice. Glancing down, he saw her legs were bare, and the clothing she wore barely covered her. Despite his appreciation of her lovely, long legs and her shapeliness, he was shocked at the scant clothing she wore—very tight, very short pantaloons and a bodice that snugged her perfect breasts. What had she been doing wandering about Hyde Park nearly naked?

"If I scream, someone will call the police," she said, breaking into his thoughts.

"If the constables come, they'll arrest you for indecent exposure," he declared.

"I'm not indecent. I'm perfectly covered up." Insult wove through her words. She tried to jerk out of his grip. "Let me go."

"No." The abrupt denial slipped out without a thought, but in the next second, he knew he should have been gentler.

The fact that the woman was wandering about nearly naked gave him pause. Perhaps she was in worse straits than he was. And she had offered help.

She halted, digging in her heels. "Look, can we talk about this? There's obviously been some misunderstanding."

Yes, there certainly was a misunderstanding. She was in possession of his ring that had been on his finger only minutes before. But he didn't have time to stop and have a polite discussion about where she had found it. Because if he didn't get somewhere safe and sit down very soon, he would likely lose consciousness. Black spots were appearing before his eyes, a sure sign he was going to pass out at any moment. And then she'd be gone and he'd never get his ring back. Unless he knew who she was and where to find her. So, he had to get her to reveal her name.

"Perhaps if I introduce myself, you might consider returning my ring," he said, forcing himself to feign that nothing hurt and he wasn't bleeding. "I am Adam Barrett, Duke of Thornhill." He bowed as best he could while still holding onto the woman's arm and bleeding from a gaping wound in his side.

Her eyes widened, lovely sapphire eyes that seemed to be the same color as the gem dangling from her ear. "Oh." Then those eyes narrowed. "Sure, you are. And I'm the Princess of Genovia. You're still not getting my ring."

Adam's patience was shredded so thin it was barely a thread. The woman was the most stubborn, insolent, aggravating creature he had ever met. With a growl, he turned on his heel, continued toward the park gate, and dragged the woman after him. She complained, but her words were merely annoying sounds that he pretended not to hear.

They finally reached the gate and stepped through. As he searched for a hansom cab, he felt the woman's shock in the stiffening of the arm beneath his hand. Glancing at her, he saw that she stared, open mouthed, at the scene before her: the carriages and drays and wagons that clogged the street, the ladies in their pale frocks out for a stroll, their parasols held just so above their heads, the gentlemen greeting each other with a bow and a lift of their hats. He wondered why she was so surprised at the ordinary scene.

She turned to him. Her face had lost all color. "What...? How...? Where's London? What have you done with it? WHERE'S LONDON?"

Like what you've read so far?
You can get
DALLYING WITH THE DUKE
Rogues Out of Time ~ Book 3
on Amazon coming in 2026...
Sign up for my newsletter for updates on new releases, contests,
giveaways, promotions, and more...
by clicking or scanning the following QR Code:

Author's Note

When I started writing this series, **Rogues Out of Time**, I kept thinking about another series I had written, **On His Majesty's Secret Service**, where each of the heroes is a spy as well as a duke. All the books are set during the Regency period, and all the heroes are titled gentlemen. Wouldn't it be fun if the men from one series knew the men of the other series?

In reality, the ton of London society during the Regency period was a small, exclusive group of people, and most of them knew each other. The boys went to school together, and the girls met at finishing school or during their first London Season. Many of them were related either through blood or marriage. So, of course, Simon, Marquis of Wildford would know Jessica and Damien, the Duke and Duchess of Wyndham, and he would know their story as well. But wouldn't you like to find out what it is? I can tell you this: It's exciting, and dangerous, and romantic. And, of course, just a bit sexy.

If you would like to discover how Jessica and Damien came to fall in love and marry, you can read about their adventures in *The Duke Who Loved me* Book 1, On His Majesty's Secret Service.

Keep reading for a Free Preview...

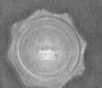

ON HIS MAJESTY'S SECRET SERVICE

BOOK 1

THE DUKE
Who Loved Me

PATRICIA BARLETTA

Free Preview 2

THE DUKE WHO LOVED ME
ON HIS MAJESTY'S SECRET
SERVICE SERIES ~ BOOK 1

LONDON, 1810

"Lady Jessica Carlton watched as the cards were dealt. Five others sat around the table in the middle of the room. It was quiet except for an occasional murmur and the hushed slap of cards. Candles glowed from the elegant chandelier, hanging over the green, baize-covered table. As silent as statues, the servants in their livery stood in their inconspicuous positions.

She watched as the players scanned their cards and tried to hide feelings of disappointment or elation. Her own cards could not possibly lose. She feigned a dainty yawn behind a gloved hand as she hid her smile. The men placed bets and play went on, as one by one, they dropped out. Only two people were left in the game. Lord Hoxly shook his head.

"Well, that's it for me," he announced as he threw in his hand. "I say, m'lady, you've the Devil's own luck this evening."

Jessica peered out from behind her black-silk half-mask, and smiled sweetly. "Nay, Lord Hoxly, the Devil has none, for Luck is a lady."

"Appreciative chuckles ran around the table as Lord Hoxly smiled his defeat. "Then may I compliment Lady Luck on her choice of companions? It is not every evening I can lose to such a beautiful victor."

"Why, thank you m'lord," Jessica said with a slight nod. "Perhaps next time you will allow me to win even more."

Guffaws came from the other players as Lord Hoxly shook his head in acceptance of his vanquishment, both verbally and at cards. They all, at one time or another, had been her hapless victims.

After gathering her considerable winnings, Lady Jessica, or Lady Fortuna as she was known at the gaming hell, bestowed a dazzling smile upon the gentlemen at the table.

"If you gentlemen will excuse me," she said as she rose, "it has been an exhausting evening. It is time I took my leave. Good night."

The men rose with her and murmured their farewells. Jessica could feel their eyes on her as she left. She knew they watched with varying degrees of interest, from gentlemanly appreciation to outright leering. She could imagine their conversation as soon as the door closed behind her."

"The speculation over her true identity.

The fact that she hid behind a mask, possibly covering some disfigurement.

Her nickname, Ice Witch, gained during one very long, very close game of faro played against one of the more notorious members of the gaming hell.

And perhaps, the conjecture once again that she was the Regent's latest paramour.

Jessica could not be bothered by such idle chatter. She wearily leaned back against the seat of the carriage which was taking her to her lodgings. She had done well playing cards this evening. Perhaps, she would have to play only once more before she had to return home to Braeleigh. A tired sigh"

"A tired sigh escaped her at the thought. There was a time when Braeleigh meant everything to her. Now, she was not quite so sure it did. The painful memories did not help.

Her mother's death, her father's remarriage to Margaret, and then her father's sudden, tragic death a year ago had combined to turn a place of peace into one of grief. Yet, Jessica would have been content to stay and try to heal her wounds and those of her twelve-year-old brother, Jason, had it not been for Margaret's cruel demands. It was because of their stepmother that Jessica was living a dual life—one of the adventuress out to win every penny she could, and one of the genteel daughter of an earl who dutifully traveled home from the city every month to visit her brother and stepmother.

She gazed blindly at the passing houses and storefronts. Normally, the excitement of the life she was living would cause her blood to pulse through her veins. The gaiety, the laughter, the concentration of the game combined to help her repress the true purpose of her sojourn in London, at least for short periods of time. "But tonight, for some reason, a depression lay heavy on her heart. It was as if something dire were about to happen, only she did not know what or when. But she could not give up the struggle of wits she sustained with Margaret. She would never let her step-mother be victorious in her little scheme."

"Jessica saw they were nearing her lodgings. Her bed, hard and lumpy though it was, would be welcome tonight. Her evening at the gaming hell had drained her. Lord Hoxly had been a formidable opponent. The Marquis of Bellingham had persisted in his advances to the point of being crude. It was a different life she lived now. She was no longer cradled in the warmth of her father's love and the companionship of her younger brother. She missed her brother, Jason, terribly, and she worried about him being subjected to Margaret, a shrew, who cared only for herself.

The carriage stopped before the rooming house where she had been living for nearly a year. Not exactly a palace, she thought wryly as she noted the stained whitewash and paint peeling off the door. Next door was the Green Dragon Inn. The sign, hanging above the door from one hook and creaking back and forth in the night wind, pictured such a creature. The poor dragon's fiery breath had turned to a pale yellow and many of his scales had flaked off with the paint. Not a very formidable dragon, she noted.

"She turned her attention back to her own lodgings. There was scant light coming through the street-level windows. The landlady had probably retired for the night and would not be pleased to be roused again at such an ungodly hour. Jessica would have to endure her dour looks and scathing comments once more. Even though the woman was paid extra for her trouble, she felt obliged to scold. At least the place was clean. And inexpensive.

She stepped down from the carriage, paid the driver and knocked. After several moments, she heard the bolt thrown back and the door was opened a crack. An eye peered at her through the opening."

"It's Jessica Carlton, Mrs. Cooper," she said, knowing her landlady's suspicious nature.

There was a grunt and the door swung wide. As soon as Jessica stepped across the threshold, the door was slammed behind her and locked. Muttering, Mrs. Cooper shambled back to her room and shut herself in. Relieved that she had been spared a tongue-lashing, Jessica started for her room. "

"The front parlor was deserted except for a mangy dog sleeping before the dying fire. He barely opened his eyes as she walked past. The candles in the sconces on the staircase had burned very low and gave testimony to the very late hour.

Jessica knew Donny would be waiting up for her. The woman had first been her nanny. Now she acted as her lady's maid. Donny's acceptance of the situation and her mothering during the time they had been in London had been the only thing that had kept Jessica sane and able to go through with her scheme."

"Quietly, she opened the door to her room. It appeared deserted. There was a single candle burning on the table beside the bed. The fire crackled brightly in welcome. Jessica tossed her wrap on the bed and went to stand before the fire's warmth. The carriage ride from the fashionable section of London where the gaming hell was situated, to the less respectable area of the city where the Green Dragon made its home, had been chilly and damp. Jessica had not wished to spend the few extra coins for a warming brick for her feet or an extra carriage blanket.

"Aye, and 'tis a God-forsaken hour ye be comin' in," Donny said from a dark corner.

Jessica laughed lightly. "Oh, Donny, stop complaining." She threw a pouch onto the bed. It landed with the heavy clink of money. "See what these late hours have brought us."

Mistress Donlin harrumphed and rose from a chair in the shadows. She picked up the pouch and hefted it in her hand. "And a good thing 'tis, too, what with ye havin' to make payment soon."

"Jessica shivered. "Better I should have to return to Margaret every month with a payment than marry that overstuffed, middle-aged baronet with thinning hair and red veins across his nose. Every time he looked at me, he made my skin crawl."

Donny lifted a loose floorboard under the threadbare rug near the fireplace and emptied the pouch into a box nestled in the hiding place. Carefully, she replaced the board and smoothed the rug.

"Aye," she agreed. "Sir Percival Lowry was no great catch for any girl. But he would've saved Braeleigh for ye."

Jessica's chin went up. "If my father were still alive, he would never have considered the marriage. He wanted a love-match for me and would have lost Braeleigh sooner than have me unhappy."

"Donny turned to help Jessica undress. "The Earl was soft where his daughter was concerned."

Jessica turned on Donny. "Just because you have been my nanny all my life, Mistress Donlin, does not give you the right to criticize my father." Even as she said the words, she knew the woman was right. Her father had indulged her, but he would never have given up his ancestral home, not even for her. That was the reason she was in London and living a precarious existence—to save Braeleigh.

Donny harrumphed. "Ye know as well as I that yer father was never in his right mind after his lady died. All that gamblin' and racin' and schemes to make money. 'Twas the racin' that killed him and the schemin' that put ye here in the city."

"Jessica shrugged and turned her back so that Donny could unbutton her dress. "With Napoleon rampaging all over the Continent and England's very shores threatened, the idea to build a new shipyard was the thing to do for a man loyal to the Crown. It was not his fault that the other investors ran off with the money and left my father with none to meet the Admiralty's orders."

"Hmph. Left you and yer brother with none, not to mention Margaret. Or have ye forgotten what it is yer about here in London?" Donny slipped a warm nightrail over Jessica's head.

"I've not forgotten. I believe I will only need one, or perhaps two more evenings at the card table this month before I have enough for Margaret. The fifteenth of the month is almost a fortnight away. I may be able to begin on next month's stipend before we leave for Braeleigh. Perhaps there will be enough left over for some of that marvelous scented soap I saw at the perfumer's."

"Donny muttered, "Seems to me y'ought to stay in and try goin' t'bed early. Ye be too thin. Next thing ye know, ye'll be gettin' sick, and then where'll ye be?"

"I'm fine, and I am not going to get sick. Margaret will get her stipend," Jessica answered as she sat before the small dressing table so Donny could brush out her hair. She knew her maid's grumbling covered up her concern.

"Ye ought to find yerself a husband to take care of ye. Ye shouldn't have to go to that gamin' place." Donny pulled the pins from Jessica's hair and began to brush the long, ebony tresses."

"I have no connection. Who would introduce me to a suitable husband? Besides, I'll not marry till I'm ready. I'll not marry someone I don't love." It was an old argument, and Jessica said the words by rote, but she meant them.

"If yer father had lived, he'd'a found ye a husband," Donny said. "And ye would've wed him whether ye loved him or not. It's a husband's place to take care of his wife an' her family. Ye wouldn't have t' be runnin' around like some strumpet all night."

"Jessica climbed onto the bed and slid under the covers as she hid a smile. "Are you suggesting that I should have been a dutiful stepdaughter and wed Sir Percival?" She knew Donny's feelings about Margaret and her scheme, but she loved to tease her.

Her nanny-turned-maid gave her a sharp glance. "Yer stepmother had only herself in mind when she came up with that one."

Jessica giggled. "Come, Donny, I thought you wanted me to wed."

"Aye. To some nice lord who'll take care o' ye for the rest of yer days." She tucked the blankets around Jessica.

Jessica sighed. "I don't think I'll ever find one of those. The men who frequent the gaming houses are not looking for wives, and the women there are not...acceptable."

"Seems t' me a young girl with a decent name and good looks ought t' be acceptable," Donny grumbled.

Jessica only smiled as she snuggled down into her pillow. "This girl with a decent name is tired, so if you are through your grumping, I'll go to sleep," she murmured.

Donny gave the blankets one last pat, then did as she was asked, shaking her head.

"But Jessica's smile faded as Donny closed the door behind her."

Like what you've read so far?
You can get
THE DUKE WHO LOVED ME
On His Majesty's Secret Service Series ~ Book 1
on Amazon by clicking or scanning the following QR Code:

About the Author

Patricia Barletta is an award-winning author of historical and paranormal romance. A former teacher of British Literature at an all-girls high school, Patricia later earned a Master of Fine Arts in Creative Writing from Stonecoast at the University of Southern Maine.

She is the author of *The Auriano Curse*, a four-book "romantasy" series set in late 18th-century Europe, and *On His Majesty's Secret Service*, a three-book historical spy-romance series set in Regency England. In addition, she has written three stand-alone historical romances set across various time periods. Patricia has published both traditionally with Kensington Books, writing under the pen name Amy Christopher, and independently under her own name. She is currently working on an exciting new three-book time-travel historical romance series.

Patricia's work has garnered numerous accolades, including the 2016 Colorado Romance Writers Award of Excellence, the 2016 Gayle Wilson Award of Excellence, and the 2018 New England Reader's Choice Award. A passionate historian, she resides in a century-old house in Massachusetts, designed by an architect to resemble a Belgian cottage. Her home was even featured in *Smaller Houses of the 1920s* (Dover Edition) by Ethel B. Power.

Patricia loves to hear from readers. You can contact her at patricia@patriciabarletta.com

Sign up for Patricia's Newsletter for updates on new releases, contests, giveaways, promotions, and more...
by clicking or scanning the following QR Code:

Complete Book List

PATRICIA BARLETTA

THE AURIANO CURSE SERIES

Moon Dark

Moon Shadow

Moon Bright

Moon Gold

ON HIS MAJESTY'S SECRET SERVICE

(Duke Spy Series)

The Duke Who Loved Me

The Duke's Dangerous Kiss

Confessions of a Dangerous Duke

ROGUES OUT OF TIME SERIES

Entangled With the Earl

Mischief with the Marquis

Dallying with the Duke